the
SILVER LINING

SILVER LINING

AUDREY LANCHO

HARPETH ROAD
PRESS
Nashville

HARPETH ROAD PRESS

Published by Harpeth Road Press (USA)
P.O. Box 158184
Nashville, TN 37215

Paperback: 978-1-963483-23-9
eBook: 978-1-963483-22-2
Library of Congress Control Number: 2025936578

The Silver Lining: A Charming, Touching Romance

Cover Design by Vanessa Mendozzi
Cover Images © Shutterstock

Harpeth Road Press, May 2025

To Mom, for all your support on this journey. I love you.

Chapter One
PRESENT DAY

In no time at all, Farrah Macon had gone from curating fine art to curing pickles.

And not just cucumbers preserved bread-and-butter style. Farrah had also helped her mom can an array of other pickled vegetables, such as radishes and beets, after she settled in her old bedroom over the weekend. She now arranged the selection on a red gingham tablecloth at the Tuesday farmers market. Though it wasn't quite open yet, it was sure to be a busy day: vendors prepped, birds chirped, and a few early shoppers ambled along the walkway.

It was hard to believe she was back.

If someone had told her two years ago—before the unraveling of life as she'd known it—that she'd be single again, living with her parents in Whitetail Ridge at nearly thirty years old, and working two jobs that had nothing to do with art, she would have scoffed at the impossibility.

She'd been so happy as a high-end gallery manager, living with her husband an hour and a half to the south in North Carolina's biggest city: beautiful, bustling Charlotte.

Her beloved career of ten years had disappeared in a flash. She humphed while straightening rows of canning jars, remembering. She'd always seen life as a series of steps forward, and she'd never imagined she'd have to start over from scratch.

Then again, this was the kind of thing that happened when others decided things *for* you.

After brushing off her existential crisis and seeing that the pickled veggies were well-organized, she focused on the next task: stocking the tables with the rest of the fresh goods from Macon Farms. She grabbed a few baskets of garden-ripe radishes and leeks, then set them on the table for display before dolloping jelly samples into little ramekins and arranging crackers and cheeses like she had so many times before. This was her first time back at Daddy's stand in years, but the body remembered.

The vinyl canopy overhead rattled in the midmorning breeze. Farrah glanced up at the sky dotted with clouds, some of them gray.

"A good rain in June sets all in tune," her sister, Macy Gatewood, said from behind her, startling Farrah.

"What are you doing here? I thought you were working." When Farrah texted her sister earlier, Macy said she wasn't sure she could escape her home office for the morning, but that was Macy. She was spontaneous and loved pulling off surprises.

Macy enveloped Farrah in a hug. At first a bit rigid, Farrah melted into the prolonged contact. The truth was, she needed it.

"Like I would miss hanging out with you on your first day back at the market booth. Pssh! Please!" Macy released her. "Besides, Mom said she could keep the boys for me while Elijah manages the business."

A husband-and-wife team, Elijah and Macy ran Gatewood Vacation Rentals, a collection of picturesque cabins dotted throughout Whitetail Ridge and the surrounding countryside, including two luxury cabins in the farther away mountain town of Boone. The business could be managed mostly from a distance. Both sisters had inherited their father's mathematical and business-oriented mind. Farrah had used these skills to manage the gallery for several years. More than manage—it had been her life's work. Her pride and joy.

"You know, I did wonder why Mom backed out on coming to the stand with me this morning. It takes a few people to run it, and I was a little perplexed when she said I'd be fine on my own."

"Sorry if that made you panic, but sometimes a little white lie is necessary to pull off a surprise. Even if she's terrible at lying." Macy snickered, and Farrah cracked a smile.

"Well, thanks. I'm glad you're here," Farrah said, relieved. "For more reasons than one. I hate to admit it, but I've been dreading facing everyone and their questions."

"I know." Macy rubbed Farrah's upper back. Her older sister's empathy was one of her most dependable traits. "I'll try to help you by fielding questions. But to some degree, curiosity is inevitable. Just remember you don't owe anyone here an explanation. It's your business, no one else's."

"I know. Thanks, Mace." Farrah glanced at her watch. "Woah, we've wasted enough time chatting."

Macy scoffed. "You can leave behind those big-city perfectionist rules, sis. This is a laid-back kind of place."

"I know, but you know I love punctuality."

Farrah set a price placard in front of each item after splitting the stack with Macy. She glanced at her watch when they were done. 9:59 a.m.—one minute early. Even if she wasn't in uptown Charlotte, she could still pursue excellence in the little things.

"Made it!" Farrah smiled at her sister and showed her the time. Macy shook her head and rolled her eyes playfully.

As her sister greeted their first customer, a woman Farrah remembered as a little girl but who was now herself a young mother pushing feisty twins in a stroller, Farrah surveyed the other market booths.

All around them, vendors had set up their canopies and tables, each with their own goods from their farms or small businesses. The beekeepers sold their honey, and the alpaca farm their yarn and crocheted goods. There were handmade gifts, woodwork crafts, beef and pork vendors, and overwhelmingly, farm-fresh early summer veggies and fruits. Farrah recognized many of the vendors from a decade or more ago, despite their aging.

Would they recognize her from a distance? Her ponytail and ball cap had given way to stylish, dark brown beach waves and bangs, and she wore a little makeup, something her sixteen- to nineteen-year-old self would have scoffed at. She didn't even look like the same person.

Yes, city life had certainly transformed her, in more ways than one.

The market's busyness grew with the warmth of the day, and it wasn't long before Farrah had to leave the partial protection and anonymity of restocking and interact with customers. Several townspeople and fellow vendors did indeed recognize her and approached her happily for a quick hug and how-have-you-been.

For the most part, she was able to politely redirect conversations that flirted with uncovering things she wanted to remain hidden. A sweet old lady she remembered from her childhood church bought some pickled beets, and a while later, a few college-aged students came by wanting to try the free samples of goat cheese with pepper jelly, but they ended up not buying anything. The area had grown, and Farrah didn't recognize some of the people shopping. This surprised her for a place as small as Whitetail Ridge.

One face, however, was more than familiar: Amy Bell. She and her husband were Farrah's neighbors at her parents' home. Although, describing them as *neighbors* was a bit of a stretch since they lived a mile down the road, even if they were the next house down. Not to mention they were more like family than neighbors.

Amy approached with a wide smile that crinkled the corners of her eyes in a way Farrah didn't recall from before. What had formerly been a mousy brown bob with a few sparse strands of gray was now adorned at the temples with two white locks. Farrah thought silver or white streaks were graceful on an aging woman. She hoped to get herself a couple when the time came.

"There's my girl!" Amy squealed, taking Farrah's hands in hers. "It's so good to see you. What's it been, three years at least?" Farrah looked at Macy, who was three clients deep. It wouldn't be fair to push off a conversation with Amy and ask Macy to handle their neighbor's shopping needs. Besides, Amy had never been one to pry, despite working behind a salon chair as a hairdresser, making her privy to the whole town's secrets.

"Three, if not four," Farrah admitted. "Things got so busy I hardly made it back home for a while."

"Your mother told me you were moving back this summer. I was surprised. I thought city life suited you."

One of Mom's gifts: discretion. She must not have given Amy any details. She was the world's best confidante, a wonderful trait for a somewhat private person's mother to have.

"It did suit me," Farrah admitted, pain restricting her voice. "It's okay, though. This is for the best." Amy's face showed only motherly affection and concern. Farrah needed to change the subject if she wanted to escape this conversation and keep her business private. "What about y'all? Still going strong with the mechanic shop?"

No more than ten days would go by each summer while she was growing up when Farrah and Macy didn't run a mile down to Amy's husband's "tractor-fixing store," as they'd called it. There, Bobby Bell gave the girls whatever ice cream he had bought on sale at Food Lion and stashed in his buzzing garage freezer. The fudgesicles were their favorite. Farrah and Macy had spent hours watching him tinker with tractors, mowers, and other small engines, and listening to his stories and corny jokes. With no kids of his own, Bobby always seemed to see them as daughters, or at least nieces.

Amy's eyes shot downward, and Farrah feared the worst. Bobby had fought cancer for years, and her stomach lurched.

"Has something happened?" The woman was so downtrodden that Farrah jumped straight to the worst-case scenario. "Did... Bobby..."

Amy lifted her face in confusion, then laughed her signature raspy laugh. "Oh, no, honey. Bobby's fine. The man's like a cat. Nine lives and all that."

Farrah laughed out her relief. "I'm sorry, you just looked so sad."

"Well, I am," Amy said, her face settling into a serious expression. "He had that skin cancer all over. Did the treatment. They say he's in remission. He likes to say he's *remiss.*"

Farrah snorted at the pun. "I'm glad he overcame it."

"I am too. But we've been left with mountains of medical debt. We might have to sell the house and rent an apartment in town. It's the only way we could get close to breaking even. You know Bobby doesn't like owing nobody."

Farrah ran some quick numbers in her head. The Bells had to be very deep in debt if they felt they needed to sell their house and land. Medical treatments were so expensive; she remembered a small surgery she'd had and the thousands of dollars she owed afterward. Of course, it hadn't even put a dent in her bank account, with her lucrative career and her husband's impressive wealth combined. She wished she still had access to that money so she could secretly pay off whatever amount Amy and Bobby owed. They were at an age when they shouldn't have to worry about sudden, unsought debt.

"I'm so sorry," Farrah managed. "I'll pray you can figure out how to keep it."

"Thank you, darlin'." Amy paid for her carrots and leeks by tapping her card on their card reader. Much had changed since Farrah ran this stand in her teen years. Technology made it easier and more streamlined than before. "Stop by and see him. Bobby thinks the world of you and Macy. Always has."

"I'll be sure to do that," Farrah said, smiling at her mother's friend as she went on her way.

"That wasn't too terrible, was it?" Macy asked, pulling Farrah into a side hug.

"I feel so bad for not keeping in touch more with these people. The Bells love us. I sent a card when Bobby was diagnosed, but I could've emailed them, or called, or—"

"No, don't go down that road," Macy said in her no-nonsense tone. It was the same tone she'd used when

Farrah started on a guilt-trip for not being in her nephews' lives. Farrah was ashamed to admit that she hadn't spent much time at all with Cash and Colton, and they were growing up so fast, now nine and almost four. Farrah hadn't even realized she was being selfish or absent at the time, but looking back with new wisdom and maturity, she cringed at her misplaced priorities.

Macy went on. "I've told people about your life and career and everything you were doing. No need to harp yourself about it. Not to mention the fact that when you did visit, nobody expected you to make time to see everyone in town. I mean…" Macy huffed as if this was the most obvious thing in the world. "Everyone here was happy for you. You had a great life going for you."

"Yeah," Farrah said, her voice strained. "*Had.*" Her eyes prickled with the threat of tears, and she swallowed against the lump in her throat.

"Hey. It's all gonna work out." Macy grabbed Farrah's shoulders, rubbing them up and down, a look of concern in her big brown eyes. Farrah wanted to say so much. Beyond the basic facts of what had happened, they hadn't really talked about what had landed her back here. It was a shadow constantly looming over her shoulder, but her sister no doubt wanted to respect Farrah's need for privacy.

Farrah thanked her sister, who went to the front table and restocked items that had been sold. Just as Macy pushed a few heavy jars of pickles to the far right of the plastic table, it buckled.

"Macy—grab it!" Farrah called from the opposite end of the market stand, well out of reach. A few pickle jars slid off the table and busted on the ground, releasing their vinegary aroma and splaying their hard-won contents across the dirt. Macy sprang forward to grab the table but wouldn't have made it.

Instead, a tall, well-built man who happened to be passing by grabbed the table, saving dozens of canning jars in the process. Macy quickly got on her hands and knees and slid the lock over the table's brace—the lock that must not have been fully in place the first time.

The man knelt to help her sister clean, but she insisted she'd handle it, though it took some convincing. Macy proceeded to thank him profusely and offered him his choice of pickle jars for free before launching into a conversation about how his father was doing.

Farrah took a few steps closer as they chatted and scrutinized the man's face, doing a very poor job at hiding her surprise.

His expression probably mirrored her own as he turned from Macy and focused on Farrah, addressing her directly with a one-word question.

"Bacon?"

It couldn't be.

Heat rushed to Farrah's cheeks. Standing before her was six feet of teenage regret. She shot a look at Macy, whose sky-high eyebrows betrayed everything she was thinking. She quickly went back to cleaning up the busted jars, leaving Farrah and James Abbott alone in conversation.

Quick, Farrah. Find your words before things get awkward.

"I-I don't like it when people call me Bacon."

Abbott's bright smile slid slowly across his face, revealing two dimples beneath his dark stubble.

"You mean other people have tried to call you Bacon besides me?"

Well, no. At least not since the sixth grade, when she got that horrible cold that left her unable to pronounce Macon correctly for over a month. Abbott had never left the nickname behind.

"What are you doing here?" Farrah asked, squaring her shoulders instead of answering him.

"I could ask you the very same thing." Abbott slid his hands into the pockets of his well-worn jeans. His smile was kind. Genuine. *Different.* The snark and cockiness he used to wear constantly had disappeared at some point in the past decade. His eyes, an unremarkable brown, sparkled beneath the shade of his bill. His dark curls peeked out from the back of the cap. "I heard you married some—"

"I did," Farrah spat out. She was almost always sociable and friendly, but the inner workings of her life were things that only a few people knew. She couldn't go into detail with him of all people, and certainly not today. Not with how things had turned out. How things were *turning* out.

"Well, where is he?" Abbott looked around innocently. "I'd like to meet the guy."

Farrah's heart raced. So much for things not getting weird.

Macy tossed the remaining soiled pickles in the trash and came to Farrah's side.

"Abbott…" Macy started, but Farrah wasn't going to let her fight this battle for her. At some point the truth would have to come out, uncomfortable or not. She stopped Macy by placing a hand on her forearm and addressing Abbott herself.

"We got divorced. I'll be back home for the foreseeable future." Farrah held her head high and looked Abbott square in the face, despite the pain and shame of the statement.

If only that was all there was to it; a simple divorce—a parting of ways—but that was merely the tip of the iceberg. The real problem was far from over.

"Dang, I'm sorry." His eyebrows scrunched together as he studied Farrah. She thought she saw either compassion or pity in his eyes. Maybe both. Macy patted Farrah's arm, excusing herself to tend to some customers approaching the booth. Farrah and Abbott walked over to the side of the canopy and stood a bit closer.

"It is what it is," Farrah said. "What about you? Did you ever marry, or…"

"Nah." Abbott cleared his throat, then pursed his lips.

Farrah waited, but it was obvious that Abbott didn't want to elaborate. He also wasn't going anywhere. He just stood there, hands in his pockets, studying her tenderly. Perhaps remembering what she was trying to forget.

"Well, what do you do for work?" Farrah asked, hoping to break the silence, and pushing through the wariness she felt at seeing him. He had gone to school in Knoxville, and last she'd heard, he'd gotten a job there. But that would've been six or seven years ago.

"Dad's ranch. Cattle and corn, same as always."

Farrah wondered how he'd ended up back in their small town after college, considering his plans to go into logistics, but she wasn't about to give him the pleasure of taking interest in where he had been for the past ten years. He certainly hadn't been calling *her*.

"Y'all still growing that genetically altered stuff?" Farrah asked, wincing.

"Yep. All your vegetables still *organic*?" He asked this with a slight head bobble, turning the question into a criticism.

For a second, she thought she saw his old snark and cockiness return, and her distrust piqued. Maybe she had felt unsure about seeing him for a reason. It wouldn't be the first time her subconscious had picked up on a nuance to protect her. Then again, there had been a few times when her gut feelings were just plain wrong.

"I'm just pickin'," Abbott said, a lopsided smile easing its way up his cheek, that stubbly jaw bringing back all kinds of memories. Her wariness melted. If she were honest, talking to him at near thirty was a lot like it had been when they were eighteen. He was handsome in his late twenties, just as Farrah had imagined he would be. "I do some of that type of farming now too. Just for fun," he added, a glint in his eyes.

Farrah realized she hadn't responded. Instead, she had been looking him over. Abbott's face was tan but flushed at the cheeks. Could he tell she was distracted by her thoughts of him?

"You're not still mad at me, right?" Abbott asked, a bit lower in tone. "I mean, we were kids. I know I acted immaturely. What teenager doesn't? Hopefully we're past all that."

Once again Farrah was reminded that their breakup had been just a bump in the road, but to her, it had completely altered the course of her life. Without her relationship with Abbott to worry about, she'd been free to study far away from him in Charlotte.

There, she'd met Connor. And the rest was history. She was glad she'd ended up with Connor. She'd loved him with everything she had. Maybe the real issue was that remembering Abbott's teenage rejection felt a lot like the sting of being served divorce papers, which had happened only one short year ago.

"No, I'm not still mad," Farrah admitted. How could she be? With everything happening now, it would have been silly to hold on to hurt from so long ago. But seeing him had old sentiments knocking at her heart's door. Things she hadn't visited for years. "I have bigger things to worry about." Farrah laughed to make this comment lighter, but Abbott's brow knitted in worry. Yet again, he seemed compassionate. Kind.

"Well, be sure to let me know if I can help you in any way."

He was being sweet, but her problems weren't exactly something he could fix.

"No, thanks. I'm good, Abbott," Farrah said, maybe a bit too coolly.

"Good," Abbott added, nodding curtly. "Glad to see you're back in your old job and doing okay." He briefly touched his ball cap's bill and turned to leave.

Maybe she'd been a little too short with him, or seemed unappreciative. She exited the protective canopy and stepped out onto the pavement behind him.

"I'm just helping here today, and maybe the rest of the Tuesdays this summer. I actually found a local job."

Abbott turned again to face her under the quickly graying sky. A fat raindrop splattered on Farrah's arm.

"Where at?" he asked.

"At the nursing home."

"You runnin' it?" he asked, and Farrah thought maybe he was joking. But no. He was completely serious. She didn't have the right degrees to run a healthcare facility. Still, she was flattered at the compliment.

"No… I…" How could she say this? He'd be surprised however it was worded. "I'm a Certified Nursing Assistant there. I started yesterday."

His lips parted in confusion. "So a CNA," he repeated. "That's very selfless of you. I guess I just assumed… with your personality and leadership experience…"

"Yeah. Things change, I guess." Farrah shrugged. Her sudden interest in the medical profession had been a surprise to many, and Abbott, apparently, was no different.

She'd lost count of the times she'd had to explain to friends and family that she'd taken the twelve-week course route to get her licensure, and it had been a necessary job change, yada, yada, yada…

It seemed completely random, but she'd have to disclose too much to explain it to him or anybody else. She folded her arms over her chest and sighed.

The raindrops fell faster, splattering around them, foretelling a thunderstorm. The splashes were cool on Farrah's bare arms. Vendors around them scrambled to cover their goods, and shoppers scurried to their cars as the pungent scent of summer showers rose from the wet earth.

"Good for you. Hey, looks like we're about to get soaked. I'll let you take shelter. I'll see you around, Bacon," Abbott said with a nod.

She managed a squeaky, "Yeah." He turned and jogged off athletically into the humid day, and then hopped into a gray pickup truck at the other end of the parking lot.

Farrah hurried back under the canopy to help pack up their things, her dark waves clinging to her face and neck with the sudden moisture. The market was closing soon anyway, and they wouldn't have any more customers in the downpour. Her hands a bit shaky, and her heart a bit fluttery, she marveled that one interaction with her high school flame had gotten her so worked up.

"I thought he lived in Tennessee. Why didn't you tell me he was back in town?" Farrah asked her sister, raising her voice over the roar of the raindrops pelting the canopy.

Macy huffed, her face painted with confusion. "What do you mean, 'back in town'? He came back not long after college."

"How would I know that? We haven't spoken since the summer after senior year, but apparently he has heard a few things about me." Farrah rubbed her clammy face and took a few deep breaths to calm her racing heart. Seeing him had stirred up all kinds of emotions. Embarrassment. Fondness. Intrigue.

"He *has* asked me about you a few times through the years," Macy admitted, filling another crate. "Casually. Maybe just being polite."

If Farrah was honest, Abbott had crossed her mind at times too. She hadn't expected to see him on her first day in public. She knew it was inevitable at some point down the road. She'd run through scenarios of how she would greet him, what she would say, safe topics to ask about, and—

"Wow." Macy paused her frantic packing to look at Farrah, who realized she was chewing on her lip in that way she did when she was overthinking something. "You're really affected by this. I'm so sorry! Did he say something about the divorce, or—"

"No," Farrah said, cutting her off. It was true that she'd been nervous when she'd first seen him, but all in all, their interaction had gone remarkably well. What was troubling her were those old, forgotten feelings from so long ago. "There's just lots of history there, is all."

Macy clicked her tongue. "You know what I think? Your emotions are all over the place. Come to my house tonight. Hang out with the boys, and after they go to bed, we can have a girls' night. PJs, popcorn. We can even have a drink in the hot tub—the whole kit and caboodle."

"Oh, Mace. I wish I could. I'm on schedule at Glade Village tonight."

Macy hummed and her eyes grew slightly sad. "Working with Mr. Mitchell?"

"No. I wish." Farrah sighed. "I'm with Mrs. Janice.

The one that likes soap operas and cats. I'm sure I'll have some stories to tell you after."

"Ha!" Macy laughed. "Here, help me load this." She handed Farrah a cardboard tray filled with pint jars of last summer's peach jam. In just a few weeks, it would be time to can fresh batches. They had just finished canning this season's cherry jams and jellies. In their line of work, the year was measured by the peak yield of each crop instead of traditional month names.

After seeing that the weather showed no signs of clearing up, Farrah sighed and stepped out from the canopy to walk to the bed of the truck. There, she shifted crates, and the cool rain drenched her thoroughly in a matter of minutes. In the distance, the thunder rolled lazily, taking its time.

Peach jam. She couldn't see that, or peach tea, without thinking of Abbott.

As she turned to head back to the canopy for a second armful of goods, she smiled as it occurred to her that for the first time in a long time, she was not dwelling on her husband and everything that had happened.

Instead, she was thinking back to that hot, humid summer when she and Abbott were eighteen.

Part of her cringed. They had been so childish. So immature. So prone to dramatic outbursts and miscommunication, as teenagers often are.

Yet she remembered with fondness that what they'd had was real.

Chapter Two

ELEVEN YEARS AGO

Farrah's tan legs carried her down the gravel road past Bobby Bell's house so effortlessly, she might as well have been flying. She reached the hydrangeas in full bloom, their deep indigo blossoms a sign of highly acidic soil, and took a sharp left down the path that years of traversing had cleared through the woods. Oaks and mountain laurels shielded her from the scorching noonday heat as the sunlight dappled the forest path ahead of her.

Her cutoff jean shorts rubbed her inner thighs uncomfortably with every brisk stride. It would be a relief to make it to the swimming hole and shed them. A relief to feel the cool water where chafing had occurred.

After only a few minutes, the glistening creek water peeked through the trunks and low-lying shrubbery along the forest floor.

"You there?" she called breathlessly, cupping her hands on each side of her mouth and smiling, giddy.

"What took you so long?" came the reply. Abbott's voice sent a shiver through her, and she picked up momentum. She emerged from the forest on the sandy bank of

Quarry Creek and grabbed her hand-crocheted, daisy-yellow top by the bottom hem and pulled it over her head, revealing a black bandeau.

Abbott whistled from the dammed-up swimming hole. The water came up to his muscular chest. His smile was bright between two dimples, and his dark curls dripped from a recent dip in the cool mountain water.

She unbuttoned her shorts and left them lying in the sand before kicking off her sneakers and peeling off her socks.

She plonked into the water that got deep quickly and dog paddled in Abbott's direction.

"New swimsuit?" he asked.

"Yeah," she said, and made it to him, wrapping her arms around his neck, and her legs around his waist.

"I like it," he said, and their noses met.

She took the opportunity to give him a kiss he wouldn't soon forget, digging her fingers into his thick, dark hair.

"Mmm," he responded, then freed himself from her embrace and set off in a backstroke. "Let's head to the log."

She caught a quick breath and dove under the water, then advanced with a graceful dolphin kick. She emerged at the log that had fallen over the creek a few years before and where Abbott was sitting, dripping wet. He extended a strong arm to hoist her up next to him.

They sat for just a moment, catching their breath from the swim and wiping the water off their faces. Abbott handed her a thermos he had balanced on the log. She took a swig. Ice-cold peach tea. She took an extra drink, just to keep from having to talk.

It was a rare thing when Farrah didn't know how to start a conversation with Abbott. Usually, words flowed with him, one of the lucky few, yet she didn't always let him in either, especially if there was an uncomfortable topic to be avoided. And today, she feared anything they talked about would take them to the inevitable conversation they had to have.

"What's got you worried, Bacon bit?" Abbott asked, gazing down at her, his skin speckled by bright globs of sun peeking through the overhead leaves.

"You know. Same old stuff." It was safer to pretend everything was fine. Daddy always did the same thing, and he floated through life, whereas Mom let herself be guided by emotions and worries, and all of life's ups and downs.

"Your sister still having issues with her new husband?" Abbott lifted his hand from the log and circled his arm around her, resting his warm palm on her hip. He scooted closer and she leaned into him.

"Yeah, but they'll work it out. They don't believe in divorce."

Abbott scoffed. "Like, at all?"

"No. I don't either. We were raised that way. Get married and stay married."

"Huh. How 'bout that. You'd think having known you since childhood and dated you for two years, I would have known that," Abbott remarked. "Obviously not the way I was raised." Farrah smiled weakly. Abbott's parents had divorced when he was in elementary school, remarried other people, then divorced those people as well a few years back.

"I'm not worried about her marriage," Farrah admitted. "I'm just a little somber."

"*Somber?*" Abbott broke into a grin and shook his head, laughing. "I swear I feel like I'm taking one of Mrs. Richards' vocab quizzes every time you talk."

"Come on," Farrah teased, punching him lightly in the side. "You know what somber means. I'm just saying... you know… It's July twentieth. Acceptance letter deadlines are looming." She dared to make eye contact, and held it. He gave her a squeeze.

"I know, Bacon." He looked over the water, his jaw squared and tight. "Have you decided what you're going to do?"

"Kind of. Have you?"

"Well, yeah. I've known." Abbott turned to her and scrunched his brow, frustration hovering behind the gesture. "I told you the week of graduation. Knoxville. Supply chain management. I want to go into logistics at Mom's company. It was *you* that hadn't decided." Abbott huffed out an annoyed laugh.

"I know. I'm sorry. You told me. It's just a lot to think about. I guess I'm nervous and it's making me avoid the topic." She was being as truthful and open as she could be.

Abbott's face softened. "You're going to have to make a decision soon. Where all were you accepted? Come on, I know you have a plan. You always do."

"Okay," Farrah relented. "I applied to UNC Asheville, as you requested, and I did get in, but—"

"That's awesome!" Abbott interrupted, sitting up straighter and motioning with his hands. "We'll be less than two hours apart. We can see each other all the time. Meet in the middle."

"But, Abbott… I'm looking at Charlotte too. You know I want to go into business, and it's just a better option." Farrah stared at the ripples wiggling across the brown creek water where her toes barely touched. She hated disappointing others and him most of all.

Abbott's face fell. "That school is like… four hours or more away from UT."

"So?" Farrah rebuffed, annoyed that he wasn't being understanding or supportive.

"So, I *love* you. I want you as close as you can be, especially if I'm getting out of this town and starting anew in Knoxville. I want you there with me. I thought I made that clear."

"So you've got our life all planned? Our future's in Tennessee?" Farrah huffed.

Abbott's face twisted in annoyance. "What's that supposed to mean?"

Farrah grunted and clenched her fists before releasing them again. "Look, I love you too. I really do. But honestly, Abbott, I feel like I'm being dragged along on this quest of yours to patch up things with your mom." Farrah wanted to say so much more, something like, *your mom, who only ever gave you the crumbs twice a year on your birthday and Christmas.* She kept that part to herself. "I'm sorry, but I think you're going to be disappointed with what you get after all this effort."

"Look, I know you have the perfect family, and you like to compare, but this isn't about Mom," Abbott protested.

"Is it not?" Farrah raised her brows and looked at her boyfriend, her blood pressure rising to match her sudden irritation. Abbott's face mirrored what she felt. "So then why don't *you* go to school near *me?*"

"Because I didn't apply to those schools," he snapped, then sighed and wiped a hand over his mouth in an attempt at restraining his temper. "Tennessee has a great program. And yes, Mom does live in Knoxville, and I get in-state tuition. We've been over all this. How can you be so detail-oriented yet forget so much important information about me?"

"I didn't forget!" Farrah spat out. Her anger suddenly melted into sadness. When she spoke, it was quieter, defeated. "I just didn't want to think about it is all."

"We've got to face this, babe. Four-plus hours is just too far. Being close is really important to me."

"But my business degree and where I get it is really important to *me*."

"So you're basically saying you've already decided on a school that's farther away, even though I'm telling you that being that far from you would kill me. Cool." Abbott looked out over the swimming hole for a spell, then slid down into the water and held onto Farrah's knees, resting his chin on his hands there and looking up into her eyes, as serious as he could be. "What do you think it will mean for us if you don't go to Asheville? How would we make that work?"

Farrah slicked back his curls with her hand and traced his cute ear with her forefinger. "I don't know," she admitted quietly.

Abbott's gasp sounded something like a sob. "What do you mean you don't know? You're the one for me, Farrah. There's nobody else but you, and there never will be."

Farrah wished she had something comforting to say, or anything to say for that matter. The proverbial cat had gotten her tongue. She could only look at James Abbott's face and worry. Here he was, pledging his whole adult life and future to her, and yet her own dreams would have to bow to his in order for it to play out the way he intended. Still, the prospect of losing him made her stomach go into freefall.

"I can't believe this," Abbott said, grimacing. He turned and swam to shore, then put on his shoes and T-shirt before cutting through the woods toward his farm.

"Abbott!" Farrah called after him to no response.

She was sad for him. She was sad for them. But she couldn't go to Asheville just because he wanted her to. She simply liked the Charlotte school better, and being the planner she was, she had done her research. If he loved her, he'd have to understand that. He'd have to let her do her own thing and wait four years to be with her. It was the only logical solution.

But all the logic in the world couldn't stop her heart from breaking at seeing him so hurt.

Chapter Three

PRESENT DAY

‎

"Where's my cat?" Janice moaned, tucked in tightly under her heated blanket.

"He's outside," Farrah offered. It wasn't true. Janice hadn't owned a cat for years, but arguing about it with her —or arguing about anything with any dementia patient at Glade Village—would only make things more difficult. The nursing home was devoted to Alzheimer's and dementia patients, who each received the care of a dedicated CNA every afternoon until their bedtime. Mornings were spent with the doctors, nurses, group sessions, and in free time in the rec room.

"It's a girl cat," Janice said, snippy.

"Sorry, I meant to say 'she,'" Farrah said, replacing Mrs. Janice's gloves on her cold, bony fingers. No matter what Farrah did, Janice never seemed to get warm. It didn't help that she always threw off her blankets and took off her gloves.

"You know, those darn cats..." Mrs. Janice started, then trailed off, returning her attention momentarily to the soap opera on her screen. Her grandson had been sure to purchase a streaming service that had her favorite ones ready at the click of a button. She liked the handsome male actors best, often quipping to Farrah that they were finer than angel fuzz, whatever that meant. About thirty seconds went by before she finished her sentence. "It's so hard to see if a cat's a boy or a girl. I never can tell."

"Mm-hmm." Farrah smiled and nodded, tucked Mrs. Janice in for the night, and turned off her TV.

Within five minutes, Mrs. Janice was sound asleep. Farrah lowered the heated blanket to number one on the dial. Hopefully she'd stay warm. She'd leave a note for the overnight nurse to check on that. But as for Farrah, her duties with the sweet old lady were complete.

Now was her chance to do her last small tasks and stretch her legs. Maybe she could even stop by Mr. Mitchell's room.

She headed to the door and clicked on the blue light, indicating that the patient was sleeping. She pulled the door to and walked quietly down the hallway. It was going on ten o'clock at night, and she'd get off work in thirty-or-so minutes. Technically she could leave once Mrs. Janice was asleep, but she preferred to make sure everything was ready for the overnight CNAs so they didn't have to do any extra prep work.

After updating charts and restocking supply baskets for her patients, Farrah used the restroom, afterward splashing some water on her face and redoing her ponytail. Her stomach rumbled. She was starving. If she knew her mom, she'd have some amazing leftovers in the fridge, perfect for an extra late dinner.

Much as she disliked being back under her parents' roof after having experienced so much success and independence, she was grateful for the warmth, the love, and the cooking. Lots of people complained about their parents or blamed them for the way they turned out; Farrah couldn't join that club. She absolutely loved her parents, and she'd had an amazing childhood full of wonder and adventure.

She turned right at the end of the main hall and waved hello to a coworker who sat munching cookies at the nurse's desk. The hallway was long, and a fluorescent light needed to be replaced, as told by its flicker over the sterile, cool corridor.

She slowed as she approached Mr. Mitchell's door. His light was blue, as she'd expected. His CNA would have left long ago. She gently pushed the door open and tiptoed inside. Silently, she sat in the seat next to his bed, willing the former teacher to wake up and talk like he had a few days ago during her first shift at Glade Village. He had really made it a pleasant one, even if she'd spent the second part of her shift trying to calm Janice down after losing her cat. Again.

Farrah folded her hands and rested her chin on them and leaned in closer, observing Mr. Mitchell's steady breathing. She hadn't cried in months, but now, watching this entirely peaceful man in perfect rest caused tears to prick her eyes. She grabbed a tissue and buried her face in it, then blew her nose softly so as not to wake him. She pressed the tissue to the inner corners of her eyes and wept freely but as quietly as she could.

"Why are you crying, my dear?"

Farrah lifted her face, and then grabbed for Mr. Mitchell's hand. "Because I'm sad," she said, fighting against a sob.

"But why?" he asked, patting her hand with his other one. "Are you my daughter?"

"No," Farrah said, laughing.

"Then who are you?"

"I'm Farrah Macon." Farrah waited to see if there was any flicker of recognition in the older man's eyes. Nothing. "I cared for you the other day. Remember?"

Mr. Mitchell's mouth fell as he tried to recall. "I don't. But I *do* know that… that…" He looked off into the air around Farrah. Maybe he'd surprise her by recalling something—anything—about his past. In the few hours she'd spent with Janice, the woman had remembered random and specific things from her younger life that Farrah knew were true from her chart, only to forget them again moments later. She hoped Mr. Mitchell would surprise her in the same way.

Finally Mr. Mitchell finished his sentence. "I do know for a fact that I've never met you."

Farrah smiled through her tears and squeezed the hand she held. "You silly goose. I've known you for years. I wish you remembered like I do. I have a lot of memories with you."

"With me?" Mr. Mitchell asked. "Maybe you got me confused with another Mitchell. My name's Byron."

"Yes," Farrah said ruefully. "I guess that's it." Mr. Mitchell's father was named Byron, while his own name was Bryan. He switched between both names as his mind willed him to. Whatever he felt was true in the moment.

He smiled back at her and closed his eyes, removing his hands from hers and laying them over his belly, relaxed. In a minute, he was snoring. At peace. None of the confusion or irritability associated with sundowning tonight, despite the multiple IVs and tubes attached to his body, which brought him no little anxiety.

Farrah wiped away the last of her tears and silently left the room. She checked once more on Mrs. Janice, who hadn't budged. Down the hall, a patient with a different care team was starting her insomniac rants. Farrah was grateful that her patients were peaceful.

Which gave her permission to clock out and call it a night.

FARRAH WALKED in the house and set down her work bag, then kicked off her clogs. The dark blue scrubs she wore were a lot like pajamas. That was one good thing about going from gallery life to medical life—no more high heels and stiff, dressy clothing. Farrah told herself this, because it was, in fact, the only good thing about having to leave her gallery dream behind. She sighed and reminded herself that her foray into the medical field was just for a short time and that she'd chosen the unlikely path for good reasons.

"Hey," whispered Mom, descending the stairs slowly and wrapping her in a hug when she reached her. "How'd it go?"

Farrah sighed. "It was fine. As good as it can be, I guess."

"I'm proud of you," Mom said, her piercing blue eyes looking right into Farrah's soul from below her salt-and-pepper bangs. Farrah didn't want to talk about her shift or her patients. Luckily, Mom sensed that. "Come on. I know you're hungry. I have quiche."

Farrah made her way through the farmhouse's cozy front living room to the kitchen in the back, where she settled herself at the granite countertop of the island on a spinning barstool. Mom would fuss if Farrah tried to serve herself after working all day. She cut a chunk of bacon-and-spinach quiche and popped it in the microwave, stopping it early so it didn't beep. Dad was a light sleeper.

Mom served her the warm dish, then sat on the stool across from her, and Farrah dug into the savory pie. "Mmm. Is that… sun-dried tomato?" Farrah asked.

"I made them myself," Mom said, preening and sitting up straight. "Oh, with the boys here, we didn't have a chance to talk about the farmers market earlier. How did it go?"

"Great!" Farrah said, then remembered. "And maybe a little awkward."

"Uh-oh. Busybodies?" Mom asked with a scowl.

"No, thank goodness," Farrah said, eyes wide. "James Abbott was there."

Mom cocked her head in confusion. "Was that the great or the awkward part?"

"Mom, you have to remember. We dated all through high school."

"And you broke up right before college. I remember. I guess I just thought that was so far in the past, and compared to what you're going through *now*, it doesn't seem so bad."

Wow. Even hyper-emotional Mom has a better handle on forgiving the past than I do.

"He broke up with *me*. Seeing him was just so weird, even though it kind of turned out all right. I think it's all coming back to me because I didn't want the breakup."

Mom reached across the island and patted Farrah's left hand. "Yes, sweetie. Just like you didn't want the divorce."

"Exactly," Farrah admitted. She downed her last bite of quiche.

"If you really think about it, honey, those two situations are night and day. Your emotions are tied up in what you're going through now. Any little thing can set them off. Even a breakup a decade ago."

"You're starting to sound like Macy," Farrah quipped,

remembering how her sister had wanted to distract her from all her big feelings by having her over at the Gatewood house to simmer in their jacuzzi.

Mom smiled. "Well, Macy and I do think a lot alike in the emotional sense." She poured Farrah a glass of water. "Look, I know you deal better with cold, hard facts, so let me shoot straight. Abbott was your high school sweetheart. You wanted different things, so you went down different paths. I know he was kind of pushy, wanting you to derail your own plans to benefit his. But he was young, and by the way, so were *you*. You've both moved on. It's nothing worth holding on to."

The way Mom described it made it seem so cold, so distant.

So juvenile.

Farrah remembered it in a completely different way. Yes, she'd moved on in the sense that she had far bigger fish to fry these days. It had been years ago, but when she thought back to how it felt to be dumped by Abbott, those old feelings fell right back into place. The sting of betrayal. Asking herself for years—before she met Connor—if she should come home and try to run into him, if she should call. Pulling his number up on her phone and almost clicking that green call button. Searching for him on social media and coming up empty—he was one of those who had opened an Instagram account in college but stopped posting after graduation.

She'd dreamed about being in his arms and thought often about what he might be doing, who he might be with. When Connor asked her out on their first date, it was her excuse to stop wallowing. And Abbott had never reached out. So why should she give up a date with a wealthy, successful man for a boy who had never bothered?

But maybe Mom's way of remembering it was also

Abbott's. Maybe everyone saw it that way: young love ending as it often does.

Embarrassment coursed through Farrah, and her cheeks grew warm. Could he sense that she was feeling all those things when they'd talked at the farmers market? Would he have felt them too?

Surely not. He'd probably have a viewpoint more similar to Mom's. Years ago, long forgotten, who even is that chick? He was probably at home laughing about running into Farrah with some gorgeous, young thing under his arm. He'd never married, but he was far too handsome to be single. Mom said he'd moved on. She wondered what she meant by that and longed to ask. But she pushed that desire deep down. She shouldn't care about Abbott at all. She needed to focus on her problems in the present.

"Thanks for the quiche, Mom," Farrah said, as she stood and kissed her mom's head before setting the plate in the sink. Dad would wake up with the clanging if she went about washing it now. She'd get to it in the morning. "I'm turning in. I think I'll visit Bobby and Amy tomorrow."

Mom's face lit up. "Oh, that's wonderful. I know they'll love that. You know about their situation?"

"Yeah," Farrah said, nodding. "She told me about it this morning."

"It's a crying shame. I hate to see people in their sixties put out like that, and over something they can't control."

"I know," Farrah agreed. "But maybe there's still a way. Time will tell."

Farrah turned and headed toward the stairs to tiptoe up to her room and crash.

"Farrah," Mom whisper-yelled from the kitchen island. "I'm sorry if I seemed a bit harsh about Abbott. You're allowed to feel what you feel."

"No, Mom," Farrah said, pawing a hand through the air to dismiss the issue. "You're right. It was a long time ago. And my emotions are fried."

Farrah turned to head up the stairs, but stopped, remembering something. "Mom, would you mind calling Amy to let her know the gist of what happened before I go see them? I don't think I can handle it."

Mom nodded with sad eyes. "Of course, honey. I'll do that tomorrow morning."

She offered Mom a smile and retreated to her childhood bedroom, exhausted. It was the same bedroom where she'd attempted, so many years ago, to make a mature decision about her relationship with Abbott. She'd been willing to compromise.

But for Abbott, like watering a long-dead houseplant, it had been too little too late.

Chapter Four
ELEVEN YEARS AGO

Farrah sat on her bed with her college acceptance letters lying before her. The setting sun painted her room a pinkish gold. Normally, she'd lie there and admire it. But tonight she had a decision to make. The deadline for communicating her enrollment to whatever university she chose was August first, only one short week away. Then in mid-August, she'd have to move to the city of her choosing. She was down to the wire. It was a lot to prepare for, and she was ready to get started.

It just didn't feel right to make this decision without Abbott.

She had half expected a nighttime visit from him on the day they'd argued at Quarry Creek. She needed to apologize—bringing up his mom was a bit of a low blow. It was a sore spot for him, and she could have handled that differently.

But she was still confused by their interaction that day. He'd pretty much demanded she do things his way and plan on building a life with him in Tennessee. While his commitment to her was reassuring, couldn't he see that she had other dreams to fulfill and paths to explore before setting her life plans in stone?

She'd sat out on her porch swing the night of their fight until long after Mom and Daddy had gone to bed. She'd waited until the lightning bugs were the only luminous things she could see. He never came. It was just her and the faithful buzz of far-off cicadas. She'd called it a night, certain he'd call the next day.

But he hadn't.

And a full four days had gone by like that.

Stubborn as she was, she wasn't willing to be the first one to cave in and call, though she did take longer-than-normal walks past the Bells' property and onto Abbott Ranch. When she saw Abbott's truck wasn't there, she'd circle through the woods and take a dip in Quarry Creek. But it didn't feel as sweet without him to swim with or talk to. If a silence of only a few days was this painful, she couldn't imagine four years.

She needed to make her choice.

UNC Charlotte, of course, was at the top of her list. She'd wanted to go there for undergraduate and then perhaps onto their MBA program, which was unrivaled. She still didn't understand what would be so bad about being four hours away from Abbott. They could still see each other a few times a year, on longer breaks from school. He acted like there was no way they could be together if they lived more than an hour and forty-five minutes apart.

His demands were unfair.

Then she remembered his face, twisted in hurt, as he forced a T-shirt over his wet chest and cut through the woods. He hadn't expected what she'd said, that she was considering another school. It hadn't been on his radar that she was willing to be far away from him. He'd already decided she should try to be close.

When he asked her what would happen to their relationship if she chose to go to a school that was farther away, she'd said she didn't know because she didn't. But did he? Could anyone know such a thing? They were eighteen years old, for heaven's sake. They were in no way ready to settle down and get serious.

But maybe Abbott was. Maybe what she saw as him being unreasonable and demanding was really him trying to build a future with her. Farrah grunted and planted her face in her hands. She had so much to accomplish before she got… well… *boring*.

She turned her attention again to her college acceptance letters. Similar, yet each leading to a different path. Just for this moment, Farrah needed to forget her feelings and focus on the facts.

How to choose between UNC Asheville and UNC Charlotte? She had her heart set on UNCC for sure, but could she study undergraduate business at Asheville first and then pursue the potential MBA at Charlotte?

Well, yes. She could. They had a good program. Of course, the professors she'd met and been inspired by on her field trip to Charlotte wouldn't be at UNCA. But on the other hand, she wouldn't lose the boy she loved.

Maybe she *was* being too stubborn.

If her being far from Abbott was a dealbreaker for him, Farrah wasn't willing to risk it. Her love for Abbott was both a feeling and a fact. It had to be included in the equation.

She couldn't just throw him away.

As usual, she had kept her college plans from him until the last minute, which had probably made him feel unimportant.

She took the letters and laid Asheville's on top.

She'd go there and stay in a relationship with Abbott. He mattered to her. She didn't want to envision her life without him. So she was willing to take a different road if it made him happy. All this, of course, if he was open to the idea of her pursuing her master's in Charlotte in the future, if she wanted to when that time came. Abbott was all about meeting in the middle, and she hoped he'd support her if she did her part during their bachelor degree years.

He needed to know all of this. She picked up the phone and dialed his home number, since he didn't currently have a cell. Abbott's first cell phone had been lost at a Friday night football game, and the second was chewed up and spit out by his standing lawnmower. His dad had refused to buy him a third one, saying Abbott would have to save up the money himself.

After a few rings, Abbott's dad, Jim, picked up. "Abbott Ranch," he said briskly. He'd probably been in the middle of something. She'd be brief.

"Hey, it's Farrah. Is Abbott around?"

"He didn't tell you? He's been in Knoxville a few days."

Farrah's heart started hard. "Did he already move?"

"Shoot, no!" Jim laughed, and Farrah exhaled. "Just visiting his momma. He's coming back tonight, last I heard. I think he said something about getting in late after the movies, but I'm not sure if he was going to an afternoon movie there or one here."

Well, it was a lead. Farrah's stomach swirled with nerves. She missed him. Her head was light with longing. "Thank you, Jim. Hey, don't tell him I called. Okay?"

"You got it, hun."

A click from his end finished the call, and Farrah

jumped up with a newfound determination. She kicked off her pajama bottoms and replaced them with a pair of jeans; her PJ tank top could double as a going out shirt, lacy and fitted as it was. After sliding on some sandals, she flew down the stairs, calling to her mom that she was going to the movies.

Dad's rusty old Bronco cranked on the first try, and she let out a relieved laugh. "Good girl!" she said, and patted the dash. In no time, she was barreling down the gravel road toward town.

It was busy on Main Street in downtown Whitetail Ridge that night, the long strip flanked with sidewalks and picturesque storefronts showcasing everything from hairdressers to antique shops to bakeries and boutiques. She drove along slowly in the evening dim, switching on her headlights to find a parallel spot to park; most of them had already been taken. As fate would have it, there was a spot right behind a red Tacoma she knew all too well. Abbott was definitely inside the theater, probably buying tickets or refreshments for the nine o'clock showing. If she hurried, she could surprise him.

She folded down her mirror and took a look at her face. The sun had invited freckles all along her nose and cheeks. She checked her teeth and when she saw that everything was fine, she grabbed the keys and a ten-dollar bill and hopped out of the old clunker, making her way directly to the 1930s Beryl Theatre.

She jogged up the sidewalk to the theater's entrance but stopped short just in front of its large glass windows. Inside, the orange glow of overhead lamps illuminated the crowd purchasing their snacks. Abbott was right there. She knew it was him, even if she could only see his broad back and dark, curly head from behind. He was so close that if he turned around, he'd see her.

The crowd shifted a bit, and it became obvious that Abbott was not alone. She caught a glimpse of his profile as he waited. She knew him enough to recognize that he was not at ease. The anxiety of their situation had not yet left him.

But that didn't change the fact that there was a curvy blonde girl standing next to him. *With* him. A girl she recognized as a cheerleader from their school.

After they'd secured their popcorn and drinks, they walked into the theater, his hand lightly guiding her on her back.

Farrah shook under the adrenaline of the discovery. Not wanting to be embarrassed by being seen by friends, she headed straight back to the Bronco with a face wiped clean of emotion.

She drove directly home, but she didn't go inside. She couldn't bear to face Mom or anyone. Her broken heart stung within her.

She sat on her porch stoop, so paralyzed by the betrayal, she probably wasn't even blinking.

Hours went by. The house lights flicked off. She could have gone in without being questioned, but she just couldn't move.

Soon, the shifting beams of headlights worked their way through the woods along her driveway before emerging from the trees and blinding her where she sat on the porch. The visitor parked and killed the engine, resulting in a placid quiet, broken only by multitudes of Appalachian insects, and the crunch of boots on gravel.

As the brightly colored spots faded from her vision, she confirmed what she already knew. Abbott was there. At once, she longed to hold him and yell at him.

He walked to within four feet of her and stopped. She couldn't make out his face in the darkness. But the soft voice he used to talk on quiet nights was the same as always.

"I've been doing a lot of thinking," he said, handing her a folded piece of paper. "I wrote it all down. I know you like lists."

"Abbott—"

"No, Farrah, listen. I don't want to hold you back. It's obvious that you have plans… apart from me."

"Forget the long-distance thing! I'll go to Asheville. I had already decided to. I called your home phone today to tell you." Farrah surprised herself by crying hot, fast tears.

"It's not all about the distance. It's the fact that you can't let me in. You hold me at arm's length. You refuse to plan with me for the long haul. You refuse to face challenges with me. Meanwhile, I… I *love* you, Farrah. I want to marry you, have kids with you. I want it all. With *you*. But if you don't feel the same way, there's no use wasting our time."

The words hit her like a truck on the highway. Her suppositions proved true. He wanted to settle down and she wasn't ready. She'd never told him this, but somehow he had picked up on the vibe.

Then Farrah grunted in frustration that she was pining over a boy who had apparently already moved on. "I just saw you with that cheerleader girl—Jincey. I went to the movies to surprise you. But you were there with her."

Abbott's silence was thick and telling. When he finally spoke, it was quiet, restrained. "That was a mistake," he said sheepishly. "I asked her out on a whim right after we fought. I thought I'd keep my word to her—she's a sweet girl—but after just a few minutes on our date I knew it wasn't going anywhere."

"Sweet? Am I supposed to be relieved by that?" Farrah

balked. "We weren't even broken up. I've been waiting around hoping to hear from you for four days—"

"You could've called too," Abbott interrupted. "You're the one that made it clear you're not in this like I am."

"I *am* in this. You know I love you," Farrah protested.

"You say it, but I'm not so sure."

Farrah was suddenly speechless when faced with Abbott's distrust. She stared up at him, her eyes now adjusted enough to see him somewhat despite the darkness.

"It's okay." Abbott huffed out a laugh. "I guess in the end these fights have shown us what we both really need. You need the freedom to do what you want. And I guess… Well, I don't know what I need. But I do know that I won't force you to keep a commitment to me when you aren't there yet." He took two steps toward Farrah and extended his hand. She placed hers in it. His was rough to the touch and warm. She wished he'd tell her he didn't mean it, pull her up to him, kiss her.

But he didn't.

He just looked at her, his face shrouded in the mystery of night's shadow. A sniffle made her think perhaps he was crying, but his voice was melodic. Steady.

"I know you'll be all right," he said. He lifted her hand to his mouth and gave it a quick kiss. Farrah guessed he was trying to be sweet, but the effect of the kiss was more like a dagger to her heart. This might be the last contact his lips had with her skin.

"Goodbye, Farrah."

Abbott turned and headed for his truck.

Farrah couldn't bear to see him go. As he cranked his engine and the jarring brightness of his headlights filled the space around her, she shot up from the porch stoop and opened her front door, then closed it quickly behind her before running upstairs to her room.

She tossed the unopened list he'd written her on her desk and crashed onto her bed. If only she had been more open with him, not leaving her worries about her college plans undiscussed until the last minute, and then doing a poor job of talking about it. He was right: she was in no way ready to promise things that would affect her entire adult life. But she also didn't want to lose what they had. Theirs was a once-in-a-lifetime type love.

Burying her head in her pillow, she had a good, long cry. Then she lay dumbfounded, staring at her ceiling until two or three in the morning.

Chapter Five

The walk to Bobby and Amy Bell's home seemed a lot different a decade later. It was longer and hotter, despite it being only ten o'clock in the morning. In Farrah's childhood years, she and Macy would have skipped or sprinted there in no time, probably holding hands, their ponytails swinging with each brisk stride.

But with less energy than she'd had back then and an achy knee that suspiciously appeared a few days after her twenty-eighth birthday, Farrah took as much time as she needed to walk along the gravel road, admiring the mimosa branches that reached toward her, beckoning her touch. But she didn't. If she reached, they'd only shy away, folding their leaves up tight against their stalks, shielding the beauty she now appreciated.

Connor had told her *mimosa* meant spoiled or whiny in Spain. How he'd come to know that, she had no idea. Their marriage was so short that she hadn't had time to fully figure him out. Indeed, it had been way too brief. And now it was over.

At the end of the Bells' gravel driveway, Farrah crested

the green, grassy hill that comprised their front yard. She followed a row of mossy stepping stones that took her straight to their cabin-style home's front door. She knocked a few times, and Amy wasted no time opening up. Her grin spread warmly across her face.

"Were you expecting me?" Farrah asked, falling into Amy's hug.

"Oh, your mom might have called to make sure I'd be home." Amy released her and winked.

Farrah stepped into the dining room, where Amy's teacup collection in the curio cabinet always impressed her. She made her way to Bobby, who stood smiling ear-to-ear at the head of the table.

At her first glimpse of his face, she struggled against a ragged breath. He had aged, naturally. His hair was now mostly white, and wrinkles adorned his forehead and eyes. But beyond the normal signs of wear and tear, a whitened web of healed scars from medical procedures blanketed his cheeks, lips, and chin. A few deep pockmarks where tissue had been extracted were now the color of his flesh but not at all natural-looking. Poor Bobby. The treatment must have been something else.

"Thanks for coming, kiddo. I know I ain't as pretty as I used to be."

Farrah gifted him a hug, fighting against the sadness of seeing his new permanent appearance.

"Let's have some coffee, shall we?" Amy said, always ready to serve, with the pot in her hand. She poured them each a cup as Farrah chose the seat next to Bobby.

"And one of the… You know." Bobby sat and waggled his finger in the direction of the kitchen.

"Oh, yeah," Amy said, then chuckled.

She returned with a fudgesicle and slid it onto Farrah's saucer.

Amy sat across from Farrah and they all three smiled, remembering.

"Thank you," Farrah said as she tore off the paper and bit off a chunk of the rich, frozen treat. "Some of my happiest childhood memories were eating ice cream while watching you tinker with the whole town's tractors."

"I always thought you two were bored to death," Bobby admitted, eyes glassy.

"No way," Farrah reassured him. "I cherish those memories." She wrapped her cloth napkin around the bottom of the fudgesicle so it wouldn't drip inside the warm cabin. Amy must not have turned on the air-conditioning. Perhaps they were trying to save every penny they could. "I'm sorry I haven't reached out a lot in the past few years, other than a card here and there. I don't really know what got into me."

Bobby and Amy smiled knowingly.

"Love got into you," Bobby offered. Amy touched his hand and gave him a look. They'd obviously gotten Mom's call, and had planned on avoiding Farrah's divorce and the aftermath in conversation.

But Farrah still appreciated his suggestion. Love had, in fact, distracted her from her roots. She'd built a new life. A different life. One she'd loved just as much as growing up in Whitetail Ridge. But it was still no excuse for not calling or visiting much in the years since she'd graduated. Especially people who had cared about her like Amy and Bobby. She had avoided her hometown due to busyness, yes, but also as a way to burn all bridges that led to where she and Abbott spent their younger years in love.

"I'm seeing things differently now," Farrah said. "I want to be involved again."

Amy perked up. "Well, you *are*. You're back at the

market and working hard from what I hear at Glade Village with Mrs. Janice, and—"

"Yeah, all that's true," Farrah interrupted. She didn't want to talk about her current life. She wanted the focus to be on their home, where she sat chatting over coffee as the warm morning rays filtered in through the dining room's picture window. Through the panes, colorful forest birds sat perched on the feeder, eating with frenzy. "But I want to do my part to help my community personally, not just professionally. I'm wondering if there's anything I can do to help you tackle your medical debt."

Bobby laughed. "Got any piles of money lying around?"

Farrah mirrored his mirthful smile. "I wish. Really, though. Maybe I could do something. As a community, we've helped others before. Do you remember when the flooding happened, and we all helped the Abbotts repair their washed-out drive?" Abbott's stubbly face and dimples flashed through Farrah's mind. She shook the image away. If the Bells noticed, they didn't let it show.

"Yeah?" Bobby said. "But I got too much pride, I guess, to let anyone pay my own debts."

"But they're not really debts," Farrah pushed back. "It's not like you went on a credit card shopping spree at your local outdoors store, or bought a new car you can't afford, or had elective plastic surgery. You owe money because you were sick, and your medicine was expensive. You had no choice: you either lost your life or accrued debt."

Amy shook her head in confusion as she laced her fingers with Bobby's. "What are you trying to say?"

"I'm saying I think the people of Whitetail Ridge might be willing to help somehow. I've seen and interacted with lots of people since coming back, both at the market and in town. Several of them have mentioned your predicament in casual conversation as we're catching up, Maxine and Joe, just to name a few. I think the general feeling is that we hate to see you lose your house, land, and everything you've loved for so long."

Bobby's cheeks reddened. "It won't be that bad." He looked over at Amy. "It'll be like when we lived in an apartment when we were first married."

Amy nodded warmly to Bobby in response, then turned to Farrah. "I know it seems like people are concerned, and we even had another person come to us with a fundraising idea one time, but I sent her away."

"But why?" Farrah asked.

"Because, honey. Everyone deals with hardships. Why should we bring everyone else into ours?"

Amy had a point. But Farrah couldn't let it go. "We have to try something. I'm not saying apartment living is bad—people do that all the time! But think about it: the apartment units in town are all two stories or above businesses and have stairs. How are you going to walk up all those steps with your bad ankle, Amy?"

Amy raised her brows and nodded, comprehending instantly what Farrah was saying.

Farrah went on. "You two have loved this home for your whole lives. How long have you lived here?"

"Forty-one years," Bobby croaked. A lone tear trickled down his cheek and he fought against a sob. Amy rubbed his back in sympathy.

"Forever," Amy admitted quietly. "We'd hate to leave it."

"Exactly," Farrah said. "And you shouldn't have to. I'm going to think of a way. I promise. At least let me try."

Bobby and Amy looked at each other with glistening eyes and tight lips. Bobby gave the first, sad nod, then Amy nodded more emphatically. "Okay. All right." She broke into a smile. "I guess I'll cancel the meeting with the realtor next week."

"I'm so glad to hear this," Farrah said. "I'll start thinking of something we can do. Maybe a spaghetti supper benefit?"

Amy and Bobby laughed softly together. Then Bobby cleared his throat. "That was the exact idea that was brought to us before. I think you might be underestimating how much we owe. You'd have to cook a whole lot of spaghetti."

"Oh, goodness," Farrah said. "How much debt are we talking?"

"One hundred and ninety thousand dollars," Amy said, eyes wide, apparently still unable to believe it herself. "Give or take. Thousands of people live in town, but even if we sold half of them a plate of spaghetti—which, realistically, we wouldn't—and made a few dollars' profit on each—"

"It still wouldn't be nearly enough," Farrah said, finishing her sentence as she realized the numbers didn't add up. "Plus, cooking that much is a ton of work. We need something more passive to generate income." Farrah looked down at her empty fudgesicle stick. She set it on her gold-bordered saucer and dabbed at the corners of her mouth before taking a sip of her coffee. Amy and Bobby also sipped and thought.

"Wait," Bobby said as he replaced his cup on his saucer. "How did we fund the driveway project for the Abbotts? Do you remember, Ames?"

"It was twenty years or so ago. But I'm fairly certain we held an auction."

"No, that don't sound right," Bobby said, swiping his hand through the air in dismissal.

"No, no! It *was* an auction. Don't you remember? People in the community donated items to sell. Mrs. Janice gave her bedroom furniture set; I remember that."

Bobby's face lit up. "Come to think of it, I think you're right!" They both turned to Farrah. "Do you think something like that could happen again? I mean, it's not like we overuse the auction tactic if it's been two decades. There *have* been numerous spaghetti suppers and carwashes and bake sales for other smaller needs, and everyone always shows up in good numbers for those."

Farrah couldn't help but chuckle. Her wheels were turning, and her brain rushed with positive endorphins at being able to plan and organize something. "I'm thinking rather than an auction, we have a raffle basket."

Amy's face sobered slightly. "A *basket*?"

"Yeah," Farrah said. "Like the ones we used to do at the farmers market stand every year before I went to college. Customers would buy a ticket for about five dollars and the winner would get the basket, full of goods worth up to two hundred, and the second-place winner got a fifty-dollar cash prize."

"We'd have to sell to everybody in this town and all the surrounding towns to even hope to make a profit."

"Or we could make it no ordinary basket—actually not a basket at all. What about a group of goods and services donated by people in town for your benefit? The biggest raffle *basket* ever," Farrah said, doing air quotes with her fingers as she said the word *basket*, "which means we could charge way more per ticket, due to the value. My computer from back then crashed, but I'm pretty sure I have a lot of papers and such in my room from the Macon Farms' raffles. They won't be a perfect match to what was on the hard drive, but it'll be a great place to start."

"You were the only teenager I knew with a filing

cabinet in their room, even in the so-called 'digital age,'" Amy said with an amused eye roll. "But, again, I wonder why the townspeople would even want to help us."

Farrah smiled tenderly and reached across the table, taking both of their hands in hers. "Amy, you've cut half the town's hair for decades and kept their secrets and empathized with their stories. And, Bobby, you kept this community's tractors and lawnmowers up and running for generations. You guys are the treasures of the town. It's time for us to give back in your time of need."

Bobby and Amy both teared up again.

"Thank you, Farrah," Amy managed.

"It's the least I can do." Farrah released their hands and stood. "I'll call you after I look through those files. Maybe I can get some ideas and remember how we did things back then. We can start there."

After quick hugs, Farrah set out for home along the gravel road.

Behind her, a vehicle crunched slowly on the rocky drive. Farrah moved over to the far left to leave room for the car. But instead of driving past, it braked.

She glanced over to see it was a familiar charcoal gray truck with its window down. Abbott's left arm hung out the driver's side window, his dark green T-shirt taut across his thick chest.

Her voice seemed stuck in her throat.

Embarrassingly, they both said, "Hey," at the same time.

Oh, gosh.

Farrah's gaze darted to her feet. Luckily, Abbott picked up the conversation.

"Need a ride?"

She glanced up at him. His cheeks were rosy under his

baseball cap, either from some work under the sun, or maybe from the same intrigue she now felt about him.

A ride. So tempting. She had some things she wanted to know… a few things she'd like to ask him.

But her logic quickly kicked in. With everything going on, the last thing she needed was to mix up her emotions, and hanging out with her first serious boyfriend might do just that.

"Thanks, but I think I'll walk."

Abbott smiled, eyes kind but noticeably dejected. "Maybe some other time then."

"Yeah, maybe," she said, making her best attempt to force her face into a neutral expression, though all her senses were heightened as she interacted with this person who was once so special to her. She wondered how different he was from the teen boy she used to know.

"Bye, Bacon," Abbott said, pressing the accelerator, his truck growling down the road, rustling up a little dust that promptly settled.

His truck advanced into the distance as she continued her mile walk home, her mind hashing out the morning, both with the Bells and seeing Abbott.

She was energized at the prospect of helping the Bells. She hadn't had something positive to work toward for so long, and she was beyond excited to talk to Daddy about her plans.

About halfway through her walk, she realized with delight that she was running.

"I FOUND IT!" Daddy exclaimed from his spot at the head of the kitchen table. Papers and folders from files they had collected through the years were strewn across the table's surface. Farrah was overjoyed he'd located the raffle basket folder, but she also couldn't believe they'd kept it for that long. They'd stopped doing the baskets years ago when the Macon daughters became too busy with college, marriage, and career.

"Awesome! Good job!" Farrah said. "Here, I'll trade you this." She'd found a picture of him with a full head of brown hair and cutoff jean shorts, probably from sometime in the early 2000s. "You really were a looker."

Daddy smiled sheepishly and grabbed the photo. "Too bad my hair didn't stick around."

Mom came up behind him with a tray and kissed his shiny bald head. "You're still a hottie," she said, and set the tray in the middle of the table on the only spot not covered with documents. She'd made chicken salad croissants and opened a bag of Farrah's favorite kettle corn. She sat on the bench next to her daughter. "Farrah, I think this raffle basket is an awesome idea. I just wonder how it will work."

"Don't worry, Barbara. Farrah and I hashed out the details in only a few minutes."

"Is that so? Do tell." Mom's impish smirk showed her amusement at her business-minded husband and daughter. She unstacked three glasses from the tray and poured lemonade in each.

"The things donated will be goods or services like cleaning, or memberships to various places, or meals at restaurants. You know, the typical things that gift cards or gift certificates represent," Farrah explained as she grabbed a croissant and then paused to take a bite, savoring the slight tang of the cranberries. "We plan on displaying the raffle basket at the farmers market on Tuesdays to build hype, so we want it to be visually pleasing and exciting—not just a stack of gift cards in an envelope. So the question became, how do we make a bunch of gift certificates sitting in a basket interesting to people walking by?"

"Exactly. How do you?" Mom asked.

Farrah went on. "Like this." She held up a paper doll she'd made in her childhood years that she'd kept in a memory box. It was a drawing she'd done by hand on thick paper and pasted on cardboard, then cut out. The result was a two-dimensional yet sturdy drawing that could be dressed and stood on its feet.

"I'll make something like this to visually represent each item in the basket to draw attention as we display it. Also, if a physical item is too big to fit, or too valuable to display in public, I can make a symbol for that too and safeguard the real items for the winner on the day of the drawing. Of course, I won't be drawing the symbols with crayons like this one. During my time at the gallery, I had to do lots of marketing and labeling. I have software I'll use to design each symbolic item, and I can print them and attach them to a foam board for cutting out."

Daddy piped in, just as excited as Farrah. "With my jigsaw, I can cut anything. Farrah will make sure each design's edges are smooth, so the cutting isn't too tedious for these old hands."

"So it'll be a literal basket full of symbols that show what items and gift cards the winner will receive," Mom remarked. "It's a great plan. Now all we've got to do is get the word out about it so we can start to raise money."

Mom and Daddy began to eat their lunch while Farrah multitasked, eating and going through the file labeled "Annual Raffle Baskets." Sheets of ticket templates were up front, which she could reference to create the new ones in Google Docs, as well as a few documents where Daddy had tallied up expenses and income from the project.

In the past, since the raffles were for Macon Farms'

profit instead of for those in need, they hadn't asked for donations but purchased the items from local businesses, and then raffled off the basket. The girls usually made a good amount of money off the project, but more importantly, it made the community happy and brought a lively energy of anticipation to the farmers market every summer. After years of going without a Macon Farms raffle, it seemed like the perfect time to bring back a new version of an old Whitetail Ridge tradition, and this time it was for a good cause.

After Farrah flipped past the first financial documents and templates, she thought she'd landed on a list of basket items and pulled it out, skimming the first few lines.

1. Abbott Ranch has been in my family for generations, but as you know, it's not where I see myself right now. Studying at Knoxville is something I have to do...

Farrah's heartbeat picked up speed. She'd stumbled upon a list, all right. The list Abbott had handed her the night he broke up with her.

The list she'd misplaced and never gotten a chance to read.

She or someone in her family had opened it and seen the first two words and must have assumed it was a list of things for the baskets, filing it away for a decade, plus some. She and Daddy were too meticulous to do something like that. It must've been Mom or Macy, who sometimes rushed through mundane tasks in order to get them done quicker. Farrah thought back to the last time they'd done the baskets.

It had been the same summer Abbott broke her heart.

"Find something?" Daddy asked, perking his head up, mouth full of Mom's delicious cooking.

"Yeah," Farrah said. "But it's not a vendor list." She folded Abbott's letter and placed it in her back pocket. She tried to act normal and camouflage her somewhat flustered state. The list had taken her back in an instant to the time Abbott ended things between them, and she thought of all the decisions and changes she'd made right after.

Daddy and Mom were looking at her from across the table, concern in their expressions.

"It's nothing," Farrah reassured them. "I'll keep looking."

Chapter Six

ELEVEN YEARS AGO

❧

Farrah wasn't quite spiraling, but her behavior probably belonged in the same family.

After Abbott broke her heart, Farrah chopped off her long brown ponytail, which Amy Bell, her lifelong hairdresser, reshaped into a piecey bob, complete with caramel-colored highlights. She then went to the drug store in downtown Whitetail Ridge and bought her first tube of mascara. When choosing between a neutral or bright lipstick, she opted for the "Hot-Pink Peony" shade. A trip to the town's high-end consignment shop got her a new-with-tags blue sundress for a third of the original price. She never wore dresses.

But today she would. Because now she was different. A new life awaited her.

Hoping to cure the emptiness she was constantly aware of despite her forced optimism, she packed away all of her memories with Abbott—the physical ones were placed in an old shoebox labeled "Do Not Read," and the mental ones were blacked out. She was good at that.

Last but not least, Farrah sent her acceptance letter to

UNC Charlotte and enrolled in their undergraduate program with a major in business and a minor in art history.

Her nineteenth birthday in early August came and went. She spent it plastering a fake smile on her face as her family gathered around her so she could blow out her candles. All she wished for was a great first semester at college. She fought not to let her thoughts float back to Abbott through a birthday wish. His birthday was only four days before hers and they had almost always found a way to celebrate together. She was hiding her emotions from herself and the whole world, and her family was none the wiser. Though she did wonder if he was thinking about her like she was trying not to think about him.

The second week of August saw Farrah and her parents setting up her dorm at UNCC, a 1980s concrete structure with linoleum floors and wooden bunk beds. Inside, Mom had left tokens from home to make it look more appealing. One of her late grandmother's quilts served as her comforter, and in lieu of a poster, Mom had blown up a black-and-white photograph of their family in front of their white farmhouse and stuck it to the wall with adhesive strips.

"Just so you never forget where you came from."

With a few hugs goodbye, her teary-eyed parents left the dorm and headed home, and Farrah collapsed on her bed, alone.

She hoped to have company soon. She'd busied herself since the breakup to avoid thinking about it. When she was alone, the thoughts threatened her resolve the most.

She distracted herself by doing a quick internet search about local businesses. She'd need a job if she hoped to afford any fun this semester. Financial aid had helped a bit, but Mom and Daddy couldn't give her what other parents probably gave their kids to spend, and she understood that. Luckily, she didn't have to go into debt, but her budget would be tight if she didn't find some sort of income.

About twenty minutes into her search, the doorknob jiggled and jolted as someone tried their key. When the door flew open, a tall young woman with a bright smile and coily black hair gave Farrah an excited hello. Of course, she knew who it was: her roommate. They'd been put in contact by the housing office and had exchanged several emails in the past few weeks to determine who would bring the fridge, the microwave, the TV, etc.

"You must be Kia!" Farrah beamed and extended her hand. "Are we supposed to shake hands in this situation?" Farrah laughed, a bit embarrassed. Kia set the duffel bag she carried on the floor and shook Farrah's hand firmly.

"Honestly, I don't know. I've never been in this scenario before either."

Kia's dad appeared in the doorway, struggling under a heavy storage tote. Farrah could see where Kia got her height and hair from. Her mom followed soon after, carrying a trash bag full of bedding and set it on Kia's bunk. Her wispy gray hair was pushed back with a beaded headband, and she wore a flowy, multicolored dress—she was highly eclectic, and her apparel stood in stark contrast to Kia's athleticwear. They introduced themselves, the dad and mom being Keith and Ginny.

"This room needs soul," Ginny remarked, sweeping her arms across the space. "It looks like a concrete cage. Except for that beautiful quilt. Is it an authentic Southern craft?"

Farrah giggled. Grandma Netty had stitched it by hand, probably in the 1970s. "It's as authentic as they come. I'm from a small town in the foothills. My grandma made it."

Ginny clasped her hands together and sang out her response. "Oh, how wonderful."

"Don't mind my mom," Kia said with a smirk. "She's an artist. It's a lot at first, but you learn to appreciate it after a while. As for me, I'm an athlete."

Farrah liked them all immediately. "You're here on a sports scholarship, you said, right? What's your major?"

"Yeah! I'm on the basketball team. And I'm doing exercise science for now. What about you?"

"Business and art history."

Keith's face lit up. "Just like me!"

"No kidding," Farrah chirped, surprised. "What did you end up doing with your degree, if you don't mind my asking? Because that's something I haven't figured out."

"*Degrees*," he corrected, but humbly. "I went on to get my masters in art history and taught here at UNCC for years. I'm retired now." Farrah had gathered that Kia's parents were a bit older. Well, much older. Keith went on. "Teaching here was how I met Ginny."

"My pieces were in an exhibit," Ginny started excitedly, as she stepped up beside Keith and took his arm, like they were still young lovers. "I usually go to all of the artist meet and greets I'm invited to. So I went, and lo and behold, Professor Ambrose was there!"

Kia shielded her eyes with her hand in embarrassment, but Keith continued the story. "I was particularly drawn to her use of tribal-looking elements in one particular painting, since my father is from Nigeria. I asked her about it—"

"And the rest is *art* history!" Ginny chortled. "Just when I thought I wouldn't meet anyone. I was forty-three the night he swept me off my feet." Ginny and Keith exchanged a loving look, beaming at each other. For just a moment their lovestruck faces made Farrah forget the sting of being dumped.

"Don't let them weird you out," Kia said. "They're actually pretty normal once you get to know them."

Farrah smiled at Kia, but she wasn't weirded out at all. Still, she understood Kia's embarrassment. Sometimes Farrah's parents grated on her nerves and acted uncool, even if her friends weren't bothered by their behavior. It was probably a universal experience for teens.

"No, it's fine, really. It's an awesome story. I hope to find someone like that someday."

Ginny brightened as if something had just occurred to her. "Kia, you should bring Farrah to my exhibition reception tonight. That is, if she's not doing anything."

All eyes turned to Farrah. "Oh, gosh. I'd love to. We still have a week before classes start, so there's nothing urgent for me to do tonight."

"Excellent!" Keith said. "It's the Oberg Gallery on Johannes Street. Casual dress. What you've got on is fine."

Ginny turned to Kia. "But you could switch out the basketball shorts for some jeans."

"Okay, *bye* guys!" Kia mock-pushed her parents out of the dorm with Ginny laughingly protesting the whole way.

FARRAH AND KIA had sampled all the refreshments and looked at all the paintings, but their reactions to everything were starkly different. Farrah could not shake the wonder of the gallery and its seemingly immaculate organization, all with the end result of visitors experiencing beauty. Kia, on the other hand, was much more interested in the prawns and cheese board.

Farrah sipped her complimentary lemonade in the

dark and moody main room of the Oberg. Industrial steel beams, painted black, loomed overhead. A polished concrete floor underneath gave the whole space an urban feel, not to mention the seemingly handcrafted bricks of varying shades with thick, coarse mortar. Farrah loved every aspect of the building. She especially loved the contrast of the rustic brick walls behind the Impressionist and romantic landscape paintings, rich in color and nuance, each illuminated with its own overhead sconce.

"How did your mom get into a place like this?"

Kia smirked and downed the last of her shrimp cocktail. With a mouth half full, she said, "Kinda easy when you're part owner."

Farrah was surprised. Ginny must've really been a big deal in the art scene. Important enough to own stakes in a gallery. She made a note on her phone to look her up later.

As if summoned, Ginny sauntered over with her glass of red.

"Did you enjoy yourself, Farrah?"

"More than enjoy—I loved it. You didn't tell me you owned the place."

Ginny sported a sly look. "Only about sixty percent of it."

Farrah looked around the building again, admiring its beauty and the peaceful feeling within. She was fascinated by the work involved with curating the exhibitions, organizing the meet and greets and receptions, double-checking placards, and everything else. It was why she was interested in art history to begin with—the museum studies aspect. Ever since her art class in high school took a field trip to chat with curators at the Raleigh art museum, she'd been hooked. She wondered, for a moment, if it might be a line of work she could one day be good at.

"Hey, Ginny," Farrah called, and the eccentric woman

turned to her with full attention. Farrah gulped in a breath, summoning confidence. "You don't happen to be hiring, do you?"

FARRAH AND KIA walked into their dorm, dodging cardboard boxes and crates of their belongings, laughing about the fact that Farrah would be Ginny's employee.

"I mean, she's only been begging me to work there since I turned fourteen and could get a worker's permit"— Kia cackled—"and now you come in *wanting* to work! You'll be her new favorite daughter."

Farrah fanned her face. They'd been rather silly on their ride and subsequent walk back to the dorms through the thick August night. "You shouldn't have been so stubborn. Rebelling against what your parents are into."

"No, I promise, that's not it," Kia said, not offended in the least, but sobering from her giggle fit. "I'm just not artistic at all. You should see me draw a stick figure. Not pretty."

"Well, it's not like I'll be doing anything artistic." At this, Farrah chuckled. "I guess I'll be getting really well-acquainted with the bathrooms and sinks of the Oberg."

Kia giggled again. "Hey, housekeeping is a start. My mom's just testing you."

"I figured so. To see what I'm made of."

"Exactly. To see if you're like other teenagers she's hired—worthless when it comes to working hard. My mom is *old school*, okay? They don't make them like her anymore."

"Well, I hope to prove myself to her. And I'm thankful. I mean, I needed a job, and—"

Farrah stopped talking when her cell phone buzzed in receipt of a text.

"Sorry," Farrah mumbled. "Let me just…" She flipped open her phone, unsure who'd be trying to reach her at this time of night. An unknown number displayed across the screen.

"It's okay, you can take it. I'm hopping in the shower." Kia rustled through a storage tote and located her body wash and sponge, then dropped them in a plastic shower caddy and headed off to the dorm's community bathroom, towel in hand.

Farrah clicked on the message:

> Hey, it's Abbott. Mom got me a new cell phone. I know you probably don't want to, but you can reach me here if needed. Did you read my list? Anyway, save my number. Bye, Bacon.

Farrah's ears pounded and her breathing picked up speed. He'd broken up with *her*. Why would he still care about the list of all the reasons he wanted to dump her?

No, she hadn't read it. Of course, she hadn't. She couldn't bear to be faced with her inadequacies, the reasons he had used to justify his leaving her. Her self-esteem was already crumbling, and she was trying not to think about her flaws. She knew she wasn't a big communicator, and that she'd messed up. It would be pure torture to feel all of that failure as she read about his decision in his own handwriting, effectively transporting her back to that recent, painful moment. She could read it down the road, when things had calmed down.

When she'd forgotten all about him.

As she thought about it, she realized she had no idea where the list was. Normally hyper-organized, she had slipped into a frenzied state after packing up any remnant of Abbott, spending time away from home, and then moving to Charlotte. In fact, her mom had to help her pack for college the day before she left, shocked that Farrah had actually procrastinated something for once. If Farrah had somehow left it out and Mom had come across it, there was no telling where she'd stuffed that list.

Her heart panged with worry. She might never get a chance to read it.

But she couldn't leave Abbott hanging.

With tears building in the bottom rims of her eyes, she saved his number, then typed out a text, and sent it:

> I didn't want to face all the things I've done wrong by reading your list. And I don't think I can keep talking with you like this. It's too hard.

A minute later, her phone pinged:

> Okay. I won't bother you. But if you need me, call. We're not enemies.

Farrah looked at the text for a long time, then selected it and deleted it.

"We may as well be," she whispered to herself, remembering his demands and his date with Jincey. She turned her phone off and curled up on her grandmother's quilt.

Chapter Seven
PRESENT DAY

Late June brought the first sunflowers to the foothills of North Carolina, and Farrah had a whole crock of them sitting at Macon Farms' market booth when Tuesday rolled back around, their happy blooms attracting people and bees alike. Macy had come to help, as she'd been doing for the past two market seasons to save her parents from having to hire someone.

Her being there was lucky, because Macy could tend to the customers while Farrah created her symbols to put in the basket they would soon start to advertise. Her task had already brought a lot of questions that morning, and she happily chatted with the folks from town who inquired, hoping to spread the word a bit early. She kept working as she talked, taking advantage of the time before her shift at Glade Village.

"Girls, girls!" a voice called, and they turned to see Amy approaching the stand, red-faced and beaming. "This is *incredible!* Word is already getting out about the raffle basket. Everyone is asking me when they can buy a ticket."

"Tickets will be on sale soon!" Farrah said, genuinely excited at the speed with which word had spread. "I've been posting on Instagram and the town's Facebook page to build excitement, and I plan on placing a small ad on Facebook that will go out locally. You can come back here and see how the basket is coming so far."

Amy snaked around the U-shaped table formation loaded with farm-made goods. She turned a crate upside down and sat next to Farrah, ogling the tray of items before them.

Farrah did a quick double take toward Macy. A crowd had formed around her waiting to be served, including a small blonde lady she thought she recognized but couldn't quite place because her oversize glasses and poofy hair obscured her face from view.

"You okay, Macy?" Farrah called. The petite blonde lady broke away from the crowd and lingered closer to where Farrah and Amy sat, as she picked up and assessed products with her back partially to them. Farrah would have to help the straggling customer if Macy was too swamped.

"I've got this!" Macy, the eternal optimist, said. Farrah shot her a thumbs up and then glanced at the blonde woman busy reading labels, no longer seeming to need assistance. Farrah took the opportunity to return her attention to Amy.

"So I'm pasting symbols I printed out to match the prize on foam board. Daddy will cut them out later to go in the basket. This one is for a free night at one of Macy's luxury cabins in Boone." Farrah held up the piece she'd just completed. It was an image of a cute little cabin with the words *Free Night in Boone* written in the center. Glued on the back of the foam board was an empty envelope where, the day of the drawing, Farrah would place the gift certificate for the cabin rental with instructions for redeeming it. Her idea had turned out wonderfully and the symbols were cuter than even Farrah had imagined.

"Oh, thank you, Macy, for donating this!" Amy said, eyes misting.

"My pleasure," Macy called back, as she rolled a client's pickled okra in old newspaper and plopped it in a paper bag among other glass jars.

"That's just the start of it," Farrah said. "Look here. These are ones we've finished." Resting in the basket were an adorable cartoon vacuum, a barbell, a poodle, and a small cutout of a lion. "We've got a free house cleaning— *I'm* offering that. A one-year membership to the town's gym, a free dog grooming, and a gift card for fifty dollars donated by the local Food Lion."

Amy was in disbelief in the best possible way. She clutched her chest and smiled, slowly shaking her head. "My word. The gym membership alone is five hundred a year. How much do you think this basket is worth already?"

Farrah ran some numbers in her head. "Wow. A lot. I'd say at least eight hundred."

"Make that nine hundred," Amy said. "I'm throwing in three free haircuts to whoever wins." She rasped out her signature laugh.

"Sounds great. I'll get to work making a barber's chair right away."

"One last thing, before I buy too many of your peaches." Amy stood and spoke a little lower. "How much do you plan on selling the tickets for?"

"Good question," Farrah said. Admittedly, she was worried about the townspeople being intimidated by her ticket price and not buying into the plan. She hoped, however, that they appreciated Bobby and Amy as much as she and her family did, and would see the ticket price as a donation to a good cause, rather than a loss if their number wasn't drawn. At the end of the day, if a family was uncomfortable with the price but still wanted to give toward the cause, they could pitch in with friends to buy a ticket.

"Originally, I had thought twenty dollars. But then Macy added the cabin, so I bumped it up to forty because I felt like that was pretty enticing."

"Yeah, I can see that," Amy said, nodding slowly, though Farrah could tell she was thinking about how some of the more traditional locals might react to a forty-dollar raffle ticket.

"But now, I'm thinking more."

"How much more?" Amy's face dropped, fully betraying her worry.

Farrah gulped back her embarrassment at having to put her friend in this situation. "Daddy and I are thinking seventy-five dollars each is a fair price."

Amy grimaced in discomfort. "I don't know, Farrah. That seems like an awful lot. To be honest, forty was pushing it."

"Well, here's the thing. I have an ace up my sleeve." Farrah reached into the folder behind her and pulled out a printed image that had yet to be pasted onto the foam board.

"Is that…" Amy gasped.

"Yes," Farrah said, surprised at the emotion in her own voice. "I didn't include this when I calculated the eight-hundred-dollar value, of course."

On the paper was a printed image of *Sandcastle Girl*, an

original Connor Dunes oil painting. It was one of his smaller works, but even so, it was worth thousands.

Farrah had a hard time even looking at the tiny, printed image. But then, she figured, Connor's work would always conjure a lot of emotions for her. She was sure that would never change as long as she lived.

"Oh my goodness," Amy said, still staring at the paper, and touching her lips with a trembling hand. "Do you need to ask him? Is that possible?"

"No, no," Farrah said weakly, swiping her hand through the air. "Connor is long gone. He probably doesn't even remember he gave this one to me." The pain of the words vise-gripped her heart and her eyes welled up with tears. She hoped Amy hadn't noticed, but she had. Her arms swung around Farrah and encapsulated her in sympathy. Farrah lingered there for a moment—long enough that the threat of crying dissipated. When they let go, Farrah was at peace.

"All right, sweet girl. Bag me up some peaches!"

Amy walked back to the customer side of the table and Farrah did as she'd requested.

After Amy had paid and walked away, the pint-size, leopard-skin-clad blonde woman sidled up to the stand and removed her oversize glasses with a click-clack of bright orange acrylic nails.

Jincey.

She still looked a lot like Farrah remembered her—she was gorgeous. But somehow, she seemed less sweet. And more… powerful. Farrah wondered how much of her and Amy's conversation Jincey had overheard as she stood nearby reading labels.

"Did I hear you were organizin' gambling?" Jincey asked, smacking her gum a few times after the accusatory question.

"I… What?" Farrah's mind raced. She was totally caught off guard by the question. A few shoppers stopped to listen, much to Farrah's embarrassment. She tried to go a different route and be friendly. "Long time no see—"

"Nuffathat," Jincey spat, flapping her hand in front of Farrah's face and, by chain reaction, jangling the many bangles on her wrist. "You can't hold a raffle without a nonprofit organization's oversight. Didn't you know that?"

Something about the way she asked that question rubbed Farrah the wrong way. Who was Jincey to come over to their stand and jump all over her case about something that didn't concern her in the least?

Macy put her hand on Farrah's shoulder to calm her and tried to take the reins.

"Aren't you the president of the rotary club? Couldn't we host it with you?" Macy asked Jincey. Farrah would hate to work with such an apparently meddlesome, spicy little woman, but if she wanted the fundraiser to go on…

"I can check the calendar, but I'm pretty sure we're all booked." Jincey folded her fingers and surveyed her nails. "You might have to call off this illegal enterprise," she said as she waggled her finger over the Macon Farms booth. "You can't just waltz into town after so many years away and upend everything, especially not illegally. My husband's police chief, you know."

That last part seemed to be thrown in as a threat. Had Farrah missed something here? Jincey's level of animosity had come out of nowhere. Farrah racked her brain to think of a reason for the woman's hostility. It wasn't like they were rivals in high school. As far as Farrah knew, Jincey's date with Abbott had been a one-time thing, and Farrah had forgiven that indiscretion since it was so many years ago and they were immature teens. Plus, Jincey was married now. For the life of her, Farrah could not come up with a logical reason to explain why Jincey was all up in arms.

"I have a nonprofit," came a man's offer. Farrah and Macy looked over quickly.

It was Abbott, sporting his usual ball cap and plaid, collared farm shirt tucked into belted jeans.

"A-Abbott, I—" Jincey sputtered.

Abbott held up his hand. "Don't worry, Jincey. We'll make sure everything is legal. I've even hosted a couple raffles before, so a bigger one shouldn't be too difficult."

While Jincey scrambled for words to redeem herself to Abbott, he turned his eyes to Farrah, and the defensiveness in his look calmed. Then he spoke again. "It especially won't be hard with Farrah's talents for planning and running things."

The compliment had its effect. Farrah didn't need a mirror to know she was blushing the color of a July foothills tomato.

"Thank you," she said sheepishly. Then she turned to Jincey, who had a feverish scowl on her face. If the choice was between the two, Farrah would take Abbott, despite their history.

"Don't worry about checking your calendar. I think I'll work with Abbott on this." She shot him a smile and his face cracked in response, his clean-shaven dimples on full display, eyes glittering with delight under his ball cap's bill.

"Well… *fine.*" Jincey angrily put back a canning jar of pickled daikon radishes she'd been admiring, as if her rejection of the Macon Farms' product was a real slap in the face to Farrah. Off Jincey stomped, swinging her hips as she went, probably en route to cause trouble somewhere else.

"Boy, *she* sure has changed," Farrah breathed out with a laugh.

"Tell me about it," Abbott concurred. "She's the queen bee around here. She's got her nose—and ears—in everything."

Macy, who had finished up with the last of that particular rush's customers, walked back to Abbott and Farrah and spoke quietly. "She's been an absolute nightmare to so many. It's like she memorized all the local laws, and she goes around informing others of their noncompliance. Rumor has it she's on edge because her marriage is on the rocks."

That still didn't fully explain why Jincey had approached Farrah like an enemy. "Well, whatever the reason, thank you, Abbott. You saved the whole benefit."

"You're welcome, Farrah." They locked eyes, but he promptly darted his away. Having known him deeply during her teenage years, she couldn't help but feel like the reaction betrayed that he was unsure of her. She was surprised at the worry that one small act of avoiding eye contact caused her heart.

If it was distrust she was seeing, it actually wouldn't be out of the ordinary. After all, they'd only seen each other a few times since eleven years prior, and for all Abbott knew, Farrah was a completely different person, and he was entering into an agreement with her under his nonprofit—which was risky. Why *should* he trust her if he didn't know her from Adam?

She brushed off those thoughts and tried a friendly, unaffected approach.

"Abbott, what does your nonprofit do anyway? I mean, besides benefit raffle baskets."

Abbott's laugh was husky. Cute. Maybe a little shy. "Shelters."

"You build them?"

"Nah," he said, with a dismissive wave of his hand.

"Anything to do with homeless shelters, or women's shelters, sometimes even animal shelters. We do different things to raise money for them, or support fundraising organizations with donations."

Farrah's heart warmed. "That's needed, I'm sure." She paused, then something occurred to her. "Is there a particular reason why you're interested in that cause?"

Abbott raised one side of his mouth as he regarded Farrah, tenderness in his eyes. "Well, yeah. A friend of mine from college lost everything in a house fire a few years back. I wanted to raise funds for him but needed a nonprofit's oversight, so I just started my own. After that, I continued with causes related to housing and shelters. After seeing what happened to my buddy, I don't think there's anything worse than not having somewhere safe to lay your head at night." Abbott offered a soft smile. "We've never saved someone's house and land from being sold before, but helping the Bells isn't too far from our mission statement."

"That's... really amazing, Abbott," Farrah managed, and Abbott gave one nod, conveying his gratitude. They locked eyes again, and this time Abbott didn't glance away, but their conversation fell off.

He seemed to realize they weren't saying anything all of a sudden. With a start, he clapped his hands together and rocked a bit on his heels. "So I guess I'll be hearing from you. I'll talk to my lawyer and see about the nuts and bolts of everything. And I might want to donate something to the basket too."

Farrah's curiosity was piqued. "Oh, really? What, exactly?"

"Well... um... a cow."

That put Farrah on edge. Abbott Ranch was one of many that supplied beef to a conglomerate, and as such, their meat was factory-raised. She understood that such practices were necessary to keep the nation fed, and in the past their farm had won awards for cattle health and clean industrial practices, but a factory-farm head of beef did not exactly give off the cozy small-town feel she had envisioned for her raffle basket. She had to burst his bubble sooner rather than later. She was too type-A to bend the aesthetic of her basket. It would be like giving out a gift card to a chain hotel instead of Macy's cabins, or like offering a franchise gym's membership rather than one to their local civic center.

"I am thankful, Abbott, it's just… we're only doing things that are—that seem…" She couldn't find the words.

"That seem…" Abbott raised one curious eyebrow and smirked, amused at her floundering.

"I'm just not sure a cow from your farm would fit in with the types of things we want to offer."

"Hmm," Abbott said and then laughed through his nose. "Come by sometime. You just might be surprised."

FARRAH CHANGED Mr. Mitchell's sheets as the afternoon sun glided in through the windowpanes, shining in long rectangles across the pallid man's frail body. She painstakingly avoided all of his different tubes and chords as she went about her tasks. He'd feel better now that his bottom was clean, and his sheets were fresh and crisp.

He'd changed so much in the past week. Less talking, more moaning. Her mind struggled to correctly categorize the changes. To her, they seemed like a regression, but in reality, his symptoms were a progression of his disease. While she moved on to sweeping his room and bagging up his trash, Dr. Smith, the head doctor at Glade Village, came in and assessed Mr. Mitchell, communicating her thoughts to Farrah as she went.

"He's got quite a rattle in his chest. It started after that last cold he had. I'm not sure if you know this, but it's not good for a dementia patient to start having lung problems."

Farrah sighed. "I know." She remembered that from her twelve-week CNA courses.

"You might want to be prepared." The doctor left the room after lightly squeezing Farrah's arm.

Farrah understood what Dr. Smith meant by "be prepared." It was part of the deal. She had come to Glade Village and to this new line of work knowing death was an integral part of it. In fact, death was included in the treatment plan: care for the individual until they passed away. In addition to being a nursing home for dementia patients, it was also a palliative care center. A patient could come into care while still somewhat lucid, as Mrs. Janice seemed to be at times, and then go on to end-of-life care in the same facility sometime later, which would be Mr. Mitchell's next step.

She'd known it was coming. His chart contained information from multiple different medical centers with clear documentation of his consistent decline and his inability to ward off illness.

His repeated lung issues.

Both Mr. Mitchell and Mrs. Janice had changed so much since their younger years. Farrah remembered Mrs. Janice as a go-getter in the community, involved in so many local events. To see her practically confined to a lift chair was unfathomable.

And Mr. Mitchell's body was completely changed. He seemed to have shrunk in stature and even his eyes had faded to gray. He was merely a shell of the ambitious man he used to be—the man Farrah used to know.

A former teacher, as he liked to be known.

Working with him and Mrs. Janice was a daily reminder that death comes to all, even the successful, even the go-getters, even the best of us.

Dr. Smith had not administered Mr. Mitchell's sleep aid, and yet, he was dozing. Glade Village was understaffed due to people taking summer vacations, so Farrah and another team member were alternating care of several patients that evening. She needed to go turn off Mrs. Janice's soap opera and get her ready for sleep.

But first she sidled up to Mr. Mitchell and held his hand in hers, watching as his frail chest rose slowly, a deep, grating rattle sounding from within. She felt as if she were the one struggling to breathe, her ribs tightening around her lungs with each of his ragged breaths. It was darn near unbearable to see.

He shifted and opened his eyes, his gaze slowly finding hers.

"Are you going to sleep now?" Farrah whispered. The room was dim and silent, but for his breathing and the low hum of his machines.

He struggled against a few breaths before he got the strength to answer. "I believe so."

"Will you dream nice things?"

"Do I normally?"

"Yes." Farrah laughed. "Go to sleep, silly goose."

"Goodnight, miss."

"Goodnight."

When she confirmed he was asleep, she slid out and changed his light color, then headed to Mrs. Janice's room. She was surprised to see a man inside with her patient, his back turned to Farrah. She wasn't aware Mrs. Janice would have a visitor.

"Oh, I—"

"Shhh," the man said gently as he turned around and held a finger to his mouth. He looked somewhat familiar, but she couldn't place where she might have seen him. Perhaps just around the halls of Glade Village. "Grandma just fell asleep."

Farrah relaxed. Mrs. Janice had been sundowning a lot lately—growing more confused and agitated near the end of the day—and sometimes it got really dicey. A visit from her grandson seemed to have cleared that up for today. Farrah made sure everything was as it should be, adjusting Mrs. Janice's lift chair so she lay a little flatter—she refused to sleep in her bed—and turning off the muted TV. Then she and the grandson stepped out into the hallway, and she pulled the door almost closed.

"She talks a lot about her grandson, Daniel—is that you?"

"In the flesh." The blond man with a sharp nose laughed and held his hands up as if caught in a crime.

"I'm so glad you came to see her. She really loves you. People here don't get a lot of visitors."

"I've been meaning to get here, but my business has had a few supply issues the past month or so, and I haven't visited like I usually do, twice a week. Have I seen you here before? I'm sure I couldn't forget a smile like yours."

Oh, goodness. The line was a little cheesy, but Farrah appreciated the admiration. In the sterile world of a nursing home, a divorced woman might find a compliment to be rather exciting.

Fleetingly, she thought of Mr. Mitchell, sick in bed. The flirtation suddenly went stale.

"I just started last week, actually. I moved here from Charlotte."

"Wow. Big move. Were you in healthcare there as well?"

"No. I… managed the Oberg Gallery." Farrah tried her best not to sound full of regret and longing as she spoke. The move had been worth it. And everything would be okay. Or, that was what she kept telling herself. She had to stay positive to keep from going crazy.

"No kidding!" Daniel exclaimed. "That must be where I know you from. Me and my friends, we're in the art scene. One's a sculptor, the other—well, it's not important. The point is my business manufactures the wooden pieces used for making picture frames. As you can imagine, we work with a lot of galleries and museums and even big box stores with framing departments. We've done several projects with the Oberg, especially framing Florence—"

"Florence Altman's watercolors!" Farrah gushed, connecting to her cherished time in that world. "Now that you mention it, I totally remember you. You dealt more with Ginny and Vlad than me, but we emailed a bit. It's so nice to see you again."

"Same to you," Daniel said, a genuine smile on his face. "So I guess you made the switch to healthcare, and all, but are you still in the art scene around here?"

Farrah stifled a laugh. *If you count making crafty symbols for a raffle basket…* "Sadly, no. My move here and the switch to healthcare was kind of abrupt, and not really my preference. Just one of life's curveballs."

"Oh." Daniel's face fell with compassion. "Sorry to hear that. Well, hey, I know this is crazy, but it might help if you've been missing art life. This Friday there's an exhibition I want to go to in Winston-Salem. A gallery I know. Would you… Do you want to…" Daniel hesitated, holding his hands in front of him like two scales adjusting their weight.

"Like… a date?" Oh no. She'd said it. The *d* word. Now things would be uncomfortable.

"It doesn't have to be!" Daniel said, trying to convince her in the nicest way. "I mean, I'm not against it. I just wouldn't want to pressure you or anything."

Farrah smiled and sighed. Poor Daniel. "I'm sorry I made things awkward. Look, the truth is, I've been through a lot lately. I was betrayed in my past relationship."

Daniel nodded, probably bracing himself for a rejection. But the truth was, she would love to get out and see some beautiful artwork. And nobody else was asking.

"I would really like to go to the gallery exhibit with you. Mrs. Janice talks so highly of you, so I trust your taste. But I do have to say, it needs to be a friend-only date."

A handful of times before marrying Connor, she'd met a man that claimed he only wanted to be friends, and then he'd lay it on thick. In her experience, a man could not be "just friends" with a woman he was attracted to. Even if this scenario with Daniel was not a full-on romantic date with roses and dinner, it was still a type of date. If anything, it was a pre-date tryout. If Daniel liked her, at the end of this friend date, he'd mention getting together again. And the next time, it would certainly be over dinner and considerably more romantic.

"That's totally fine," Daniel said. "Want to meet there around six? Here, put your number in my phone. I'll text you the address."

"Okay," Farrah said, and bumped her phone with his. She accepted his contact. "I'll see you there Friday, I guess."

"Yeah. Sounds good." Daniel flashed a pearly grin, then gave a quick look to his grandma one last time through the crack of the door. He nodded to Farrah once before heading through the main exit.

Farrah breathed deeply in and out, massaging her temple with her hand.

Dr. Smith, having finished with a patient in a nearby room, surprised Farrah by walking up beside her.

"You don't look so good," she said.

Farrah chuckled in disbelief at what she was about to say. "Yeah. I think I just got asked on a date."

Chapter Eight

❧

"Farrah, can you meet me in my office?" Ginny asked from the hall, surprising Farrah as she restored an illustration on what had been a normal summer workday.

"Sure. Be there in a sec."

Farrah peeled off her cloth gloves and stashed them in her leather work tote. She had worked as custodian at the Oberg for two years during her undergraduate degree, then Ginny had taken a chance and let Farrah come on as an intern and later, a part-time assistant. In the year since she'd graduated, she had worked as Ginny's full-time managerial assistant—and loved every minute of it. She had no plans to leave or work elsewhere, especially since her dream of attending grad school had shifted. She didn't need an MBA for gallery work. Her art history degree suited her just fine.

It certainly wasn't the first time Ginny had called her to the management office. More than a boss, Ginny was like a work mom. Sometimes office visits were to bounce ideas off Farrah about her professional or even personal life, especially since she'd lost Keith to a heart attack last year.

Farrah fully expected this when she stepped into the office and closed the door behind her, finding Ginny staring out the steel-framed, industrial window that gave her office a fully urban feel. The summer sun poured in warmly through its panes.

Ginny kept her back to Farrah, hugging herself around the waist of her bright, multicolored smock. "I'm getting old," she said matter-of-factly.

"No, Ginny…" Farrah pleaded.

"Oh, it's not like that," Ginny said and giggled. She whipped around and invited Farrah to sit as she took a seat across from her. "No, I'm not feeling philosophical today. It's a fact. I'm sixty-nine years old. I'm tired."

"I'm sure you are. You always work so hard," Farrah offered.

"So do you. You started out scrubbing our toilets and cleaning up after our events. I was testing you, you know. And you proved yourself to me again and again. Your senior year in college as a part-time assistant went flawlessly. Now this past year, with you helping me plan and execute these exhibitions full-time, it's become obvious to me that you have a knack for this line of work. You're more than a sidekick. More than a trainee."

Farrah stuttered with excitement at Ginny's praise. "Well, I… um, thank you, Ginny."

"Well, you're welcome. It's well-deserved. And furthermore, you're like family to me. You were there for us through losing Keith, and you and Kia have been inseparable for years. I want to have someone I can trust… someone whose vision is closely aligned with mine."

Okay, what was she getting at?

"Have someone where, exactly?"

Ginny's face cracked into a smile. "Here. At the Oberg. I want you to be manager in my stead."

"Wow." Farrah gasped. "What about Vlad?" Her coworker, the son of Russian immigrants and an artist, had been at the Oberg for almost as long as she had.

"Oh, I have him tapped for handling the financial parts —grant writing and accounting. That's what he studied, after all. But you… You'd be perfect as manager. So, what do you say?"

Farrah couldn't think of answering anything other than that she'd love nothing more. She had adored everything about helping run the gallery. While her training had been extensive and thorough, she hadn't known Ginny was preparing her as her own replacement. She had never imagined a promotion, at least not so soon.

"I'd be honored."

"Oh, good!" Ginny clasped her hands in front of her and laughed a breathy laugh. "I was scared you'd say no, so I had a list of things to convince you. It'll be more money, but also a bit more responsibility. I'll step down from all of my duties. Of course, I'm retaining my part ownership, but we can talk about that down the line."

"Okay, so where do we start? A new contract?"

"Yes, for sure, a new contract. But practically, after that step is done, you'll plan your first exhibition entirely by yourself, and I'll be here to walk you through it. You already know so much, but this will give you a hands-on try at doing things from the ground up."

"That sounds amazing." Farrah could hardly believe it.

"And after I step away, you'll be fully prepared. Vlad will be here, and we will have our two college interns and the maintenance crew, as well as the other owners on call. You're going to do splendidly." Ginny rose from her desk and walked over to Farrah and hugged her. "I couldn't be happier to have you taking this position. Well—if it was

Kia, maybe I would've been happier. But we both know she grew up to be anti-art." Ginny scoffed.

Farrah giggled and squeezed Ginny tight before letting her go. "Ginny, thank you. I am so excited about this opportunity. I look around this place and see my whole future and what I want it to look like."

"That's wonderful, hon."

"But when you step away, you'll have a lot of time on your hands. What are you planning on doing?"

"Oh, traveling, of course. I used to go to Europe every summer up until my mid-forties when I settled down with Keith and had Kia. I think I'll go back. I still have a few friends in France. And I'll try to make all of Kia's games."

Kia had taken a job after graduating college as head girls' basketball coach at a huge high school in Charlotte known for winning cutthroat championship games against the best teenage ballers in the nation. Her landing that job was no surprise, considering her UNCC women's basketball career had been such a success.

"That sounds amazing," Farrah conceded.

"And I'll come see most, if not all, of your exhibitions." Ginny smiled, a nostalgic twinkle in her eyes. "I was just like you, once," she said softly. "So young and full of potential. Brimming with hope."

"I hope to hold up as well as you have, both in success and resilience through the ups and downs of life."

"Well, I'll tell you the recipe. Prayer and patience," Ginny said, her eyes misting. "Prayer and patience is the key. No matter what life throws at you."

Upon hearing the news of their daughter's promotion, Farrah's parents strapped three-year-old Cash, who they were keeping for the day, into his car seat and drove down to Charlotte to have dinner with their girl.

"I guess this means you won't be moving back to town anytime soon," Daddy remarked.

"No, Daddy. But you knew that." Farrah placed her hand on his shoulder where he sat in her small apartment's living room. Her little nephew played with blocks on her rug.

"Yes, he did," Mom affirmed from the rug. "We knew that the moment you moved down here. City life is for you."

"And we're so proud of you," Daddy said. "Besides, Whitetail Ridge is clearing out. Times have been rough these past few years and it seems the younger generation— your crowd—is opting to take work elsewhere. Even the Abbott boy took a job in Knoxville working for his mom."

Farrah tried to hide her surprise. It sounded like Abbott's plan had worked out after all. She hoped he could find what he was longing for—a healthier relationship with his mom.

She started to question her father, to ask how he knew that, but as she had so many times over the past several years, she willed her self-control to dominate her curiosity. She didn't need to worry about Abbott. She'd moved on. Apparently, so had he.

She chose to be happy and in the moment with her family. It wasn't every day she got to play blocks with the world's cutest three-year-old. She plopped on the rug and started building a tower, then realized she hadn't responded to her dad's comment about Abbott.

"I hope he'll be happy there," Farrah said quietly. And she meant it.

Chapter Nine
PRESENT DAY

A my's raspy laugh greeted Farrah midday Thursday as her neighbor opened her front door and then gave Farrah a squeeze.

Farrah was all too happy not to be alone today, the one-year anniversary of walking in on Connor with his lawyer. His icy look had said it all. She hadn't even had to ask what the papers were on his desk. His betrayal of their vows pierced through her yet again as she remembered.

Mom and Dad were at a vegetable expo until later in the afternoon, when Macy and Elijah were going on a romantic getaway for a few days, and the boys, Cash and Colton, would spend those nights with their grandparents and Farrah. And in just over twenty-four hours, Farrah would go on her friend-date-thing with Daniel that she already regretted committing to. For now, visiting Amy and Bobby—and talking about the so far successful raffle idea —would be a great escape from both the morbid anniversary and the nerves in her belly about tomorrow night.

Amy shuffled her out to their back deck that overlooked the rolling green hills of their back yard, framed by a forest of pines and oaks.

Framed. Frames. Daniel. Ugh. I'm not ready to date.

She quieted her mind with a shake of her head and a deep breath; then she plopped onto a teal-colored Adirondack chair next to some potted geraniums, blooming bright red. From the porch's covered roof hung vibrant ferns and impatiens in mossy baskets. This was the type of back porch she could really relax on.

Amy settled on the plush outdoor sofa beside Farrah and handed her a glass of sweet tea with a lemon slice adorning the rim. "Did you get any new items for the basket?"

"Oh, yeah! A voucher for one free outfit—top, pants, and shoes—from Louise's Boutique on Main. She was so sweet when I went by asking about a donation, so I went ahead and bought some jeans to support her business. She really wants me to come see her baby goats for some reason."

"Oh!" Amy laughed. "Louise is a sweet one, for sure. You should take her up on that. A local girlfriend would be good for you."

"Maybe I will," Farrah said, filing away the idea as a serious consideration. She missed Kia and remembered she probably needed to call her and check in. "As far as other donations, we got a few restaurants throwing in gift cards, like Thirteen Bones and Speedy Lunch. And that health store, The Herb Garden, threw in a fifty-dollar gift card too. The response has been amazing. I got a reply to almost all of my emails, and I've been welcomed so warmly in person. The community is really coming together."

"That's great news," Amy admitted. "Do we need anything else?"

"I don't think so. I was going over our donor list this morning, and I think we're set. I went ahead and posted updates on social media that we're no longer accepting donations—for this basket at least. I think we have the perfect amount of everything. Anyone else who wants to help can buy tickets. I put up a few flyers around town with information and—"

"Um, you call that a flyer? I've seen them. They're works of art!" Amy grinned. "And the basket is too."

"Thanks so much, Amy. I tried to put the flyers in popular spots in town to help build interest. We'll start displaying the basket on Tuesday at the market." Amy nodded in understanding, and Farrah realized they were a person short for their meeting. "Hey, where's Bobby?"

Amy squinted and pointed far off. "Over yonder somewhere. He always did the mowing in the middle of a summer's day. Probably caused all his health issues. At least now he wears a wide-brimmed hat."

Farrah squinted. In the distance, a lawnmower was barely visible driving behind a row of bright pink crepe myrtles. "I guess you'll have to let me know how he's feeling about all this."

"I can tell you now. He's tickled to death. At first he was shy about asking for help, but that changed to awe and gratitude when he heard the number of people coming forward to donate."

"Just wait till we start selling tickets next Tuesday. So many people have asked me, people I haven't seen in years are coming out of the woodwork, excited to collaborate."

"Fantastic. And is everything coming together okay with Abbott's nonprofit?" Amy asked.

"Yep! Just waiting on a contract to make everything official."

"I'm so glad he stepped in to help us." Amy reached

over and clasped Farrah's hand. "Next Tuesday is going to be a great day. I really have hope we'll be able to keep this home and land." Her eyes were glassy as she smiled. "Thank you, Farrah. When a person doesn't have kids, they don't know who'll be there for them. I sure am blessed to have a neighbor-niece like you."

Warmth flooded Farrah's heart with Amy's sincere gratitude. She squeezed her hand and smiled back at her.

Suddenly, they heard a man calling Bobby's name from the side of the house. "Oh, probably a mechanic customer," Amy said. "Let's go see what this is about."

Farrah hopped up behind Amy, following her as they walked down the deck stairs and around toward the driveway. Green-and-white hostas with soft, purple blooms threatened to take over the sidewalk. Amy rounded the corner first and delightfully cried, "Abbott!"

Farrah's heart fluttered, the unbidden reaction surprising her. *It's just Abbott*, she tried to tell herself as she approached. *We've grown up, and everything between us was a long, long time ago.*

She emerged and Abbott's eyes locked on her.

"Hey." He exhaled the word, seemingly surprised to see her. His ball cap was gone, and his dark curls were tight and wet. A few drops of moisture glided down his reddened face. He held a greasy black tractor part in his hand, his nail beds and fingertips dingy and his work shirt soaked with sweat.

"You look like you need a dip in Quarry Creek."

Abbott, apparently not expecting Farrah's lightheartedness, gasped out a laugh and shook his head. "Nah. No place for a grown man like me. I think only teenagers go down there to mess around."

The reference was not lost on Farrah, and sparks shot

up from her heart to her cheeks. Amy seemed none the wiser and skipped the topic entirely.

"What's wrong?"

"I need Bobby to check if he has a replacement for this part. Ain't no rush. I've just been tinkering with it today and it's not fixable without a new piece."

"I'll leave it on his work bench," Amy said, promptly taking the part and heading down the sidewalk, then disappearing into the large, metal outbuilding with the "Bobby's Tractor Mechanics" sign over the door.

Farrah and Abbott looked at each other as she thought about maybe saying something. She was just about to ask him about the cow he had mentioned at the market when Amy returned, wiping her soiled hands on her gardening apron.

"Do you need to borrow a tractor for this evening?"

"No, ma'am. But I thank you," Abbott said. He turned to Farrah. "Since you're here, how about you come by my place in about twenty minutes? I've got the contract from my nonprofit ready. You'll need to sign it before you start selling tickets."

Amy's gaze shot between Farrah and Abbott, as if she were figuring out that a slight tension lay beneath the surface of the conversation.

"She'll be there," Amy said before Farrah could react. "I have a few haircuts to do at the salon, and we're about done here. I'll drop her off in a few when I head out." Amy's salon was on the iconic Whitetail Ridge downtown strip. Her great-uncle, Floyd, who had passed away many years before, owned the building and left it to Amy. There, she installed a women's hair salon and named it Pink Floyd's in a nod to one of her favorite bands, her favorite color, and her beloved great-uncle.

Abbott smiled ear to ear at Amy's decisiveness. "Farrah, is that all right?"

"Um, yeah," she managed. Alone, with Abbott, on his farm. What would they talk about? Business, she hoped. There was always the cow donation topic, if all else failed. "I'll see you in a bit."

"Good! I'll go hop in the shower." Abbott climbed back in his truck and backed out onto the main gravel road, then lifted two fingers in a lazy, country-boy goodbye.

"He's a *good* man, Farrah," Amy said. "Give him a chance."

"Amy, that seems a little out of nowhere. I've only seen him a few times since a decade ago." *Besides,* Farrah wanted to say, *I gave Abbott a massive chance when we were teenagers.*

"Out of nowhere, my foot," Amy protested. "You think his offer to shield you with his nonprofit was disinterested? Ha! It puts him close to you." She moseyed back up the sidewalk. "I'm going to freshen up before work. You're welcome to wait for me inside."

Farrah followed Amy in, her thoughts whirring. She had changed a lot in eleven years. Had Abbott? She couldn't deny that there was something between them—the tiniest of sparks hovering below the politeness of their conversations. Perhaps just a memory of the chemistry they once shared. But it was nothing to explore, and her heart still belonged to Connor, as much as she didn't want it to. As much as she knew it would be easier if she forgot him like he'd forgotten her.

As Amy went about getting ready for her afternoon of clients, Farrah finished her tea.

She caught sight of Amy's wall calendar and remembered that Kia's baby shower was this coming Saturday, and Farrah was scheduled to work at the nursing home.

Kia was around seven months along by now. Farrah's heart squeezed, and she fired off a text to Kia, her best friend in life:

> I wish so bad I could be there Saturday. I'll be there in spirit. I love you guys so much!

She sighed deeply. She'd never missed any of Kia's important events, including her bridal shower last year and her wedding a couple months later, even though her own life was unraveling. She'd set all her problems aside and been there for her friend. Now, for the first time ever, being there for Kia was impossible.

Three pending dots popped up, and soon a text came through:

> Girl, I completely understand. Please don't worry about it. You know Mom invited half the city, so I'd be too busy to talk much anyway. Take care of yourself and we can celebrate in the future, just us two.

Sadness overwhelmed her as she replied:

> Yes. When this is all over, you'll have me back. I'm so sorry. Enjoy your (and baby's) day!

WHEN AMY DROPPED Farrah off at Abbott's house, he greeted her on his front walk, hands casually in his pockets and a calm smile on his handsome face. His hair was still wet, though this time from the shower, and as she approached him, the clean scent of line-dried linens and a hint of spice floated in the air. The afternoon sun beat down on them, its warmth comforting to Farrah.

"Thanks for coming. Shall we?" He motioned toward the door, then led her into the house. They stepped into the living room with oversize couches and a nice, stone fireplace. The kitchen had been completely redone in the modern farmhouse style that she adored. It was bright and white and clean.

Together, they walked across the oriental rug spread over new hardwoods and into Abbott Ranch's offices. Farrah half expected to see Jim, but he wasn't there.

"Where's your dad?" she asked.

Abbott laughed a bit sardonically. "Fourth marriage. He'll be back, I suspect, even though he did say this time he'd found the one. And 'the one' happens to have the nicest home in Whitetail Ridge and a fancy pension from her late husband. Thankfully he went ahead and transferred the house to my name."

"Oh, wow," Farrah said, unsure what to say in response to the bitterness in Abbott's tone. She'd always liked Jim on a personal level, but the man's ways of doing things were indeed questionable. "So that's why there are so many changes."

"The kitchen and floors? Yeah." Abbott stood by his desk and leafed through a few documents, then pulled out one in particular. He offered Farrah his leather desk chair and handed her a pen. He leaned down beside her, and the spice of his cologne or aftershave teased her nose.

"So this is the contract my lawyer drew up. I hope you trust me enough to know I'm not screwing you over. I'm not asking for a cut of anything. This is a pro-bono type contract. But still, I'll walk you through all the items because I know from experience that you don't read lists."

Farrah whipped her head sideways to look at him and

her heart climbed to her throat. Her shock at his comment was probably displayed on her face. He met her gaze with a smirk that evolved into a laugh.

"Lighten up," he said, grabbing her shoulder and giving it a gentle squeeze. She let herself relax as the corners of her mouth also quaked with a threatening smile. His face was a foot from hers, at best. Being so close to him made her heart beat harder. In the passions of youth, they'd spent a lot of time looking in each other's eyes, not embarrassed or ashamed to talk closely to each other's faces. It seemed something from that soul tie remained.

"Well, I *am* sorry about that."

He glanced at her mouth before settling again on her eyes. "Took me a while to get over that one, but I eventually did." He laughed softly at himself, kindness in his eyes as he shook his head.

Farrah tried to remain calm and unaffected, but she had to admit, she was pleased that he also had some hang ups over their breakup, and it wasn't just her.

"I know. It was immaturity and stubbornness on my part, but then I actually lost the list. Honest. I think my mom filed it away wrongly. In fact..." She reached in her back pocket and pulled out the list. She'd read it the day she'd stumbled upon it, then kept it with her.

They both stared at the wrinkled paper. On it, Abbott explained in numbered points how Farrah was right about his desire to fix things with his mom and how he wanted to go to Tennessee and work for her, and that it wasn't fair of him to expect Farrah to uproot her own plans to support him in that dream. He went on to say that the pressure of sustaining his family farm weighed heavy on him as an only son, and he and his father had had a few explosive arguments about his desire to break free. College and trying something new was a now or never type thing for him.

He'd written about his desire for Farrah to be more open with him, how he hoped to remain friends with her during college and maybe try their relationship again after school was over, but that nothing they wanted was lining up. He'd said he wanted the best for her, even if that meant UNCC, and that he loved her, and it was just a goodbye for now.

In his final point, he promised he would give her his new cell number soon, but other than that, he'd let her handle the communication. He wouldn't force himself on her. She only had to say the word, and he'd be out of her life forever.

Abbott humphed, amused. "So you found it."

"Yeah, a few days ago. I've only read it a thousand times since."

"And what did you make of it?"

She ran her hand over the list, smoothing out the paper containing its seven handwritten items. "It was very mature. I should've read it then. Especially the last part."

Farrah recalled, cringingly, that first night in her dorm when Abbott held up his part of the deal by texting her so she'd have his new number. What could've been a four-year friendship, then more, had ended when she "said the word" and cut him out, until now. She'd decided as a teen that they were enemies, and yet as an almost thirty-year-old woman, she could hardly muster any negative feelings about the man at all. Time had gone by, and she simply wasn't upset anymore.

Reading the list brought regret, but she had to face it. In contrast to her personal guilt fest, Abbott laughed lightly as he perused it.

"You know what?" he said, voice low. "This is holding

us back." He grabbed the list and tossed it into a tray labeled "to shred."

Farrah exhaled her tension and closed her eyes tight for a few seconds. "I'm sorry, Abbott," she said, with only the contract before her on the desk.

Just then, the front, shorter layers of her hair broke free from her claw clip and flopped in front of her face. With his right hand, Abbott brushed the wayward strands behind her ear, lightly tickling her nape with his rough fingers, perhaps unintentionally. Heat rushed to her face.

"Sorry. Habit," he said under his breath, his hand still hovering near her head, tentative.

Under other circumstances, perhaps Farrah would have given in to the excitement of being close to him after all these years—the boy she used to love. But she remembered her current life and flinched away, refocusing on the contract.

Quickly, as if burned by a hot cast-iron skillet, he yanked his hand back and cleared his throat. "I'll just go through the points quickly."

He pointed at the first sheet. "This is the financial breakdown. As I mentioned, the Bells are getting one hundred percent of the net proceeds as a charitable donation from Abode, which is our charity. The IRS considers raffles a form of gaming, so we actually do still have to pay taxes, but whatever is left after that—What?" He looked at her, a quizzical expression on his face.

Farrah let out a giggle she'd been holding in. "I just think it's clever how you designed the Abode logo to look like your name, Abbott. The *d* and the *e* fit into two large *T*s, and the *b* has a shadow, so it looks doubled. It's cute. And dare I say, crafty?"

Abbott placed a hand on his chest as if bragging. "Well, thank you. That was all *my* doing, believe it or not."

He flipped to the second page. "Here are the ticket prices —seventy-five, right?" Farrah nodded. "Great. And the sales locations. You said we'll do Tuesdays at the farmers market."

"Yes, and I'm calling around about other locations that may be able to sell tickets. Amy will sell them at her salon, of course, and I was thinking the café in town might also be a good spot. I dropped in for coffee yesterday and tons of people asked me about it. Maybe we could even make an appearance there to promote it. You know half the town seems to go in and—"

"An appearance? Like, together?" Abbott's creased brow was probably meant to camouflage a bit of hopefulness, or at least it flattered Farrah to think so.

"Well, yes. I was hoping so. Isn't there some sort of stipulation in here that if I'm under your nonprofit, you have to be involved?"

"All that is here, on the last page." Abbott flipped to the spot. "The by-laws. It mostly details the drawing, which in North Carolina, has to be in-person. As long as you're operating within my NPO, you'll be good to sell. I'll vouch for you, if questioned, that the raffle is being officially run by Abode. You're signing here as a volunteer with my organization."

"Oh," Farrah said, realizing. "So we don't have to be together at events."

"I mean, we *can*," he corrected, a bit too eager. "I have no problem with that. Let's do it. The café thing." He nodded, brows high, trying to reassure her.

"Let's for sure do that," she said, giving him a smile that seemed to put him at ease.

He started going into the legalities of Farrah volunteering with Abode, a few other clauses that might affect them, as well as more specific tax information. But she could barely pay attention anymore. She kept glancing at his strong, masculine jaw covered with a five o'clock shadow where teenage patchiness had once been. His skin, once entirely smooth, now boasted fine, curved lines at the corners of his eyes, evidence of years of laughter. Season after season of working his ranch and taking in sun had allowed some sunspots across his nose and cheeks, barely darker than his skin color.

Other things hadn't changed in eleven years: his perfect row of white teeth. His dimples that popped out when he pronounced certain words.

The kindness in his eyes.

Even if she wasn't in the market for love, she told herself, she could still admire a fine-looking man. Kind of like the "look but don't touch" policy at the Whitetail Ridge annual antique car show and sale.

It was a fact. Abbott was handsome.

Good for him.

"So, if you agree, sign here as an official volunteer and co-chair of this event." She did. "And here as a witness, next to where Amy and Bobby will sign as beneficiaries." She signed again. "It was a pleasure doing business with you." He stuck his hand out and she stood and shook it firmly, looking him straight in the eyes, where she could tell a question loomed—some things definitely hadn't changed in eleven years.

"Are you thinking of something?" Farrah asked.

"Yes, actually. About the café," he said after releasing her hand. "I don't have plans right now. Let me buy you a cup of coffee, and we can talk to Donna or whoever is on shift about the fundraiser."

She thought about the week ahead. She'd promised to spend some time with her nephews and do farm chores on Friday morning, and then she'd committed to going out with Daniel tomorrow night. She worked Saturday and Sunday at Glade Village, and the café was closed on Mondays. Tuesday would be the farmers market and their first ticket selling day, which would be busy, and she was scheduled again to work that night, as she was the bulk of next week. Today, Thursday, was practically her only free time for the next little stretch, and it certainly made sense to go.

She gave a deep, good-natured shrug. "Sure. Why not?"

Abbott's smile mirrored her own. "Great. Let's head to the truck."

She followed him out of his house and into his garage, where he locked up behind them. As much as she wanted to shield her vulnerable heart and focus on her current situation, the idea of simply sitting and chatting with Abbott after this successful private meeting was actually comforting to her. She was no longer nervous about how they'd get along. She'd known him so well eleven years ago, and she was curious to learn what had changed in that time and if a friendship might bloom where love had once been.

Chapter Ten

❧

"Gosh, this place hasn't changed at all." Farrah held her thick stoneware mug as she glanced around the room. The hot drink was comforting, even during summer, because Donna always kept the air-conditioning turned down low.

The café's peach-colored walls were like a patchwork quilt of framed newspaper articles about the local prides and joys of Whitetail Ridge. Forever a plant lady, Donna had pothos, snake plants, and peace lilies in every nook and cranny and along many shelves. The eighties-era golden sconces above the pleather booths illuminated the long, narrow business with a warm glow.

"I think it's been the same since '85. Just more plants and picture frames," Abbott said from across the table, as he stirred the contents of two small creamer cups into his coffee.

Farrah laughed, taking in the quirky nostalgia of the place. Donna entered from the back and approached their table.

"Farrah, darlin'." She opened her matronly arms, and

Farrah rose to give her a squeeze. Donna's close-cropped, curly gray hair tickled Farrah's cheek as she hugged the plump woman. Farrah released her, and then sat. "I heard you came in yesterday. I was at an appointment, and I'm so sorry I missed you. Here, just made these. On the house."

She placed a plate with two sticky buns and two forks on the table.

"Wow. Thanks so much, Donna," Farrah said, her stomach rumbling. She'd had a late breakfast and skipped lunch.

"Well, did you find yourself on the wall?"

"I made the wall? What for?"

Donna clicked her tongue. "Come on." She grabbed Farrah's arm and walked her over to a frame in the back corner among other historic town happenings. It was a picture of Farrah from the local paper with the headline *Whitetail Ridge Woman to Manage Oberg, Charlotte.* She remembered doing the phone interview with Chuck Branson that led to the article and had seen it at her parents' house on a visit back home, but even so, Farrah's chest seemed to clench at the surprise of seeing the article framed on Donna's café wall. Being promoted at the gallery was such a proud moment for her, and she was touched to see that it had been for the town as well.

"I feel so important," Farrah joked.

"Well, you are," Donna replied, and the two walked back to the booth, where Donna continued chatting. "What you're doing for Bobby and Amy is just wonderful. You know I've gone with them to the Church of Christ for decades. We're like family."

"We actually wanted to talk to you about that," Abbott said, then explained their idea to sell tickets at the café. Farrah told Donna what her and her serving staff's responsibilities would be.

"Count me in!" Donna said gleefully. "We'd be honored to be a selling spot. I'll do my best to spread the word. I'll even reach out to Chuck at the newspaper."

"Oh," Farrah said, remembering. "Actually, I emailed him a couple days ago but haven't heard back. I was planning on emailing again or maybe calling tomorrow."

"What's today, Thursday?" Donna said, momentarily grabbing her chin and thinking. "He'll be in tomorrow morning for breakfast. I'll tell him to get back to you. I'm sure he'd love to promote this too. He and Bobby were old hunting buddies before Bobby got so sick."

"That's so nice of you. I appreciate it." With Farrah's busy schedule in the coming days, having Donna's help and direct line with the local newspaper was a relief. Farrah intended to get some press to create more buzz and the sooner the better.

"Let me know if you need a refill. I'll leave y'all to it," Donna said, then ripped off and placed the check for the coffee on the table before turning to go. "Heaven knows you two have plenty to talk about."

Donna walked off, stuffing the order pad into her apron and leaving Farrah and Abbott alone.

"What did she mean by that last part?" Abbott asked Farrah, then drank from his mug.

"I guess that eleven years is a long time and we have lots to catch up on."

"I'd agree with that." Abbott smiled, but suddenly Farrah grew wary. She was unsure how much from her past she wanted to disclose at this point. Today was the first real time she'd spent with him in over a decade. Until this moment, she'd seen their small outing for coffee after their contract meeting as a bridge to friendship, but more importantly, an escape from her complicated reality. She really didn't want to relive her hardships right now, and she was relieved when Abbott spoke up again, saying, "Ask me anything."

Farrah settled her gaze on him, comfortable across from her in the booth. He smiled when she didn't speak right away. The truth was, she didn't know where to start, so she rattled off the first thought that popped in her mind—something she'd wondered about since seeing him at the market that first time.

"Okay, I'll shoot straight. Why are you back? Daddy told me years ago you went to work with your mom in Knoxville, and I know that was your plan after we graduated."

Abbott sighed through a smile. "How do I say… you were right?" He laughed, a genuine, deep sound that made Farrah remember the boy from her past, made her feel like she still knew him. "Mom's not able to be what I want her to be. Let's just put it like that."

Farrah's heart twisted. "I'm sorry. That must have been hard to figure out."

"Yeah, maybe. I don't know." He took his fork and squashed the sticky bun with the side of the utensil, wiggling it until a chunk of bun broke free. Farrah did the same and ate. She immediately tasted the honey, pecans, and cinnamon—scrumptious.

After a moment, Abbott went on. "I forgive her, though. I've lowered my expectations. If she says something is going to happen, I know it probably won't. That type of thing. It's better that way."

"For what it's worth, I wish I had been wrong."

"Yeah. Me too," Abbott said, and Farrah studied his face as they finished off the buns. She could see the pain written across his forehead and the little boy inside him with a heart wound the size of Texas when his mother left.

Tears pricked her eyes, but she forced them away with a few rapid blinks.

"Look at it this way," Farrah said after composing herself, glad he hadn't noticed. "You get to be all those things you never had in your parents when you have your own family someday."

Abbott scoffed. "I'm not sure that'll happen."

"What? Why?"

Abbott smirked at her in a way that said, *Come on now, be serious.*

"You're a catch!" Farrah said, despite herself.

"Well, thanks, but I'm also pushing thirty. That's like sixty in a small town like this."

"That's *not* true," Farrah said, laughing in disbelief. "Hey, you're normally not so pessimistic. What happened to that golden retriever boy I knew who always looked on the bright side?"

Abbott seemed to think a while and then downed the rest of his coffee before speaking again. "Let's just say life has dealt me a few blows since then."

The way he flitted his eyes to Farrah and then away from her told her she was likely one of those hard hits he was referring to. She wondered if Abbott had fully processed their breakup, the idea of her not wanting to commit to forever with him. That, combined with his flaky, unreliable mom, had caused some trust issues she was now seeing.

"I never meant to hurt you all those years ago."

"I know," Abbott said. "Same here. I look back on it and see that we just wanted different things."

"Exactly. We were so young."

"We were," Abbott said. "But we're here now, aren't we? How awesome is it that we've circled around and now we're back, hanging out, talking like old times, but as adults? It's… nice."

A smile came unbidden to Farrah's face. "It is. Really nice." She locked eyes with Abbott, memories of old feelings flooding back.

Just then, Donna came by the table, interrupting them and breaking their connection. "Farrah, honey, I hate to interrupt, but I just flagged down Chuck. He said he'll take your statements now at the newspaper building so he can run an article by Monday. He said he's pressed for time."

"Oh, perfect!" Farrah said, then turned to Abbott, looking at him apologetically, then back to Donna. "I'll go right over."

Donna nodded, then headed to tend to another table.

"I got this," Abbott said, swiping the check, and they both stood.

"Thank you," she said. "I'm going to head out." She jerked a thumb over her shoulder in the direction of the door. "Daddy can pick me up later. This was really nice. We should do it again sometime."

"Yes, we should," Abbott said. "And… well, I look forward to seeing you again at the Tuesday market."

Farrah nervously pulled at her necklace. "Yeah. Okay." She couldn't help but feel that he had wanted to say something different but opted for the safe option instead. Maybe he was feeling what she felt—small nuances of old emotions trickling in, defying the logic that it was the worst possible timing for such a thing to happen.

She looked into his eyes, which winced as he chewed on his lip and considered her. He was definitely holding something back, or worried in some way.

"Is… everything okay?"

He slid his hand into his pocket and nodded. "Yeah. Right as rain. I was just wondering if…"

"If?"

"If you were doing anything tomorrow night. Because I'm not. And if you're not…" He motioned between them with his free hand, letting the unfinished sentence hover.

Farrah sighed deeply. "I'm sorry. I agreed to go out with a man Friday night, just as friends, but still. I really don't want to go. It was a moment of weakness. He was flattering me."

Abbott squared his shoulders and spoke boldly, though his cheeks gained color and there was a slight tightness to his voice. "If you don't want to go, then hang out with me instead."

Farrah melted under his assertiveness. She liked that option much better, as did her heart, which was about to pound out of her chest, but she had to be fair to Daniel. "He's a nice guy. And we're just going to Winston to a gallery. I'll be fine."

What she said was the truth. She left out the fact that she was sure her date with Daniel would stay in the friend zone. She wasn't so sure about time alone with Abbott, considering all the thoughts and emotions coming back to her after the one short day they'd spent together.

"I know you will. You're always fine," Abbott said, his sad smile and glistening eyes almost too much for Farrah to bear. "Anything happens, you call me, okay?"

"Okay."

With one last nod his way, she headed out the café door and down the sidewalk to her interview with Chuck Branson.

FRIDAY ROLLED AROUND, and Daniel texted her at five as she was sliding on the brand-new jeans she'd picked up at

Louise's shop in town. Her white eyelet top and gold sandals completed her summery chic outfit.

I'm sorry, I'd just feel so guilty if I didn't drive you. Pick you up at Glade Village at five-thirty?

This was already sounding more like a date, but at least he wasn't suggesting picking her up at home. Glade Village was close to the highway they needed to take, and thus, convenient as a meeting and parking spot.

Farrah glanced across her quilt-laden twin bed and out the window. She spied her large cargo van. It wasn't the best on gas, and her hourly pay was much less than what she was used to making in the art business. Riding with Daniel instead of meeting in Winston would definitely be more practical in the economic sense. She scolded herself internally for putting off trading in her van for something more efficient, yet she held on to hope that one day she could return to gallery life and would need the storage space. She shrugged off the feeling, and the worry, then texted him back:

Sounds good.

Time flew, and before she knew it, Daniel was pulling up at Glade Village in his adventure-style SUV. He hopped out quickly, blond hair slicked back, and opened her door for her, then handed her a rose.

"Honest to goodness," he said, his loud voice booming in the small space of the car where they were buckling up, "I picked it from a bush on my front walk. I swear I didn't buy it."

The gesture was sweet, and Farrah couldn't help but smile.

"You just mentioned you were betrayed, and I thought, even if we're on a friend date and wining and dining is off-limits, I can still show you what it's like to be treated right. No man should ever mistreat a woman."

Farrah allowed Daniel to be wrong about her relationship. Other than one decision made without consulting her, Connor had never mistreated Farrah. Quite the opposite.

The drive to Winston was short because of Daniel's enthusiastic and knowledgeable conversation. Farrah couldn't help but think that Daniel was the perfect guy— for someone else. She had absolutely no romantic spark with him. Still, she'd give the experience a chance. She had to start dating at some point, and getting back on the horse tonight with a super nice, professional guy was a great way to get her feet wet.

They pulled up to the gallery and Daniel hopped out to open her door once more. They walked a short way to the door, where a folding sign welcomed visitors, reading, "Appalachian Touch: Local Landscapes and Portraits." Daniel had no doubt chosen a great exhibit. Farrah was not familiar with Winston-Salem's art scene, since she'd been too busy growing the one in Charlotte to hop around to other towns. Still, this was right up her alley.

Daniel opened the gallery door for Farrah and stepped in behind her.

Farrah glanced at the wall to their right and it seemed there wasn't enough oxygen in the room. Her heart pounded behind her eyes and she crumpled on a nearby bench. Along the wall was a Connor Dunes collection of mountainscapes and cabins and lakes. She couldn't handle it on that day, so close to the unfortunate anniversary she longed to erase.

She couldn't stop crying. Daniel was saying something, trying to figure out what in the world was happening.

"What's wrong? Are you okay? Have I done something—"

"No," Farrah said through her tears. She managed to stand and pulled Daniel to a corner so as not to cause a scene. "You couldn't have known. The artist was my husband. It didn't end well."

"Connor Dunes… your husband." Daniel's shocked face suddenly drained of all color, and he looked absolutely mortified. "Wow, I'm the biggest jerk on the planet. Farrah, I'm so sorry. Connor was always so private, and then he just dropped off the radar. I swear, I didn't know."

"It's okay. Really. You didn't do it on purpose. And I know you want to see it, so you stay."

"No, I'll take you home." Daniel fished his keys out of his pocket.

"Daniel, I insist." There was no way she could sit with him in awkward silence in his car all the way home. She also feared his inevitable questions about what happened to their marriage and what happened to Connor that made him disappear. She hated talking about it. Heaven knew, enough people had asked her already. "Really. I know a café around the corner. I'll have a friend pick me up there in no time."

Daniel looked over at the exhibition, considering Farrah's conditions. "I just don't think that's right of me."

"But I'm asking you to stay and let me go. I need to get out of here, and I need to be alone. It's just been a really tough year and now this. I'm so sorry."

Daniel relented, pocketing his keys. "Okay. Just promise you'll text me when your friend picks you up. I'm not leaving Winston until I know you're safely on your way home."

"Okay, thank you," Farrah said, relieved. She hugged Daniel quickly, probably catching him off guard, considering the surprised "Oh" he let out. "You're a good guy, Daniel. Please don't feel bad about this."

He gave her a rueful smile. "It's hard not to. I'll see you around at Glade Village, I guess."

"Yes, for sure." Farrah swiped at the last of her tears and walked quickly out of the gallery—she couldn't stand to be around Connor's paintings any longer than necessary.

And she knew exactly who she needed to call.

"Bacon?" Abbott answered on the second ring.

"Hey. Come pick me up?"

Abbott laughed into his iPhone, a muffled, airy sort of chuckle. "I'm already on my way."

Chapter Eleven
FOUR YEARS AGO

"To another successful event!" Ginny squealed, raising her glass to clink with Farrah's and Kia's. The bustling room and chatter of the delighted crowd at the Oberg Gallery drowned out any chinking noise the flutes had made.

"The best one yet," Kia said loudly, over the room's booming noise.

"Oh, I agree wholeheartedly. Best ever. I still can't believe we got a Rehlinger," Farrah gushed, feeling loose. She'd gotten the provincial landscape by the famous German artist on loan at the last minute and it had drawn quite the crowd. She'd even dressed to match the painting, her amber blouse hanging loosely off one shoulder, matching the golden fields, and her black skirt resembling the murky lake of Rehlinger's *Dark Waters by Wheat Fields*.

Ginny teared up suddenly and slurped in a wet breath. Kia and Farrah reached for her in support. "No, I'm fine. It's just… Keith would've been so proud."

"I know, Mom," Kia said and side-hugged Ginny. "He

wouldn't have believed how successful the Oberg has become. It's just amazing."

Ginny nodded in agreement, but then something caught her eye and she perked up. "Is that…?" She squinted and looked across the room, shifting to one side to try to get a better look. Her hand darted to her mouth and her eyebrows shot up in surprise. She motioned for the girls to draw in closer to her, which they did. "Oh my word. You guys. It's Connor Dunes!"

Ginny was referencing the one and only landscape artist from North Carolina to have "made it big." Some people, though not Farrah herself, would call him a sellout because he had branded merchandise: puzzles, mugs, greeting cards. His placid beach images were printed on funeral home keepsakes and in vacation-town gift shops. He was one of the very few artists to be successful on a commercial scale. And as a result, he was dripping with money. Consumers couldn't get enough of his eye-pleasing creations.

But there was absolutely no mistaking his talent. Before he made it big, he was called "The Modern Monet." He had single-handedly revived the wonder of *au plein air* painting, and impressionism in landscape. Farrah had heard from colleagues about him, seen documentaries about his work, as well as read online articles—but rarely had Connor given an interview or appeared on screen. She never would have been able to pick him out of a crowd, but Ginny, being heavily involved in the art world, potentially could. Farrah would love to meet him. To think he was really in her gallery, though? She didn't believe it for a second.

"No way," Farrah said. Ginny was prone to practical jokes and all sorts of mischief. It was likely she was tricking her for a laugh.

"No, really, I promise! Kia, look!"

Kia stood on her tiptoes and, as tall as she was, saw over nearly the whole crowd. When she crouched back down to Farrah's level, she was breathless. "That's him! I'm sure of it! I heard him speak to an art class at UNCC with Mom one time. I remember him."

"So, what do we do?" Farrah asked, now frantic.

"I think," started Ginny with an impish smile, "the manager and curator of this fine exhibit should introduce herself. Who knows? You might get a painting on loan from him for the next show."

Farrah swallowed hard. She was able to pause her emotions and plow through whatever needed to be done, but to socialize with the rich and famous? She wasn't sure she was up to it. "But you're the owner."

"Bah, I don't do anything anymore," Ginny said with a flick of her wrist. "Go." She made a shooing motion with her hands.

Kia looked at Farrah too. "You heard the woman. You know she doesn't take no for an answer!"

Farrah downed the last of her glass and set her sights on the relaxed, sandy-haired man across the room. She made her way to him through the crowd more easily than she'd expected. As she approached, his sea-glass-green eyes fixated on her.

"Connor Dunes?" Farrah said as confidently as she could, extending her hand to shake his. His sandy hair was sun-kissed, streaked with blond. His tan face crinkled at the corners of his eyes with the lingering handsomeness of middle age.

He shook her hand and nodded, a polite smile on his face. He was used to being approached by fans, no doubt, and he didn't seem interested in getting into a long conversation. Farrah would have to set herself apart.

"I'm Farrah Macon, the curator of this exhibition and manager of the Oberg. Do you like the collection so far?"

Connor's eyes opened wide, relating his surprise. "Let me congratulate you. You've done a wonderful job." His voice was deep and smooth, attractive. He took a step closer to her to be heard over the noise. "Even with all my travels, I've never seen a Rehlinger in person."

"I'm glad you saw it first at the Oberg. Maybe someday we can get a few of your works on display. We're an up-and-coming gallery and, as you see, we have great exposure and attendance to our events. This is one of our livelier ones, because of the band. Normally things are much calmer."

Connor rested his hand gently on her elbow and moved closer to her ear. A scent of fresh cedar drifted her way, close as she was to wherever he had patted on his aftershave.

"Mind if we step outside? I can barely hear you, but I want to talk more about this."

Farrah nodded, butterflies invading her belly. She guided him to their outdoor patio, which featured a railing overlooking a city park, flanked with apartment buildings. A few couples were conversing on the patio as night fell and the first lightning bugs zapped their neon-yellow signals across the humid park below.

"How does a young thing like you take control of a gallery like this?" Connor asked, and laughed. "I mean, I'm sorry, but I'm so impressed."

"*You're* impressed?" Farrah asked, flattered beyond words. He was the famous one, and yet, he was praising her.

"Absolutely!" Connor exclaimed enthusiastically. "I want to talk to you about something—not my commercial stuff. I want to start a new series without anybody knowing, so I can escape the fame factor. Maybe even go indie again under a different name. I've moved back to this area, which is where I lived for a time years ago, and I've been taking day trips to the mountains. Occasionally, I'll stay a night or two in a rented cabin. You know, Asheville, Cherokee. I'm doing some mountain scenes, lake scenes, and the like. I think it could be a whole new aesthetic."

"I'm sorry, Mr. Dunes, but your name is synonymous with beach landscapes. I have to be honest."

"Exactly," he lamented. "I'd have to come up with an alias."

"Connor Peaks?" Farrah jested and half expected him to ignore the quip. Instead, he looked at her and the most genuine laugh escaped his lips. His smile was kind, his green eyes alive. His joy, contagious. Farrah shared in the laugh. "I mean, you could also do Connor Hills, or Connor Slopes. Sorry—I'm a goofball."

"That's okay," he said, amusedly shaking his head. "I love it. Usually curators are so…"

"I know," Farrah said, having worked with many of them through the years. Museum personnel certainly had a type, though she'd met a few fun ones. "I'd love to work with you on this, though. In all seriousness. The Oberg will gladly take your indie, pseudonymed paintings."

"I'm glad to hear that. And I'm excited. I'm at the age where I have had my success—my *peak*, if you will—and now I want to do what I want. My parents died of genetic heart and lung diseases well before their time, and that makes me think a lot about how fast life goes by. I want to be able to say I did what I wanted to while I was alive. It's something I've really been focusing on for the past few weeks. Seizing the day." Farrah affirmed his philosophy with a soft hum, and Connor's eyes drifted off to the park, now quiet, heavy with night. "And that brings me to this.

How old are you?" His voice quaked with some sort of hidden tension.

"Twenty-five? Almost twenty-six."

He chewed on his lip and looked down at her, searching for the words to proceed. She knew what he was getting at. And she wanted him to just go ahead and *say it*. She felt it too. The whole time they'd been talking, an electricity lurked behind every little thing they said. They matched wits. They clicked. They liked each other.

She hadn't felt this way in a long, long time. Not since Abbott.

"Well, I'm *forty*-five. Is that too old to ask you out?"

It was a little unconventional, yes, and Daddy wouldn't like it, seeing as he was only seven years older than this man. But she knew about Connor from all she'd read. They were of a similar background as far as faith and family were concerned, and his reputation of being kind, sincere, and level-headed preceded him. Nobody in the business ever had anything bad to say about Connor. And besides, she was sure her parents would get over it. She was an adult, after all, and all her other decisions had been excellent so far.

The justifications held strong. She wanted nothing more than to pick Connor's brain and get inside his heart.

"Age is just a number," Farrah said and smiled.

Connor reached down and took her hand.

"What do you say we do something crazy?"

Her planning mind screamed no. But her heart pounded a fervent yes.

"Like what?"

"Dinner tonight, beach tomorrow."

Farrah squinted at him skeptically. The beach was four hours away, which meant staying overnight. She wasn't really *that* type of girl. Connor understood and raised his eyebrows to give his defense.

"Sorry, let me explain. I have a beach house in the Outer Banks with a separate, attached apartment, where I would stay. It's a common thing for me to paint at the studio at the beach house, as well as invite friends. Look." He fished his cell phone out of his back pocket and opened his camera roll, swiping through it to show Farrah several of his recent models—one that looked to be a male friend about his age, whom Connor had painted fishing on a pier. Next was a lady model, very pretty and also in her forties, wearing a lilac sundress.

"That's my long-time friend's wife," he explained, as he swiped to a snapshot of the breathtaking portrait he'd done of her sitting in front of sand dunes.

That's a convenient explanation, Farrah thought, still skeptical. But then, the next photo Connor flipped to was a selfie he took with the same woman, now snuggled up to her husband, their three faces beaming in the photo.

"And here's my studio," he said. The picture showed an eclectic array of paintings in differing stages of being finished. Paint was splattered on all surfaces, and it was definitely a frequently used space. After seeing all this evidence, Farrah was inclined to trust Connor.

Connor put away his phone. "I just want to see you at the beach. Wear something white. You can pick up shells or build a sandcastle, and I'll paint you."

Farrah was lightheaded from the attention. It was a total pinch-me moment. Not only did she get to see this master artist paint, but he'd be painting *her*. A warm breeze floated through the humid night air, displacing her brown waves.

"I'm in," Farrah said, a thrill coursing through her. "I'm totally in."

It was too hot to have chills, but she had them. All over.

FARRAH GROGGILY OPENED her eyes on the twelfth consecutive morning she'd woken up at Connor's beach house, cocooned in soft blankets. She was grateful Ginny had allowed her to take her allotted two weeks' vacation on such short notice, and she'd explained the situation to her parents, who were surprisingly supportive. They trusted her, they'd said.

The sunrise's earliest light eased in through the gigantic picture window in the master bedroom where she stayed, coating the room in orangish pink. She placed two bare feet on the pine floors, then wrapped a light blanket over her shoulders and headed for the balcony. Hovering over the placid blue-green ocean, the sun was an orange orb lazily making its ascent. The sea breeze tickled her hair, and a hand touched her shoulder.

She spun around and fell again into his arms. He breathed her in.

"Coffee?"

"You know it," was her daily reply.

She settled on the outdoor furniture and wrapped the blanket over her legs. Connor returned soon with a tray supporting two mugs, a full French press, and creamer. He took the seat beside her, and they watched the sunrise in awed silence, holding hands amid the salty smell of ocean tides. When the French press's time had elapsed, he pushed down the press and served her coffee, just how she liked it. She sipped. Placid. In love.

"I was thinking I'd take you to breakfast this morning. There's a place I know."

"Oh?"

"It has excellent cinnamon buns."

"You don't have to tell me twice."

"I knew you'd love that." He *did* know that about her. He knew practically everything about her. In the almost two weeks since they'd met at the gallery, gone for drinks, and taken off on their impulsive, carpe diem beach trip, they'd barely stopped talking long enough to breathe— except during the peaceful morning sunrises over the Atlantic that held their attention captive. They'd talked about both of their family histories, where they see them- selves in five years, if they wanted kids or not—he didn't, but that was fine with Farrah. She had her two sweet nephews to love. Besides, she knew many men who hadn't wanted kids when they were single, but changed their minds when they settled down with the right woman.

The past two weeks had been an extended adventure with zero red flags, and all the fuzzy feelings.

Farrah had never fallen so hard so fast.

Well, she *had*. But that was a long time ago, and in the end, it had resulted in heartbreak. She'd let all that go, and now she was free to love again.

"There's something I want to show you first, before we get ready."

Connor stood and offered his hand, and the two walked to his outdoor easel, draped with cloth. Connor removed the shroud, and *Sandcastle Girl* just about took Farrah's breath away. She'd only gotten peeks of it on those first few days on the beach as he drew and then painted a rough outline. After that, he'd moved it to the balcony and had been working on it painstakingly for days.

In the image, Farrah reclined leisurely on the sand, propping herself up on one elbow. With her right hand, she built a small sandcastle, adorning it with sea glass she'd found. Both her brown hair and white dress flowed behind her with the beachy breeze.

The canvas was a feast of color, despite being of a simple subject matter. The curator in her couldn't help but pick it apart, much like an editor might do to a book they wanted to read for fun. Still, she was in awe of Connor's craft. Her white dress was impossibly bright; it looked like a light was installed to shine right on it. But then again, it *wasn't* white, it was sort of pinkish, maybe lilac, and definitely navy blue in the shadows. Her face, a red and brown and cream montage of brush strokes, still conveyed her bone structure and features somehow. Her hair contained twenty or so colors, but all tricking the mind into thinking it was a woman's brown hair being kissed by the sun.

"You're incredible," Farrah said, breathless. She turned, falling into Connor and kissing him hard. "I'm honored. They used to call you the modern Monet, but this almost looks like a Sorolla. I love it."

"It's yours," Connor said. "It's not for sale. This was a work of love. I love you, Farrah."

Her heart beat faster. It was the first time he'd actually said it, but his tone and demeanor proved the statement's truth. She looked into his greenish-blue eyes, sandy blond lashes framing their kindness. He reached into his back pocket and pulled out a handkerchief, then handed it to her.

She unfolded the antique, embroidered hankie trepidatiously. Inside was a simple rose-gold band with a matte, teal stone, not too different from the colors of Connor's eyes. Nothing ostentatious. Just like she would have wanted if she could have picked it out herself.

Perfect.

"Is this… sea glass?" she asked, smiling in wonder.

"Yeah, I might have snagged it from the castle you

were building and taken it to the local jeweler." Connor paused, the salt air thick with potential between them. He cleared his throat and restarted with a more serious resolve. "I want to make an honest woman out of you," Connor said. "Farrah Ann Macon, will you marry me?"

In all her teenage fantasies, she'd imagined things playing out so differently when she was proposed to. She'd imagined a bouquet of flowers, a big diamond, a man—specifically, Abbott—dropping on one knee while a secret photographer documented the moment. She thought she'd squeal, tremble, giggle, or maybe cover her mouth in shock.

But now that it was really happening, all she was experiencing was peace. Connor was her match. Her partner. She'd noticed it from the very first moment they started talking. It had only been twelve days, but she wanted twelve more, and twelve more, and twelve more, forever. She didn't think she could *ever* get enough of Connor, not in a million years. Their age difference had only been a topic of discussion on the very first night they met. Over dinner, they'd hashed out what people would think, and came to the conclusion that it didn't matter to them at all. That seemed ages ago. This was now, and she was sure.

The past several years, and growing into her role at the Oberg, had changed Farrah. She had become a woman who was less wary of commitment. In contrast to her late teen years when Abbott had professed his love to her, she was sure now that she could have both love *and* the life she wanted. When she looked at Connor, she was certain.

She'd rarely been so sure of anything as she was of a future with him.

"Yes," Farrah said, extending her hand and allowing him to slide the ring on her finger. "And, Connor? I love you too. I will love you—forever."

Chapter Twelve
PRESENT DAY

Farrah climbed into the passenger seat of Abbott's pickup truck, overwhelmed with relief to be somewhere safe. Not that she had been in any physical danger at the gallery or with Daniel. But she had been at risk of losing her cool, of spewing her pent-up feelings that she'd worked so hard at camouflaging. She didn't know what that would look like, and quite frankly, she didn't want to find out.

Especially not in public.

"Where to?" Abbott asked, patiently regarding her.

Her options were endless, but nothing came to mind.

"I don't care, just drive."

Abbott smiled and cranked the truck.

She sent Daniel a text as Abbott pulled out from the café and merged onto I-40, then 52 North. Farrah looked over at him while he drove. Right hand relaxed but in control, a loose grip on the top of the steering wheel. His collared shirt's sleeves were rolled up to his elbows, exposing forearms tanned from hours of working at his ranch. He had shaved, and his hatless head of hair had been tamed with wax. Farrah stifled a chuckle as she wondered if he'd gotten ready to go out on the off chance that she'd call. Hoping to be the backup. What would he have done if she hadn't called? Just sat at home looking perfect?

"What?" Abbott asked, looking at her amusedly with a half smile, one dimple popping up fleetingly.

"You look good," Farrah said, a little too matter-of-factly.

"So do you," Abbott shot back. He turned his face, now rosy, back toward the road. "Date from Hades?"

Farrah groaned and briefly covered her face with her hands. "He took me to my husband's exhibition."

Abbott didn't skip a beat. "Wow. Dude had no clue, did he?"

"Bless his heart," Farrah muttered, and meant it. "He's the nicest guy."

"Anything there?" Abbott asked, his voice quaking with momentary insecurity.

"Nothing. Not even a spark. And it was a friend date, so…"

Abbott exhaled pent-up tension and laughed through his nose.

"For the record," Abbott said, "I would *never* do what he did."

Farrah laughed. "I'm sure you wouldn't." It might even have been impossible for him to do so, because he wasn't into anything artsy when she knew him before, and she suspected a gallery date wouldn't have crossed his mind in the first place.

"I know what you need," Abbott said. "A strawberry cheesecake milkshake from the Grill Out."

How he remembered her favorite milkshake flavor from their local fast-food hotspot after a whole decade,

Farrah had no idea. She giggled and laid into him. "It's not '*the* Grill Out.' It's just 'Grill Out.' You country bumpkin."

"The Grill Out. The Wal-Mart. The Food Lion. They've all got 'the.'" He smirked and laid a heavy hand on her knee, giving her body a playful shake, then promptly removed it, which was probably for the best. Still, Farrah couldn't help but relish the short, mischievous touch after so long without any affection from a man.

Abbott merged into the right lane to prepare to exit. In his truck, with the green summer trees flanking them, and the warm air rushing in from the cracked windows, she was eighteen again.

"Come on. I'm buying. Say yes."

"Okay, but I'm paying. I insist, because you got my coffee the other day." Abbott glanced her way with a slightly furrowed brow, as if he were going to argue, but he eventually relaxed his face in surrender. As drawn as she was to Abbott, she needed to not let old dating behaviors pop into their budding friendship. Her heart was vulnerable, and it would be too easy to get carried away.

"Fair enough," he ended up saying.

And it *was* fair. This wasn't a date, and he owed her nothing. He couldn't dispute it, because that would mean he wanted this evening to be more than it was: a friend helping her out when she was in a pickle. Something told Farrah he wasn't yet confident enough to be assertive about whatever they were. He was still trying to figure out who she was as an adult.

Abbott pulled off the exit on University Parkway and into the Grill Out drive-through line. Farrah reached into her purse, retrieved her debit card, and handed it to him, his fingers brushing hers as he received it. Their eyes met briefly.

Gosh, he was handsome. He'd missed his calling as one of Mrs. Janice's soap opera stars.

"Finer than angel fuzz," Farrah said, remembering the older woman's comment. Abbott looked at her like she'd lost her mind. He ordered their takeout, turning his broad back to her as he leaned his head out the driver's side window to address the crackling speaker.

No, she hadn't lost her mind, but if she wasn't careful, she'd be in danger of losing her heart.

———

THEY'D FEASTED in the truck on burgers and shakes while heading north to home, and they'd just passed the welcoming sight of Pilot Mountain, positioned just so on highway 52 North that it seemed to rise up from the middle of the road. Before Europeans arrived in North Carolina, the native Saura people had called the mountain *Jomeokee*, or great guide, due to the enormous rocky pinnacle on top that could be seen for miles and used as a landmark or lookout.

Passing Pilot Mountain meant they were just about home.

"Where you wanna go?" Abbott asked several minutes later, as he drove slowly down a historic section of Main Street in Whitetail Ridge. Large homes lined the street with plenty of windows and wraparound porches. Many of the houses featured granite elements, due to the nearby quarry. The sunset filled the sky with the orange-and-pink brush strokes of the Master Artist.

"Not home," Farrah said as Abbott turned down the main thoroughfare, past 1930s storefronts rented to trendy boutiques, gift shops, and salons—including Amy Bell's.

She eyed the Beryl Theatre as they passed and remembered the night they broke up. "Anywhere but home."

Mom and Daddy were keeping the boys overnight. The house would be hectic, and they'd want to know about her night out. If she returned home now, they'd ask why it had ended so quickly. They were excited for her and hopeful since she had agreed to go out with a friend despite her circumstances. What had happened would be a letdown, and she wanted to save them the pain tonight. Tomorrow after everyone had rested, the story was bound to be less impactful.

"My place?" Abbott asked.

Time froze for Farrah as she weighed the implications of such an offer.

"Not like *that*," Abbott blurted, eyes wide. "We won't even go inside. I want to show you a few things in the pasture."

He was *so* cute. She couldn't help but grin, though she fought it. "All right. The Abbott Ranch it is."

"There's no 'the,'" Abbott corrected, giving her a sideways glance.

"Exactly," Farrah said, smiling out the window as they left town and turned toward the backroads. Eventually, Abbott drove past her house, then past the Bells,' and turned into Abbott Ranch's drive. The warm wind whipped at her long hair the whole way, the summer night making her feel alive.

The gravel driveway was long, practically a road in itself. He parked the truck outside his house and shut off the engine.

She opened her own door and followed Abbott through the darkening evening to his front porch, where he fumbled with the keys, grumbling that the porch light had burned out. After he succeeded in opening the door, he said, "Wait here."

He jogged inside and returned with two pairs of rubber boots and two flashlights, then closed the front door behind him and pocketed his keys.

"These are Dad's, but his feet are smaller than mine, so they shouldn't be too big." Farrah put her feet in the boots. They were enormous on her, but she didn't care. "Okay, maybe they're still gigantic. Did your feet never grow after the fourth grade or something?"

"Don't worry about it," she said, grabbing her flashlight. "Are you taking me down to Quarry Creek?"

Abbott let out a surprised laugh. "No. Something better."

He flicked on his light and led the way. They walked through the yard toward the forest line. "This is a shortcut."

Darkness had fallen quickly, and the air was heavy with humidity. Farrah pocketed her flashlight for a moment and felt for the hair tie on her wrist. She swept her sticky waves back into a messy bun with a few shorter pieces falling down to frame her face.

Abbott advanced, snapping twigs and rustling underbrush, sure of his path. Farrah turned her beam back on, a bit frightened. With her left hand, she reached up and grabbed onto his shirt, and he let out a small laugh.

"Don't worry." His voice was low and familiar, taking her back to their teenage days. "We're almost there."

They soon emerged from the thick Carolina woods into a pasture, and Abbott hopped a metal gate, then extended his hands for Farrah to do the same. "It's not close enough to zap you," he said, referencing a wire that must've been nearby, strung along the fence somewhere in the dark where Farrah couldn't see. She climbed the gate and placed her hands lightly on Abbott's shoulders, not missing the firm and warm feel of him under his shirt. He grabbed her waist and helped her hop down on the grass, letting her go right away.

Necessary touches, Farrah told herself. She'd needed help getting down.

In the dark, they advanced to the unknown location through the pasture. "Watch for patties," Abbott said, and Farrah darted her light to her rubber boots, where a greenish-brown mush adorned her heel.

"Too late."

Abbott chuckled quietly.

Farrah didn't mind her messy boots. She was mesmerized by the landscape she'd gone so long without appreciating at night. Along the darkened horizon, hilly tree lines resembled ocean waves. Lightning bugs blipped their Morse code all around them, darkening and then flashing for a spell before darkening again. Nature's lullaby, the humming violins of tree critters, engulfed the whole landscape with long, rhythmic pulses. The aroma of pasture grass and earth filled Farrah's lungs with each breath.

"It's beautiful out here."

Abbott agreed with a hum. Then he slowed down and talked even quieter.

"This is what I wanted to show you," he said, breathing a little heavy, and motioning around with his free hand, while his other directed his light beam at different things. "This whole pasture is for grass-fed cows. If you noticed, it's on the complete other side of our operation."

"Wow," Farrah said, staring out at a group of bovines that Abbott's beam illuminated, all brown and black. Some lay on the ground in a deep sleep. Others blinked and looked about, and still others stood chewing. A few friendly moos greeted them, and Farrah couldn't help but laugh with joy.

Abbott went on. "I understand my dad's ways, certainly. And they've made a good income for us. But I want to take things in a different route. These cows get a little grain from time to time, depending. Other than that, they just graze all day and night. Hay and grass."

"I'm sure that special treatment makes them happy," Farrah said.

"Oh, they are. I treat my girls *real* good," Abbott said confidently.

Suddenly, Abbott squinted in the direction of the cows, attempting to shine his flashlight farther toward the back. "Come with me. I think I see something."

They skirted around the sleeping cows to the back of the pasture, light beams bobbing up and down haphazardly, until Abbott stopped a bit closer to one cow and shined the light directly on her.

"Oh, man," he said, joy overtaking his voice. "We have a baby!"

Farrah squinted toward his beam. Close to the tree line stood a mama cow and a nursing, newborn calf.

Abbott crouched and walked slowly, motioning for Farrah to follow. His breathing was excited, and he laughed at the spectacular moment. Farrah shined her light on the pair so Abbott could assess them.

"Good job, Trixie," he said to the mama cow, as he stepped closer. "One week early."

The calf left nursing and approached Abbott, not fully sure about him but also not afraid. Abbott held out his hand and the little thing sniffed and nuzzled with its precious, wet nose. Abbott squatted and inspected the calf, while petting its head.

"It's a bull," he said, his deep voice a low rumble, but

still relaying his exhilaration. He turned back to Farrah. "Come pet him. What do you think about all this?"

Farrah approached the bull calf and caressed its soft face. "Oh, I'm in love."

Once Abbott saw that everything was in order, he led Farrah out of the pasture and to his old, beat up, red Tacoma—the same one he drove in high school, now relegated to a forgotten lot behind the barn. He opened the passenger door and grabbed a sleeping bag and a quilt. There were also some canned drinks and a few packs of Nabs.

"You should lock your truck. Someone might break in and steal your, ahem, *valuables*." Farrah giggled.

"Hush," Abbott joked. "Help me."

Together, they spread the sleeping bag and quilt in the empty bed of the Tacoma, then climbed in and sat side-by-side. Farrah was surprised at herself, crawling in the truck bed beside him without a second thought. It seemed too easy. Too natural. She didn't want to come off as too eager.

But, man, she was lonely, and late at night after an emotional day, it was getting harder to keep her resolve intact. Though her mind and spirit knew it was the worst possible time to draw closer to Abbott, she feared her flesh was too weak and vulnerable to resist hanging out with him more like a couple and less like friends.

Above them, in the pitch-black summer sky, the cloudy glow of the Milky Way arched across the heavens, smattered with uncountable stars.

"Sometimes I come out here and just look up. Think about life." Abbott's hands were behind him, propping up his body, as were hers. His thick chest rose and fell with a placid breath.

"What about life?"

"Just where I'm going with the ranch, mostly. How to break it to my dad."

Farrah furrowed her brow, attempting to decipher what he'd just divulged. The distant, flashing lights of a plane flitted across the nightscape, causing Farrah to be excited for just a moment, before seeing that it wasn't a shooting star. Maybe they'd be lucky enough to see one.

"Break what to your dad?"

Abbott groaned out a sigh. "I'm—*we're*—turning thirty soon. And I guess I've just realized that I've put all this pressure on myself to sustain this legacy of his that I don't have much interest in pursuing anymore." Abbott paused and Farrah waited patiently in the silence. She knew him well enough to know he wouldn't stop talking until he'd gotten the full feeling out in the open. When he picked back up with his confession, he was quieter, as if he was afraid his dad might be near enough to hear.

"I'm just burned out with the factory stuff. The cramped, muddy pastures. The long, smelly chicken houses. I want to pursue this grass-fed thing, maybe add in some highland cows, do goat milk stuff, high-yield organic crops. But I'd need more land. Honestly, when I heard Bobby might sell his forty acres, I was almost excited, before my morals kicked in."

Farrah couldn't blame him. "Did you ever tell your dad any of this?"

"I hinted at it once. But he kind of shut it down, told me my place was with the family business, doing things like we'd always done them. I suspect his harsh reaction to my idea was because he took my college studies and attempt at working with my mom personally. Like I was turning my back on him." Abbott paused a moment before continuing. "He and I are so different. He's not much to look up to. Kind of a womanizer, kind of money focused. I'm not interested in that. It's tough, but it looks like I'm going to have to break up with my own father, in the business sense."

Farrah thought about zinging him by saying that he was good at breakups, but decided against it. Her mind, however, turned to the night he broke things off with her, and the different paths their lives had taken.

"You ever think about us when you come out here alone?" Farrah's voice seemed tiny, powerless. Like a twinkly Christmas light among burning red giants.

Abbott skipped a few beats, and just breathed. "More than I care to admit."

"Just recently, or—"

"Mostly in the beginning. But yeah, since you've been back. I'd be lying if I said…" Abbott's speech trailed off into silence. "I guess you could say I had a little trouble moving on from you at first."

"Didn't you date anybody?"

"Not at first. But then, when I'd healed a bit, I dated just about every eligible girl in Stokes and Surry counties. Now they've all gotten married, had kids, or moved away."

"Any of them serious?" Farrah's chest squeezed with sudden, surprising jealousy, which she tried to brush off. Abbott and she were nothing. She had no claim on him anymore. She shouldn't care if he had loved anyone else. "With you, I mean?"

"Not really." His voice was restrained, almost bitter. "None of them measured up to what we had. I was lucky to get a third date before the illusion wore off. We had a good thing going back then, Bacon."

He wasn't wrong. A shiver ran through Farrah. "Surely in college there were girls…"

"No. I stayed single. It was better that way." Abbott's voice cracked and fell away. It was a while before he started again. "In the back of my mind, I was always hopeful that you'd call."

Her heart panged.

What he'd said was true: she hadn't called.

She'd always seen it one way: that Abbott had broken *her* heart. She hadn't considered that he'd have substantial heartbreak as well, or that he'd still have trust issues based on her actions after all these years.

Regret pierced through her stomach. He'd waited four years for her. Why hadn't she read that stupid list? Why hadn't she done what he'd asked and kept him in her life, been patient for a few years, and then seen how things went after college?

Her mind flitted to Connor. Did she regret him? Absolutely not. But she also hadn't expected things to end up like they had. From whatever angle a person looked at it, this was an extremely complicated situation—and far from a normal one. Here she had a man in front of her, opening up, insinuating that he wished things could have been different for them. And now the other man was long gone, and as she'd slowly accepted, he would never come back, even though the aftermath of that situation was far from over.

"I do wonder what would have happened if I had read your letter and ended up calling you. I mean, I got married and everything…"

Abbott shrugged as he looked up at the sky. "Maybe it was supposed to happen that way."

"Yeah," Farrah offered, and the thought brought her peace. Thinking that this was the plan for her life, and she needed to go down this road to learn and grow from it, made her feel that maybe, no matter how difficult it had been, it hadn't been in vain.

Abbott turned to look at Farrah, holding her gaze. "And call me crazy, but maybe this was supposed to happen too."

"This?" Farrah asked. "Us?"

"Yes, us. Look at us. Here we are, after all these years, in the bed of my Tacoma, in the same town where we started. I'm not saying everything is perfect for you now, or that I don't have my own stuff to work through, but..." Abbott paused, watching her. His gaze flitted to her lips, and he moved her ponytail behind her back, letting his hand rest on her shoulder. The feel of it was warm and rough. "Maybe we were supposed to find each other again."

Abbott leaned closer, until he was only a few inches from her face.

"I missed you all these years," he whispered, squeezing her shoulder. "I know things are complicated." He leaned in more. "And I know I shouldn't do this..."

Lonely for touch and almost trembling, she lifted her hand to clutch his shirt over his chest. "Maybe you should," she whispered.

Abbott—both at eighteen and twenty-nine—absolutely *never* missed a cue. His strong arm pressed her close, and he dipped his face to hers, lingering over her mouth, before lightly touching his lips to hers. The kiss was warm. Tender.

Energy coursed through Farrah, and she reached up, digging her fingers through his curls like she used to do, like she'd never stopped doing it. He pressed his mouth to hers again, stronger this time, hungrier.

"No!" she suddenly gasped, in spite of herself. Abbott

flinched back and quickly took his hands off her body, breathing hard as he watched her, worried.

"Connor," she groaned, and then wept, covering her face. "I can't do this to Connor."

THE HOUSE WAS dark when Abbott dropped Farrah off back at home, everyone having gone to bed hours before. The walk through the pasture and the truck ride were quiet, tense. She couldn't bear a second more in such a thick silence, so she had him take her home instead of to her van halfway across town at Glade Village. She'd worry about that tomorrow.

She'd caught a glimpse of Abbott's disheveled face. He was beating himself up. She could tell by the way his jaw twitched.

The truth was, she was blaming herself too. She knew better than to get involved with anyone right now, even if it was Abbott, even if it was fate, as he'd suggested. Her heart wasn't stable enough. Macy had told her, and so had her mom, that her emotions were all over the place and anything could set them off. Now her own panic during their kiss had shown her just how shaky she was.

How fragile.

Tiptoeing toward the staircase, she spied her two nephews sleeping on the pullout sofa where they'd probably dozed off watching a movie, and she melted. Their sweet innocence took a little bit of the night's sting away.

Guilt and fear overwhelmed her. She changed into her pajamas and crashed on her bed, grabbing for her phone, which she'd ignored the whole time she was with Abbott. In it, were texts from Kia with pictures from her baby shower prep. Her husband, Travis, and Ginny were there, of course. They had a cute theme—baby safari.

She also had a text from Daniel thanking her for letting him know she was safe, and saying not to worry about it after she had apologized profusely. Then came his own string of apologies. *I didn't know, I had no idea, I'm so sorry, I never would've...*

Finally, a text from Macy, who never texted unless she had to. She only called. Indeed, Farrah checked her missed calls and had four from Macy. She'd felt her phone vibrate during her evening with Abbott, but she'd ignored the calls when she'd seen they were just from Macy. She had more interesting things going on than a phone call with her sister.

All at once, she remembered that Macy and Elijah had gone off for a romantic few nights away. If Macy was calling Farrah while on her trip, it had to be a big deal.

Farrah's heart plummeted as she opened the text:

> Farrah, it's important. Jincey is going around hinting that our basket isn't legit. She's said all kinds of things, one being that you or Abbott are trying to profit from it and that the way some of the items were acquired was sketchy. Know anything about this?

Farrah could hardly contain her fury and confusion. Jincey was like an annoying little gnat flying around her face, except the gnat was trying to thwart plans and ruin reputations—and for no apparent reason. What had Farrah ever done to Jincey? It seemed outlandish that the woman could still be upset about not being able to snag Abbott the summer after high school, which was the only reason Farrah could come up with for her outrageous, mean-girl behavior. Normal, mature adults just didn't act like that.

This turmoil inside Farrah was not a good thing to feel before sleeping off an already emotionally wild night.

She stumbled down to the kitchen to make herself a relaxing tea to calm her nerves, then drank it quietly while observing the sleeping angels in the living room. All this tension—Abbott, Connor, and Jincey—would have to be dealt with tomorrow.

She finished her tea then quietly grabbed a pillow and a throw and snuggled onto the sofa bed next to her littlest nephew. In his slumber, he reached around and hugged her arm. He was so warm, so soft, so tiny. Even the sound of his shallow breaths was filled with sweet innocence. She would've liked to have had her own little ones by now. But it wasn't in the plan.

Heavy with sleep, Farrah drifted off, thinking of Connor.

And thinking of Abbott.

Chapter Thirteen
THREE YEARS AGO

O n a summer Thursday evening, Connor stopped by to see Farrah at work. They were catching up in the Oberg's management office as a few remaining guests roamed the gallery under the college intern's surveillance before closing time in fifteen minutes.

Perhaps it hadn't been the best time to bring up the topic of children, but a year had gone by since their Bahamas destination elopement a month after Connor's proposal, and everything else in their lives had been coming along nicely.

Except for growing their family.

Farrah had been fine with the idea of not having kids for a few months. But things had changed. Maybe they had for him too. Or, maybe she could convince him.

"I mean, just *one*," Farrah said as she carefully stored some loaned pieces in a designated locker for an artist to retrieve later. "I don't mean five or anything. I couldn't handle that. Maybe not even two."

Connor clicked his tongue and shook his head, settling his hands on his hips. Despite several years living in Charlotte and focusing on mountain landscapes as his subject matter, he still wore a breezy linen shirt unbuttoned at the top and khaki shorts. He was beachy to the core.

"I thought we settled this already."

"Not really," Farrah said, wrapping a piece in bubble wrap. "To be honest, the one time I brought it up I noticed that you kind of changed the subject." She'd let it slide because of how new their relationship was. But they'd had enough of the honeymoon stage. She was ready for the next step. A child would complete their family. And she wasn't getting any younger. Neither was he. "My biological clock is ticking, is all."

"You're not even twenty-seven!" Connor exclaimed, laughing in shock. Even when they bickered, their tone was light, lovey. Connor had endless patience and humored Farrah's perfectionism and ambition. "Your biological clock has plenty of years left. At least ten, if not more."

Farrah locked away the last art piece, removed her cloth gloves, and sauntered over to Connor. She rested her head on his neck and hugged him around his taut waist. She hated to compare, but he had a slighter build than Abbott. It was a relief to her neck because she didn't have to bend over backward—literally—to kiss him, like she had with Abbott in high school.

"Honey. You're forty-six. If we wait ten years, you'll be fifty-six. Come on!"

She broke down in laughter at what that might look like, but it was muffled against the satisfying texture of his shirt. He smelled like sandalwood and cedar. She breathed him in.

He patted her back lovingly. "It wouldn't be the first time," he offered. "Abraham."

"Oh, don't start with the Bible stories!" Farrah scolded in mock frustration and Connor laughed genuinely. "I just mean… I don't think I can be on this earth and not have *one* kid. It's an experience I want to have. You know?"

She stayed in their embrace but felt Connor's stillness in return. She sensed him pulling away emotionally.

"Farrah," he said sorrowfully. It was the way he said her name when what he had to say wasn't good. When he had to tell her no. Or when he had to stand firm, even though he hated disappointing others—especially Farrah, whom he loved more than anyone. "Why don't we have a seat?"

Farrah pulled away and looked at him, cocking her head in confusion. Sweetly, he nodded, encouraging her to sit on the leather sofa over a cowhide rug right in the middle of the spacious office.

When they were settled next to each other, he took her hands in his, then hesitated and studied her fingers, his mouth agape while he searched for the right words.

"Farrah, I… can't give you what you want. In that regard."

Farrah shook her head, trying to make sense of his seriousness. A baby would be a blessing. Did he not think so? Did he not see the urgency of doing this now rather than later?

Or had something happened to him that would make conception impossible?

"Are you incapable?" Farrah whispered since the door wasn't fully shut. "Or did you have a procedure or something?"

"It's not that." He ran his hands through his sandy blond hair and sighed, then rubbed them up and down on his face. "Remember what we talked about on our first date?"

"Yeah?" How could she not? She had hung on his every word over food and drinks at Litro. The bar was one of Farrah's favorite rooftop locales with an extensive tapas menu. That first night, she and Connor had talked for hours before he'd dropped her off at home, and then returned to pick up her and her suitcase the next morning for their impulsive trip to the North Carolina Outer Banks.

"Then you'll remember I told you my parents died very young from awful diseases, and that's why I didn't have kids in my first marriage, or plan on having any in the future."

Farrah scrunched her brow, thinking back. She remembered the conversation, certainly, but she hadn't thought it was as set in stone as he was letting on now. While she'd respected that he didn't want kids and been okay with it at the time, she'd thought he might come around, like she was warming up to the idea now. Most single men would never want children without a faithful woman in the picture. She thought settling down and building a life together would bring about the desire for kids naturally.

And she wasn't quite sure what his parents' unfortunate deaths had to do with any of this.

"What do you mean when you say your parents died *very* young?" she asked, needing stats, numbers, dates. Enough with the vagueness.

"I mean they were only forty-nine and fifty-eight."

It was a blow, for sure. She hadn't asked about it again after that first date because she hadn't wanted to upset him. She wouldn't want to talk about it if she'd lost her own parents—not for a long while.

"Okay… And you're scared you'll leave your children fatherless like you—"

"No!" Connor snapped, then jumped up and started pacing the room. "No," he said, calmer, an apologetic look about his troubled face. "I'm sorry. This topic gets me a little uptight."

"Connor," Farrah said pleadingly, holding her hands out, palms up as if to beckon him back to her on the sofa. She'd never seen him like this before. So distraught and disheveled.

He turned instead and supported himself with one hand on the windowsill, looking out over the city as he spoke. "Farrah, they died horrible deaths from genetic diseases. They suffered. My mom died of cystic fibrosis—it's a lung thing. And my dad had genetic cardiomyopathy that led to congestive heart failure. I'm not positive, but I'm pretty certain my grandparents died of similar things. I never met them. They were all from a tiny town in Kentucky. Anyway…" Connor shook his head. "You're right that I don't want to die young and leave a kid behind. But I also don't want to pass on a death sentence to an innocent little baby." He choked on this last word. Farrah had seen him play with kids before. He loved them.

She grasped desperately for a positive take on all this. "Well, my family and I are all healthy, as far as I know. Both of my nephews are perfect. I mean, what are the odds that you'd pass something down?" Her voice was thick with the threat of tears, and as soon as she voiced the question, she realized how naive she sounded.

Connor didn't respond, perhaps on purpose, because she wouldn't like what he had to say. He just looked over at her from the window, sadness seeming to pull his handsome face down toward the floor.

She couldn't help it. She blinked and the tears pelted onto her slacks. It was a real no, and she was crushed.

Connor stepped quickly to her and took her hands, pulled her up to face him, and placed his forehead on hers. "Farrah bear, am I enough for you? Will you be happy if this old man is all you get?"

She drew a shuddering breath, swallowing the lump in

her throat. "I made a vow to you. This is part of it. And you're right—you did bring this up on our first date."

"Because I was absolutely serious about it."

"I see that now," Farrah said. Connor had been upfront the whole time. He was being real with her. She wasn't sure why she had expected him to change suddenly after a year.

"Genetic diseases," Farrah said as she thought. "Have you gotten yourself tested for anything?"

Connor closed his eyes and exhaled. "I hope you understand, Farrah. Maybe you won't, because no one can unless they're in this particular situation. The thing is, I'd rather not know."

She nodded, lips pursed, tears streaming. She couldn't judge him, though she longed to know if he was a carrier for anything. If he wasn't, why were they not having children? They could be so happy with a little one. Of course, birthing wasn't the only way to become a mother. She cleared her throat and tried one last time.

"What about adoption? Or fostering?"

Connor removed his forehead from hers and smiled softly, wiping the tears off her cheeks with his thumbs. "We can talk about it," he said, but the sadness in his eyes prevailed. Farrah could read his thoughts almost perfectly about most situations. He was thinking of dying at fifty-eight like one of his parents had and leaving behind a ten-year-old.

Suddenly, his face took on a livelier look. "In fact, maybe we can talk about it tonight," he offered. "Isn't the gallery closing now? Let's go to Litro again."

Farrah grinned, then her analytical mind took over. "Think they have reservations on such short notice?"

Connor smirked, raising one brow. She chuckled in embarrassment. Of course. Connor Dunes got a table whenever Connor Dunes wanted a table. It wasn't every day that a world-famous artist turned into a local, and the city of Charlotte seemed happy to oblige him whenever possible.

"Honestly, Connor, I'm just overjoyed that we're doing something on our anniversary." Farrah grasped his shirt and pecked him on the mouth. "I was beginning to think you'd forgotten."

His face said it all. The man could not lie. His eyebrows lifted up and he scratched the side of his head.

"Oh, you could have been one lucky dog, right now," Farrah said, shaking her head and crossing her arms, then cackling. "You should've just gone along with it."

Connor circled his arm around her waist and grabbed her hand, starting up an impromptu waltz-like dance in the middle of the office. "Of course I remembered! See? I planned this elaborate dance!"

"Typical man," Farrah said, giggling as Connor spun her. "But this one stings. I mean, this is our *very first* anniversary."

"To be honest, our wedding is a blur to me," he admitted.

"Me too," Farrah said, stopping in front of him and hugging him again. "It all happened so quickly. But now we have the rest of our lives to make memories."

"So many memories," Connor repeated, kissing her gently, almost making her want to go home instead of out on the town. "Grab your bag. The sunset waits for no one."

Connor was right. And there was no better place to see it than from Litro's rooftop bar.

Chapter Fourteen

PRESENT DAY

The sweltering summer air caused Farrah's tank top to cling to her lower back as she positioned the raffle basket on the Macon Farms table at the Tuesday farmers market. It was certainly too early to be so sticky and hot. The weatherman had put out an advisory for all vulnerable age groups due to the heat wave. Farrah was relieved she didn't need to worry about Mr. Mitchell and Mrs. Janice since they'd be inside the cool air-conditioning of the nursing home all day.

Despite the heat, the market was full of people, old and young alike, most of them crowding around the booth, checkbooks, debit cards, and Benjamins in hand. Many patrons fanned themselves with whatever they held, trying to circulate the stifling summer heat. Farrah wiped her brow and dreamed of her pool back home in Charlotte. She and Connor had bought the place after they got married. She also remembered the swimming hole in Quarry Creek. But at this point, she'd pour a glass of water over her back and call it enough.

"We'll open in a few minutes. Let us get our payment

system set up," Macy announced to the eager, chattering crowd, as Farrah set about turning on the register and logging into Abbott's NPO account. He'd shown her the system on Sunday night at her dining room table. It had been strictly business. He'd barely made eye contact with her as he factually went through the login steps, and he'd even talked more to Daddy and Mom than he had to her. She'd see him today, and she hoped they were more comfortable around each other. She'd make the effort.

As Macy and Farrah set out their last products and opened for the day, Farrah spotted a group of ladies chatting together quietly as they stood in the space between two vendor canopies over to the right. At first, Farrah thought they were just taking advantage of the shade the canopies offered while they waited to buy raffle tickets.

Their low conversation and darting eyes couldn't mean anything good. Farrah's stomach twisted when she recognized them as Jincey's friends, or at least people she'd seen Jincey with on other Tuesdays. The heat of embarrassment crept up her cheeks.

She swallowed her nerves and pressed on. "I'll take the first raffle buyer here," she announced with a friendly wave. Macy announced that she'd handle the farm product sales, and a short line formed in front of her. She used her phone to process payments, and Mom helped pack orders from behind the stand. Amy stood off to the side of the booth, chatting and greeting ticket buyers, thanking them for their contributions. Bobby wasn't there because of his wariness at asking for help. He'd opted to assist Daddy extracting and storing Macon Farms' honey instead, which would be a long process.

Farrah was greeted with an interminable line of friendly faces, most of whom remarked how happy they were to help the Bells. Some went in together on the price or split it three ways, and others bought multiple tickets—two, three, four. The constant transactions and ripping of ticket stubs caused time to fly by.

She'd needed Abbott's help with the people paying with cash and checks, so he could create receipts in order to have a paper trail in the case of an audit or refund. With Abbott not there yet, Macy was having to work both positions. Mom and Amy stepped in where they could, but even so, they were scrambling. Sweat streamed down Farrah's back underneath her ponytail.

"Sorry I'm late," Abbott muttered when he finally appeared and slid between Farrah and Macy. He was sporting an Abbott Ranch T-shirt and shorts. It wasn't lost on Farrah that his arm had met hers with a brief bump as he cleared a spot to take cash.

"Thank God you're here!" Mom said, then flitted to the back of the booth to continue helping Macy with farm goods sales.

"Where were you?" Farrah asked as casually as she could, trying to seem relaxed as she took payment for a ticket from the local high school principal.

"Damage control," Abbott responded gruffly.

The ticket line split between Farrah and Abbott, but even so, the queues seemed to only grow larger. They'd known it would be busy but hadn't imagined such a stellar turnout.

"You-know-who?" Macy asked, leaning toward him so Farrah could also hear. Farrah scoffed and handed two tickets to a purchaser, trying to hide her frustration.

"Yeah. She's also spread rumors that I'm taking a cut, I guess because it's under my nonprofit. When I confronted her, she completely denied it. Said she meant nothing by it. Acted all innocent. I told her if she said anything else she'd hear from my lawyer."

"I bet that set her off," Macy said and snickered as she grabbed a roll of quarters. "She's the type that has to have the last word, whether she's right or wrong. And if all else fails, she'll remind you she's a 'Taylor.'" Macy placed air quotes around the word *Taylor*, referring to the fact that Jincey had married Jake Taylor, Macy's high school friend and a distant cousin of a popular mayor in Whitetail Ridge. Though it was said that Jake didn't share the man's panache or people skills.

"I don't know. I think it will blow over," Farrah said. "I mean, look at this line. Our ticket sales are strong. I've tried to keep a rough count, and I'd say there have been over sixty or seventy sold already, and it's only the first day."

Abbott abruptly stopped sorting bills and turned to Farrah, wad of cash in hand. His eyes seemed desperate when she met them. Worried. "Farrah, you don't know Jincey. This isn't going to just blow over."

"But, why? What in the world is her motivation?" Farrah's stomach flipped with worry. Macy and Abbott exchanged a look.

"I've got this. You guys talk," Macy said, shooing them to the back of the stand and motioning for Amy to come help with tickets.

Abbott seemed nervous when they reached the back and faced each other, and Farrah was truly confused about what was going on.

Abbott wrung his hands like he did when he had to apologize for something and he didn't know what to do with them. "I wasn't completely honest with you the other night."

"About..." Farrah sensed a bomb about to be dropped. She prepared her logical mind. She'd had enough plot twists with Connor that she'd learned to compartmentalize them neatly into practical, rational places, and keep her emotions separate.

"I *was* serious with a girl once. A few years after college. After I heard you'd married."

"Jincey?" Farrah's face distorted in shock as she whisper-yelled her enemy's name.

"I know, I know. It was a bad decision. We went on that one teenage date, then kind of tried again as adults. She got really into me, really quickly. And she pressured us to be more. She even mentioned ring shopping way before it was on my radar. We were only serious for a few months, and mostly because she declared it. But she wore the pants in that relationship."

"And every situation since." Farrah groaned and wiped the sweat from her brow. "You jilted her and now she's set on vengeance." Farrah giggled at how ridiculous it was, and Abbott cocked his head in confusion. She couldn't pick on him after he'd been so vulnerable, but she found it humorous that something about his breakups caused women to spiral, and in Jincey's case, end up out to get him.

"I don't know why you're laughing, but yes, you could say that. She started dating Jake the Cop right after and pinned him into marrying her."

"I love how everyone calls him Jake the Cop instead of just Jake."

"Well, Just Jake is a farmhand for Ruby's Produce."

"Oh my word," Farrah said, laughing and covering her face.

"So you're not mad?" Abbott asked, his puppy dog eye game strong.

"That was forever ago. I mean, it does complicate things now for the basket, though our turnout today seems promising. I hope it stays that way. Bobby and Amy need this money. I don't understand why she can't put the past behind her and stop meddling for the greater good. It's so frustrating."

"About that," Abbott said, grimacing again in apology.

"There's more?" Farrah asked. "I mean, besides just being jealous of you and me being… friends?"

Abbott's eyes narrowed at the last part of her comment, but he didn't address it. He didn't need to. She, too, was wondering if they were still just friends. Or if their hearts had decided otherwise, once they recovered from the panicked kiss situation, which they still hadn't discussed. This wasn't exactly the place to talk about such things, neither was her parents' kitchen table Sunday night with them present. He went on, focused on Jincey.

"A while back, Jincey presented a fundraiser plan to the Bells, and it didn't go over well."

Farrah gasped. "The spaghetti supper!"

Abbott's eyebrows rose. "You know?"

"Yes! I mean, I talked about it with Amy. She never told me it was Jincey that had suggested it. She just told me it would never work due to the amount they owe."

"Jincey took that rejection hard. She even changed hair stylists. She'd gone to Amy since she was a little girl."

Farrah humphed knowingly. That was a real passive-aggressive snub, especially in the South.

Abbott went on. "And to make matters worse, she brought her idea to me to see if I would help convince the Bells, since they're my lifelong neighbors and all."

"And you refused?"

Abbott nodded sheepishly. "Yep. And then you showed up after all these years with this great idea that everyone jumped behind, including me and the Bells, and, well, you catch my drift."

"You think it's a great idea?" Farrah asked, hanging on his approval.

"Well, yeah." Abbott's face brightened. "You've always had great ideas. I'm just sorry she can't see it due to all the pot-stirring she's doing." Abbott looked out over the crowd wearily.

"Now I'm no longer surprised she confronted me like she did about the NPO stuff." Farrah dabbed at her glistening face with a hankie. "It was a personal vendetta. Did I tell you that last week she was not-so-secretly eavesdropping on my conversation with Amy about the basket? I'm pretty sure she knows who all gave what. I'm nervous for those people. I feel like she'll use that information against me or them somehow."

"Maybe. But look on the bright side. Aren't you glad I was there to save the day with the nonprofit thing?" Abbott asked with a silly smile. "Just kidding. This is kind of all my fault." He groaned out a sigh. "I'll try to get her to come around before the drawing."

Farrah wanted to reach out and touch his arm to comfort him but refrained. Instead, she reassured him with a smile. "It's not your fault. It's hers. You really did come through for me." He met her gaze and returned her smile. "Try your best with Jincey. We only have two weeks, and look." Farrah motioned behind Abbott. He turned and looked where she indicated—Jincey hunched and whispering with some of her friends, pointing to the Macon Farms' stand.

Abbott pulled out his wallet and handed Farrah three hundred dollars. She savored the moment his hand brushed hers while interchanging the bills, wondering if he felt the same.

"Put me down for a few tickets," he said gruffly. "I want to lead by example." He looked back out at Jincey as she gossiped, stress all over his face. Abbott always carried everyone else's weight, even when he didn't need to. And now he carried the weight of Bobby and Amy's financial need. He was probably beating himself up about his role in endangering the fundraiser, though they had been entanglements he'd gotten himself into far back in the past with no way of knowing how everything would play out.

But Farrah couldn't dwell on how he was feeling for too long. They had customers to serve and time was running out. Farrah had a busy day ahead of her, harvesting summer veggies back at the farm, and then sitting with Mr. Mitchell for the afternoon to night shift at Glade Village. She'd have to deal with Jincey another time. She still held on to hope that it would all blow over.

"Come on," Farrah said to Abbott. "Let's go get your stubs."

"Wait," Abbott said, catching her arm as she turned. "Don't we have something *else* to discuss?" The look in his eyes was serious but concerned. He was referring to their kiss.

She glanced at Macy, who was definitely within earshot. "Not here. I'm sorry."

He nodded good naturedly, and they walked back to their sales positions at the front of the canopy, and Farrah focused on her tasks instead of her feelings. Abbott immediately jumped to work, doing the same.

In the distance sounded a rumble from an afternoon summer storm. Daddy's vegetables would have a very happy day.

THE RAIN POURED HARD against the windowpanes and the thunder rumbled overhead. Farrah adjusted Mr. Mitchell's blankets, the room dim from the heavy clouds outdoors as evening approached. It was the perfect day to take a nap, especially after harvesting and cleaning vegetables with Daddy before the storm came. She laughed to herself when she thought about asking Mr. Mitchell to scoot over so she could lie down and sleep. The idea was outrageous, of course, and she'd never do that.

He'd been napping on and off all afternoon, exhausted from his congested lungs. He now had a heart monitor, oxygen tubes, and two IVs, one for medicine—antibiotics and anti-anxiety meds—and the other for nutrients and hydration, since he had little interest in eating. The bruised skin over his arms broke Farrah's heart. She wasn't sure how much longer he'd be her patient. Almost every time she saw him, he showed a marked deterioration. But she chose not to dwell too much on that. For now, she was content to listen to the storm and sit by his bed. She curled up in her chair as she watched him, overcome by the comfort the showers and rumbles offered.

She must have drifted off, because she woke to his gurgling voice and his hand reaching out. She sprang into action, taking his hand as he always expected, and looked hopefully into his eyes.

"Why are you still here?" Farrah was able to make out the question after he tried to say it three times.

"Shh, don't talk. It's too hard on you. I work here, remember? I'm here to take care of you."

"Why?" Mr. Mitchell whispered, phlegm rattling, and then he broke into a wet cough.

"Because I need a job, like everyone else. Didn't you have a job?"

He nodded while rounding up his coughing spell. Farrah wiped the foamy spittle from the sides of his mouth with a tissue, then tossed it into the nearby bin.

"I was a teacher," he managed to answer, then rested his head back on his pillow.

She smiled. He had remembered something.

She shoved the newborn hope down deep. Mr. Mitchell would not recover from his dementia. It was a blip of memory, probably because his mind was fresh from a nap. He would succumb to his illness and not remember anything one day. But today, he had remembered.

"What did you teach?" Farrah asked, giving his hand a slight squeeze.

"Math," Mr. Mitchell said after thinking for a while. Farrah laughed and shook her head. They sat for a moment, just being present together. Then he posed a question to her again. "Why are you taking care of me?"

Farrah couldn't stop the tears that fought against the borders of her eyes. They streamed down slowly, lazily. "Because someone I loved got very sick, and I couldn't save them. So now I'm paying it forward by taking care of you." She held his hand a bit tighter.

"You're a nice person," Mr. Mitchell said in a raspy whisper, then closed his eyes and dozed off, completely weakened by the infection in his lungs.

"Thank you. Go ahead and get some sleep."

She tiptoed out and changed the light above his door. Her phone buzzed in her pocket.

After pulling it out, she read Abbott's text:

Meet me at Donna's? They're open till 10.

Farrah checked the time on her phone. 9:12 p.m. She texted him back:

Sure. See you in five.

ABBOTT PULLED on the handle to the café, but it didn't budge.

He groaned. "So much for being open until ten."

"Look," Farrah said, pointing to a handwritten sign in the window: "Closing at 8:00 p.m. this week only—Some staff on vacation. Sorry for the inconvenience."

"Well, how do you feel about a walk along Main Street?" Abbott asked, offering Farrah his arm. She took it.

"That'll be fine." They started their stroll down the sidewalk, streetlamps illuminating intermittent patches of concrete. Farrah asked about Abbott's afternoon, then they chatted about the raffle, updating each other on what they knew. Minutes later, they were almost down the whole strip. Every shop and store was closed due to the late hours. They passed Louise's and Pink Floyd's, the candy shop, and the bookstore.

"Is that music I hear?" Farrah asked, perking up. "*Nineties* music?"

"Yeah, I think it's summer karaoke night on Tuesdays and Thursdays at Pour Outcomes, the brewery up on the corner. Feel like singing?"

Farrah snickered. "I feel like *listening* to some singing. If they don't mind my scrubs." That line got a smile from Abbott. "And I'd love to sit." She glanced at her clogs as they walked. Comfortable as they were, the morning spent on her feet at the market and in the garden had caught up with her, and her arches and heels ached.

They approached and Abbott opened the door to the fairly busy brewery taproom. With not much to do in Whitetail Ridge by way of entertainment, summer events like this were always a hit. Some families with kids were there, but it was mostly couples and a few older townspeople.

They walked through the crowd, giving quick hellos to a few of the patrons. Farrah recognized one of her mom's friends, a local florist named Maxine, as the current singer of Abba's "Dancing Queen." Farrah waved at her and got a wink from the stage in return before Maxine hit the chorus again.

Abbott found a table for them near the back, away from the loudest speakers.

"Sorry, man," called a college-aged boy, probably working a summer job while back home. "You have to order to sit at the tables."

Abbott tipped his hat to the boy in recognition, then turned to Farrah. "Water? Tea? Something else?"

"Water's fine."

Abbott hopped up and headed for the bar, then returned with two bottled waters and a cardboard container of aioli fries with two forks.

The garlic was pungent, and Farrah's stomach rumbled. She hadn't eaten since around three o'clock—a hastily made turkey sandwich and a banana. "Gosh, that smells amazing."

"Dig in," Abbott suggested, handing her a fork.

She stabbed a fry, wiped up some of the aioli and a bit of parmesan cheese, and took a bite. Wonderful, but zingy. "My breath is going to be so bad after this. Sorry in advance."

She took another bite, then caught the look on his face. His cheeks were rosy. At once, she worried that he thought she was talking about another potential kiss.

"Oh!" Farrah corrected, mouth half full, shielding it with her free hand. "I mean, not that it matters if my breath is bad. Just saying."

Abbott laughed, obviously knowing where she was going. He groaned good naturedly and then rubbed his eyes, a self-deprecating smile still across his face.

"Farrah, do you know how bad I've suffered these past few days? I was too embarrassed to even text you. I know it's been awkward. I'm so sorry."

"No, *I'm* sorry. I told you it was okay to kiss me, and then I just freaked out."

He looked at her tenderly from across the table, eyes glistening. "I don't ever want to make you feel that way. I should have listened to my gut." He breathed deeply in and out as if taking courage. "Look, I'll shoot straight. I feel a certain way about you. But the way you reacted to that kiss, even though you did want it at first, made me think that… maybe you're not exactly ready."

Farrah paused her fork, despite her hunger. Her lip quaked a bit as she considered what he had said. "That's because I'm not." She set her fork down and reached over for his hand, placing her fingers over his, scooping them into the hollow under his thumb. "Abbott, I feel the same way about you. Believe me, I do. Every time I see you, I'm filled with this desire to know you as an adult. It's just… well, you would not *believe* everything I've been through in the past few years."

Abbott took a long swig of water with his free hand, contemplating. He gave her hand a slight squeeze. "That's another thing. Part of the reason I didn't text you was to clear my head and think things through. Every time we've been together these past few weeks, you've asked me about my ranch and my projects, my nonprofit, and my parents. You asked me why I moved back, what all happened in Knoxville, my plans for the future. I feel like you know everything about adult me. And yet…"

Farrah could guess what he was going to say and braced herself.

"I don't know anything about adult *you*. And now we're back in this town together, and we kissed, and you haven't even told me what happened all these years you've been gone, other than you got married and worked at a gallery and now you're divorced."

"*Managed* the gallery," Farrah said under her breath.

"Okay," Abbott said enthusiastically. "Managed. See? I didn't know that." He rubbed her fingers with his thumb. "Bacon, I'm just scared we're going in our old circles again."

"Meaning?" she asked, meeting his eyes, the quake in her voice surprising her.

"Meaning that you left me out emotionally as a teen, and I'm scared you might fall into those patterns again. I won't be able to bear it."

"No, I've grown up a lot since then." She'd have to prove it to him and be honest about where she was emotionally. She would push past her comfort zone because he deserved that.

"I met my husband when he came into my work, and we were extremely close. We did everything together for several years. My marriage… and why it ended… it left me shattered. That's why I called out my husband's name after you kissed me. I still feel linked to him. Like I was cheating on him." She choked back a sob, regaining composure in short order. "I'm sorry. I'm really trying here. I just can't get into the specifics right now. Can't let myself feel all that."

"That's fine," he said, tentatively. "I'm a patient man when I need to be, but I do wonder if there will come a time when you *can* feel all that. When you *can* get into specifics and let yourself open up." He paused and they locked gazes, seriousness and concern behind his expression. "Look, I just don't want to be jerked around." Abbott shrugged, his eyes wide and sincere. He let go of her hand and she returned it to her lap. "I don't want either of us to waste our time."

Hurt squeezed Farrah's heart, perhaps at Abbott's last statement, which sounded a lot like a reason for them to stop hanging out.

"My time isn't being wasted. It's been wonderful to reconnect with you."

"Is that what you want?" Abbott asked. "To reconnect with me?" His expression was earnest.

If Farrah was honest with herself, she did want something to bloom between them. But despite these budding feelings, she was in no way ready for love. Not yet. Not until she achieved the closure she needed to move on.

"It's not about what I want at this point. Things are really complicated right now. It's about what I need, which is for you to be patient. Be there for me and wait on me. Be my friend. I *will* tell you everything, and I *will* let you in, I promise. But I need to get through this last stretch."

He looked at her warily, as if he didn't believe her at all, and she couldn't blame him.

"Do you trust me, Abbott?" Farrah asked, and he winced slightly.

"I want very badly to trust you," Abbott admitted. "I want with all my heart to believe that you won't keep me at arm's length this time around. Or whenever our second round comes. Whenever you're ready for it."

Farrah nodded. "What can I do to earn your trust until then?"

Abbott thought, then spoke. "Exactly what you did tonight, but all the way. Open up, be a woman of your word. Let me in. If you're telling me there's a future for us somewhere down the line, let me in."

"I *will* let you in," she repeated, and she meant it.

A half-hearted smile turned up one corner of his mouth, exposing a coy dimple briefly. "Okay," he said and nodded, his face drained of emotion. "Okay."

He smiled again, but Farrah could tell by the way his glassy eyes searched her face that he was in no way fully convinced.

A new singer took the stage with a rendition of "Neon Moon."

"That's enough of this heavy stuff," Abbott said. "Wanna dance?"

"Can friends who like each other but aren't in a relationship yet because of life complications dance?"

Abbott laughed, then stood and walked over to her side of the table, and extended his hand. "Pretty sure our setup is unprecedented, so I'm going to go ahead and say, *yes*, they can, just not too close and all over each other."

She slid her hand into his and walked with him to the dance floor, where she placed her free hand on his shoulder. He did indeed keep a safe, platonic distance.

Farrah studied the navy-blue checkered pattern of his shirt as they swayed with the music. "Hmm, plaid and scrubs. Nice combo."

"Everyone here is *so* jealous," Abbott added, provoking a giggle from her, then he gave her a spin.

The dance was just what she needed to get her mind off the twist that had serendipitously brought her back into Abbott's arms, yet distanced her from her beloved Connor.

Chapter Fifteen
TWO YEARS AGO

Farrah sat in the management office of the Oberg with Kia and her new boyfriend, Travis. She liked him better than any guy Kia had ever dated. The best thing? He was a teacher at the school where Kia coached, and he was obsessed with basketball. She saw their potential as a serious couple, so after they'd met at Litro one night a few weeks prior on a double date, she invited them over to the gallery for macarons from Tillie's Bakery, a favorite corner spot about a block away.

"I like your little French cookie things," Travis said, then popped one in his mouth. "But just wait till you taste these bulgogi tacos I brought from Sizzle. Better than my mom used to make."

"It's a fine combination." Farrah laughed, and Kia rolled her eyes lovingly at her beau. Travis made it clear that he'd always show up with his own food because, in his words, it was hard to keep a six-foot-seven man fed. She appreciated the gesture, and as she bit into the taco, complete with sticky rice and kimchi, she hummed out her approval of the flavor explosion. "Oh, that's good," she said, nodding emphatically, mouth full. Kia and Travis also dug in.

"Should we save some for Connor?" Kia asked carefully, as if walking on eggshells, a slight grimace on her face.

Farrah sighed and checked her watch one more time. He was super late, again. They'd agreed to meet as soon as the gallery closed, since it was a more convenient midpoint. "I'm not sure. Let me call him."

He answered, thankfully, on the first ring, and Farrah paced the hallway outside the office as he gave his explanation.

"I'm sorry, babe. I know. I remembered our date at six with Kia and Travis, but I just can't get out of the studio. It's that darn copyright mess I'm in." He sighed heavily and Farrah's anger melted.

Connor had hired a ghostwriter to create a devotional journal inspired by his paintings. The guy had used titles and phrases from songs without getting permission and without letting Connor or his agent know that he'd used lyrics. When Connor read over the final proof, making his last tweaks, he'd assumed the italicized portions were just pieces of poetry the man had made up. Never in a million years did he think the ghostwriter was using lyrics without obtaining the rights to do so. He learned otherwise when a lawsuit arrived in the mail a few weeks after publication, suing the daylights out of him. The legal proceedings had been going on since Christmas, and it was now the beginning of summer, with several more months of battle in sight.

"I know," Farrah said, consoling him. "I understand. We'll be all right if you can't make it."

"I hate this so much. You're the last person I want to let down. Honestly, this gives me chest pains."

Farrah breathed slowly, in and out. She hated when he said things about his health. She wasn't ready for him to get sick, to have any type of genetic illness come up. Wasn't ready for his heart to give out.

He still refused to get tested for anything, adamant that he would rather not know, even after a year of Farrah encouraging it. Unable to sway him, she had to settle for supporting him, even though it made no sense to her.

"Listen. It's okay. I have some tacos and macarons for you. I'll just come by the studio after we're done so you can eat. Take all the time you need."

"Farrah, thank you, honey." Connor breathed out a sigh of relief. "I don't know what I'd do without you being so understanding."

She rejoined her friends after finishing the call. "He can't make it," she said, and their faces fell. "He's got a lot of legal stuff going on. It's the ghostwriter that screwed him over, the thing I told you guys about last week."

Travis and Kia had been great listening ears while Farrah vented out the struggle. Travis had studied pre-law before getting his North Carolina teaching license. He'd offered Farrah some good advice as someone who had dabbled in the language of legal matters.

"What's he doing to fight back, exactly?" Kia asked, worried.

"His lawyer is on it, I guess," Farrah said, taking a sip of her drink.

"Whew. I hear music cases are tough," Travis remarked knowingly. "Hopefully the lawyer is good at what he does."

"*She*. Erin Matthews."

Kia clicked her tongue. "So he's spending a lot of time with a female lawyer, alone inside his studio?"

"It's not like that," Farrah said, swiping the issue away with her hand. "Connor would never cheat."

"Says every wife ever cheated on…" Kia set her taco down. "Did I hear you say you were going to his studio tonight to take him food? Best to go when she's there. You need to meet this lady. See if she's a threat or not. We can hang out another night." Travis nodded in agreement.

A small doubt rose up in Farrah's mind. She didn't want to be wrong about Connor, but at the same time, she didn't share her best friend's wariness of men. Kia was always untrusting. Ever since her college boyfriend serially cheated on her, she often assumed the worst about the men she dated. Travis had earned her confidence after proving himself repeatedly. But that didn't change the fact that Kia didn't trust other men.

Still, what could be so bad about meeting her husband's lawyer? Even if Kia was wrong about Connor, getting to know the woman he was around all the time seemed like the most obvious thing to do.

"Good idea. When y'all are done, I'll head out."

"We're done," Kia offered, shooting Farrah a supportive but concerned look. "This is important."

***

"Farrah," Connor gushed, when she walked in the door of his messy artist studio turned legal office. He got up and walked toward her, kissing her on the cheek, and gladly accepting the food she'd brought him. "Erin, Mark. This is my wife."

Mark looked up from his laptop where he was fervently typing—but just for a split second. He acknowledged her with a quick "Hi." Erin, on the other hand, stood up from her work and made her way to Farrah.

"Pleased to meet you," Farrah said, taking in the bombshell redhead standing before her with a perfect hourglass figure. She was tall and lean, wearing a suit that was tailored to fit just right, the skirt of which landed seductively about six inches above her knees and perfectly showcased sleek, athletic legs. She was glad this Mark guy —another lawyer—was here, but he seemed to be pretty absorbed in work. And Erin… *didn't.*

"I've heard so much about you," Erin said, smiling big. "I've been to your gallery and seen you there but didn't want to bother. When I'm off the bench, I'm actually pretty shy." Erin giggled as if this were some great anomaly. "Come in! Sit!" Erin motioned to plastic table they'd set up with documents strewn all about it.

The juxtaposition of Connor's beautiful scenes cluttered all over the room on various easels, and the tacky, plastic table put her on edge, as if Erin had cheapened the studio's beauty with her makeshift, mass-produced office supplies. Not to mention that there was something about another woman inviting Farrah to come inside and sit in her own husband's studio that rubbed her the wrong way. Still, she tried to keep an open mind. But she didn't sit.

"I'm good," she offered.

Connor unpacked the food, setting it before himself on the table. "Thanks, babe."

"Oh, yum. Thank you so much, Farrah," Erin said gratefully. But Farrah's tummy tightened. The food wasn't for Erin or Mark, though there was certainly enough for all three of them. She glanced down at Mark, who had an empty Chick-fil-A sandwich bag and red waffle fries container next to him.

He wouldn't be eating tacos and macarons.

Farrah couldn't help but feel that she had just catered a

date for her husband and another woman. She suddenly felt sick to her stomach.

"I'm going to get home," Farrah said, and Connor picked his head up, confused.

"So soon?" he asked, cutting into his bulgogi taco with a plastic fork and knife to-go set.

"Yeah, I've… got some reading to do." It was a believable lie. She often saved articles on artists so she could study the creative scene and stay on top of new talent and what might drive crowds to the gallery. Tonight, however, she was all caught up and didn't have any research left to do.

Connor abandoned his tacos and rose, walking to her. He embraced her and gave her a warmer kiss on the mouth, right in front of Erin, who seemed to pay no obvious attention. Farrah had made sure to look.

"Are you sure you're okay?" Connor asked, talking low to protect their privacy. "Do you want to step outside? We can talk about it, or—"

"No, no," Farrah interrupted. "I'm just going to head home. I'll see you later tonight."

The stinging in her heart was the same pain she'd felt the night she saw Abbott with Jincey at the movies, but ten times greater. She hoped there was a logical explanation. She hoped what she thought was happening, wasn't.

"WHERE IS HE?" Mom asked from the tall table at a gallery soiree a few weeks later. She was staying with Farrah and Connor for the weekend, having wanted to see the exhibition Farrah had put together of early twentieth-century-inspired Appalachian handicrafts. All along the walls were baskets, quilts, portraits, and whittled objects. It was truly a special collection, and Farrah was proud of it.

She'd wanted Connor to see it firsthand on opening night. He had gone from supporting Farrah's every move to being distant, self-absorbed, and scatterbrained, not even coming to one of Farrah's biggest soirees of her career. She couldn't wrap her mind around the change.

His time with Erin Matthews had not reduced at all. In fact, they spent more time together, supposedly trying to "finalize the case as a team." Farrah had gotten so tired of hearing him say that as if it was an excuse to miss important events.

Mom must've noticed the tension between them and the sour look on her face when she asked where he was. Ginny sipped her glass of red and kept quiet. Farrah shrugged, and her mom shook her head in disappointment, lips pursed into a thin line.

Farrah couldn't stand it. She left the table to avoid losing control of her emotions. She stepped out onto the balcony where Connor had first asked her out and pulled out her phone. No missed calls. No texts.

She called him, fighting tears.

He took much longer to answer than usual, and when he did, there was background noise. A woman's voice.

"Where are you?" Farrah asked, much angrier than she would have liked to sound.

"It's a crazy story, baby. We came to the studio to really finalize the case, since the ghostwriter is now blaming us, and I could not for the life of me find my studio keys." Farrah rolled her eyes and trembled as she tried with everything in her to control her anger.

"We?" She spat out the question, incriminating him forthright.

"Erin and me, yes," Connor said, a bit sheepishly. "We're meeting Mark and some others in a bit."

Farrah was uncomfortable with the attractive lawyer's almost daily presence in their lives. For Farrah, the honeymoon was definitely over, and Erin had a lot to do with that feeling.

Connor went on. "So when I couldn't find them, we drove back to the house, and they're not there either, so we're back in her car."

"You took her to *our house?*" Farrah seethed.

"Well, yeah? To get the keys."

Connor's innocent, nice-guy performance was so good it was almost believable.

Now Farrah's whole body, including her voice and hands, shook with adrenaline and fury. "That's a really shoddy excuse, Connor. Nice try, though."

"Wait, what are you talking ab—"

"We already talked about it earlier this morning. You know we agreed that I'd bring the keys here with me, so you wouldn't be tempted to go to the studio. So you would make sure to be here to support me in one of my biggest themed shows yet. And that you could go to the studio after."

Hot, angry tears streaked down Farrah's cheeks. How could she face her mother and Ginny and every other gallery patron after such a tense moment, as if nothing had happened? She couldn't. Maybe it was time to confide in her mom instead of hiding it. She seemed to share things only when she got so full of pressure that she had no other choice, except exploding.

"Did we talk about that?" came Connor's voice, meek.

"Don't act like you don't remember."

Silence on the other end.

When he spoke again, his voice was grainy, hollow. Tired. "I need the keys, babe. We have work to do."

"I'm sure you do," Farrah said. "You and your best buddy can come get them."

Connor was silent again, as was Erin in the background. For a moment, Farrah feared she was on speaker, but then again, she didn't care.

"All right," Connor mumbled. "We're on the way."

About a half hour later, after Farrah had told her mom just enough, Erin pulled up and double parked, allowing Connor to hop inside.

Farrah handed him the keys, forcing what she hoped was an icy look in her eyes.

"Farrah… honey…" Connor pleaded.

"This is a big night for me, Connor. It would have been nice not to have to beg my husband to be here in support of me."

His face fell. He sighed and slumped his shoulders. He looked tired. Older. "You're right. Let me give the studio keys to Erin. She's got all my statements and shouldn't need me until the actual week of the trial. It's just exciting because we're so close to finishing this case. But they can do it without me."

Connor did as he'd promised, and it made Farrah feel a little bit better. But thoughts of what might have happened if they'd gone to the studio alone that night gnawed at Farrah's mind. She hated feeling like she couldn't trust her own husband.

Like somehow she was losing importance in his heart and in his mind.

Chapter Sixteen
PRESENT DAY

Farrah knelt in the garden picking hornworms off the tomato plants and plunking them into a bucket of soapy water.

"Well, I declare! I'll give you a dollar for each one you get!" Daddy called from the other side of the garden, his wide-brimmed straw hat bobbing as he hollered.

Daddy was irate. He hated the worms that ate just enough of the blossoms and fruit to ruin the crop. He'd slaved away in the greenhouse for an early germination and painstakingly covered the plants at any risk of frost after transplanting them, and he wasn't going to lose them to some ugly, terrorizing worms. That was how he put it, anyway.

Farrah secretly thought the worms were pretty. Bright green with colorful markings—and, yes, a horn—they blended in with the fuzzy stalks of the tomatoes, and it was quite a job to find them. Every once in a while, with her face close to the fresh stalks, she'd jolt with surprise at finding a stealthy hornworm mere centimeters from her face, chomping on a leaf.

"Got another one!" Farrah called as she tossed it into the bucket with a *plop* and a splash.

"It's too bad we're too classy to eat them. People say they're good."

Farrah snorted, then wiped the sweat from her brow with her gloved hands. They were at the stage of hard, repetitive labor that made everything seem funny. Daddy had kept her laughing all morning under the hot sun, despite his outrage at the invader worms.

She touched her shoulders to gauge her sunburn, and the spot she touched briefly turned white. She'd had enough rays for today.

Farrah darted her eyes upward, shielding them with her hand. Indeed, it was a clear-sky Friday. And Farrah had no plans other than working in the garden and spending the afternoon on her shift at Glade Village.

"That's enough of this," Daddy said, then stood and cracked his back. "I can't handle any more of this bending down stuff."

"Planning to work on the peach trees next?" Farrah asked.

"I believe I'll head that way. You coming?"

Farrah was about to say yes, until she noticed Amy and Bobby walking across the field that separated their properties. "I would, but I believe I have visitors."

Daddy nodded and Farrah took an inventory of herself. She wore Abbott's old ball cap from his high school baseball days, paired with cutoff jean shorts and a dirty, once-white tank top now sticky with sweat. Luckily, Bobby and Amy wouldn't mind that she looked a fright.

As Farrah worked to reach a stopping point and called hello to their guests, Daddy shook hands with Bobby and gave Amy the typical, "I'd hug you but I'm sweaty," explanation and shrug, which she shooed away with a friendly wave. He excused himself to continue his work, and Farrah approached the Bells.

"You caught me working," Farrah said, but her light-hearted demeanor darkened quickly upon seeing the worried looks on their faces. "What is it? What's wrong?"

Bobby sighed and Amy looked downward. "Can we sit and chat?" Bobby asked.

Farrah led them to the porch where, surprisingly, a bit of breeze blew, though the air was still thick with heat.

Amy and Bobby took the two wicker chairs while Farrah settled herself on the swing, but she didn't push herself leisurely back and forth. The Bells' seriousness had her worried. Bobby was the first to speak, and the crease between his eyes was deeper than she remembered it.

"We know you done all this with the raffle to help us," he said, gesticulating with his hands and looking for the right words. "But what people are saying is kind of getting to us. I guess I'm feeling kind of embarrassed." Amy stared at her feet, clutching her husband's hand. "It ain't easy to come here and say this, but I think we should call off this whole basket thing."

Farrah's heart jumped to her throat, and lightheadedness, whether from the heat or the shock, threatened to overcome her. "What?" She'd have to give so many refunds, not to mention the mortification she'd feel at failing at something she'd done just to help.

Amy spoke next, compassion in her hazel eyes. "We know the rumors aren't true. We trust you. It's just—"

"Is this Jincey again? Last I heard, she was saying Abbott was taking a cut of the proceeds, which is not the case. He was planning on talking to her again, even though he already confronted her once."

Amy pushed air out between pursed lips. "Good luck with that. Jincey's a hard one to nab. She's always sticking her nose in other people's business but rarely leaves a trace of anything that could actually prove her guilt." Amy looked at Bobby, who nodded as if giving her permission to go on. She looked at Farrah cautiously. "I think you need to know… she also said a few things about you."

"What kind of things?" Farrah sat up tall, and the swing creaked with her movement. Her heart pounded so heavily she could hear its dull throb in her ears.

"Well, she said some of the things you put in the basket weren't necessarily obtained legally."

Farrah's jaw dropped and she thought frantically, trying to pinpoint something—anything—that could have been stolen or otherwise wrongfully obtained. Angrier than Daddy was at the hornworms, she fervently shook her head.

"It's not true. Everyone donated everything whole-heartedly. All the townspeople want to help, except Jincey. She has a personal vendetta against me for having the winning fundraiser idea, and against Abbott for breaking her heart—twice."

Amy snickered briefly, but pulled it together by touching her lips.

Farrah leaned forward, entreating them. "Why would you want to give up on the basket? We've already sold so many tickets."

Amy and Bobby looked at each other sorrowfully. "We know you've done everything right," Amy said. "But we're just worried about how this will reflect on our reputations."

Farrah immediately understood. Amy and Bobby were active members of the community. They volunteered at church, and Amy cut half the town's hair. And there was no other tractor mechanic like Bobby this side of the

Appalachians. The midsize agricultural town turned to him to keep their farms running smoothly. These were the reasons they deserved to have a benefit in their honor—but now it was also the reason they were nervous. Any tarnishing of their squeaky-clean reputations would mean losing the trust of the community. No amount of charity could ever make that worthwhile.

Farrah took a deep breath. "I know you don't want to be associated with anything dramatic or negative, and I understand that. But look at it this way—the people who truly know Abbott and me realize that those rumors are false. And the people that believe Jincey are probably not the type of people you want in your life anyway." It was the best Farrah could do, even if it fell short.

"My father used to say that a good name is all you have," Bobby said. "I'm not willing to lose that by association. Even if it means I have to give up my house."

Disappointment coursed through Farrah. Then, once again, she fluctuated to anger. "It really eats me up that she's doing this. I'm going to have no other choice than to go to her and give her a piece of my mind and demand she stop this. If I did that—if I stopped her—would you consider going on with the benefit? I can go talk to her today."

"No, honey. Don't do that," Amy pleaded, shaking her head at Farrah. "She's slick, and you'll end up in a bind. I don't want that for you."

"But I don't want you to lose your house and everything you've worked for all these years. I mean, look at Bobby's scars," Farrah said. "Isn't that enough?"

Amy and Bobby exchanged another look, this time with tears in their eyes. A fresh breeze blew across the porch, momentarily scattering the stifling heat.

"Just give me a little time to handle it. Please. I think I

have a better idea about how to stop her and keep all of our reputations intact. Her husband's a cop, right?"

Amy's head perked up and she furrowed her brow. She let out one, raspy huff. "Jake ain't got no control over that woman. She's more determined than a squirrel after a nut."

"I'm not talking about control," Farrah said, a sly smile working its way across her face. "I'm talking about the law."

FARRAH HAD WANTED to look put together since she needed to confront Jake, so she'd dragged out an old curling iron from under Mom's vanity and gone to work on her hair. She opened her makeup bag and ran mascara over her lashes, worked some blush into her cheeks, and added a nice rosy gloss over her lips. The colors complemented the freckles that had surfaced across her nose from working in the garden. She wore a pink sundress and brown leather slip-on sandals. Last but not least, jewelry—which she hadn't bothered with since the divorce—was the icing on her cake.

When she caught a look at herself in the mirror, she was giddy with joy. She was revitalized. She felt like herself once again, for the first time since losing her life partner and the gallery. She'd gone too long without self-care, opting for messy buns and old, comfy clothes or scrubs from work. She made a mental note of how good she felt and decided it would be beneficial to her grief to get dolled up from time to time.

Into town she went and parked her cargo van at the Whitetail Ridge police station, then waltzed right through the double glass doors. For the first time in a long time, she turned heads, as several daytime cops were on duty, some at their desks, and a few hanging out by the water cooler, including one man she'd seen a few times patrolling the town. He was older than her by about five years, but she remembered him from their childhoods, as he'd been friends with Macy. He turned and looked at her, scrunching his brow in scrutiny and puffed up bravado. He was the one.

"Are you Jake the Cop?" she asked the short blond man with matching transparent eyebrows and eyelashes. A sandy blond mustache shielded almost his entire mouth. It wiggled up and down animatedly when he talked.

"Who's asking?" He placed his hands on his hips, appearing to snarl.

"I'm the woman running the benefit for the Bells. Your wife is slandering me around town."

Jake the Cop guffawed. "Slander. That's a pretty hefty accusation." His body language communicated his annoyance. His water-cooler buddy adopted a bewildered look after hearing the tense interaction and escaped to his desk. At once, Farrah felt a little attacked but also a little silly for trying to get Jincey's husband on her side.

"Uh, no sir. She's the one accusing *me*."

"Of what, exactly?"

"Amy said that someone said—"

Jake held his hand up. "Nope. I need names. Who was the third party that heard Jincey say these things, if not Amy?"

"Well, I don't exactly know. Jincey's claiming that we've included things in the basket illegally, and that could damage Amy and Bobby's reputations, as well as mine and Abbott's."

At the mention of Abbott's name, Jake's eyes narrowed. "Do you have any proof of the damage that *could* have been done?"

The way he mocked her tone and body language when he said "could" irked Farrah. She answered through gritted teeth. "I guess I don't. Some help you've been. Have yourself a nice day." She turned to storm off, then caught herself and spun back to face him once again and tried a calmer tone.

"Can you at least tell her—as someone she loves—to stop stirring up problems?" Farrah's shoulders dropped and she hung her head. "I'm begging you here as a real person, not as an enemy, even though Jincey wants to make it that way. The Bells *need* this benefit, and she knows that. She's dead set on trying to ruin it just because they went with my idea instead of hers. If you can't support me with the law, please try to talk to her as her husband."

Jake's eyes seemed tired and just the slightest bit sad. He leaned back on the large metal desk behind him and tinkered with a miniature American flag that he plucked from his jar of pens.

"Jincey and me don't talk about anything beyond how our days went and what's for supper," he mumbled, abandoning his self-righteousness and ego.

Farrah wasn't sure what to make of his sudden openness. "I'm sorry," she muttered.

"It's okay. I love her. But after the wedding and our daughter being born a year after, I guess we just grew apart."

"But surely you could get through to her."

Jake the Cop laughed through his nose and shook his head. "Jincey is going to do what Jincey wants to do. And beyond that, she's protected by free speech up to a certain point, unless slander is proven and reputations are hurt, resulting in less business and other losses. But you don't have evidence of slander, and you can't prove any damage has been done. All I can do is wish you luck. And all you can do is hope she stops."

Defeated and deflated, Farrah thanked Jake and turned to go. She had promised Bobby and Amy she'd protect their reputations, and now she was leaving without having accomplished that. She dreaded facing them to let them know Jake hadn't been any help at all and she was nowhere closer to saving the raffle.

As she opened the glass double doors and stepped into the warm sun, Jincey stopped in her tracks on the sidewalk in front of Farrah with a scowl on her face. Today she wore a zebra-print bodysuit and large hoop earrings. Her hot-pink lipstick matched her new nail color—for once, not orange. She chewed her gum with angst as she gave Farrah a once-over and brushed past her, hugging files to her chest. As she walked in to see her husband, Farrah heard her squawk, "What were you talking to *her* for?"

That couldn't be good. Seeing Jincey had definitely not been part of the plan.

She brushed it off and walked hastily to her van, searching for her keys in her small straw handbag that Connor had bought for her from a street market in Charleston one year.

"My, my," came a crooning male voice with the slam of a truck door. She spun around and came nearly face-to-face with Abbott, who refrained from touching her but seemed to take in her appearance with reverence. "I just stopped by the Bells' and they told me you had some sort of plan here. I came to be backup, but I guess I'm not needed." He gave her another once over. "Look who got all prettied up to see Jake the Cop."

Farrah giggled. "I was trying to talk some sense into

him about Jincey." She'd had a few other run-ins with Abbott during the week and they'd all gone pretty well. While balancing the pain over Connor and the adjustment to her new life, she still couldn't get him off her mind. She'd been afraid that she'd ruined things by not opening up to him when he'd asked her to, but lately it seemed like he was making an effort to give her the benefit of the doubt and trust that she'd open up when the time was right, as she'd promised.

His patience made her think more with each passing day that she was approaching being ready to date him.

Abbott's face sported a grin. He took Farrah's hand and her heartbeat picked up speed. "I just can't stand it. You look too good. Come out with me."

Farrah swallowed hard. She didn't stand a chance against her feelings now. Not when he put things so clearly. "I have to work a short shift from two to six."

"After."

"Where?"

"My place."

Farrah chewed on her lower lip for a moment, while he looked down at her and grinned, dimples flexed. Despite still feeling like she was betraying Connor, she was inclined to say yes. She wanted more than anything to be at Abbott's house after work, talking with him, sharing in his company, feeling special. Connor was in her past, even if she hadn't fully accepted it yet. She needed to allow herself to act according to that truth.

Farrah swallowed hard. "Okay." Her stomach flipped, like she had gone bungee jumping for a millisecond. The decision was spontaneous, and she hoped it was the right thing, that she wasn't too vulnerable and hurt to make progress with Abbott.

His smile grew wider, his brown eyes glistening with excitement. "Okay," he whispered back.

She didn't feel completely ready to move forward with Abbott. But her heart was drawn to him in an inexplicable way.

Sometimes, Farrah reasoned, the heart had to win over the mind.

Chapter Seventeen

PRESENT DAY

"I used to be so pretty," Mrs. Janice groaned as she watched the soap opera stars pine for one another on the screen. The blonde bombshell main character finally told the hunky co-star the truth about how her evil identical twin sister had played him for his money. "Well, I think I was," Mrs. Janice added slowly.

"Do you want to look at your pictures?" Farrah asked.

"I have pictures?" The woman's eyebrows pulled her wrinkled face upward in delight.

"Oh, yeah," Farrah said, laughing. Mrs. Janice was absolutely precious to her. "You can look at them if you let me wheel you out to the covered patio. It's warm there."

Mrs. Janice was often paralyzed by fear. She never remembered the patio, so she never wanted to go unless there was an incentive. But Farrah had the hardest time keeping Mrs. Janice warm in her room, and the afternoon heat would do her good.

"I reckon that'll be all right," Mrs. Janice said.

"Good girl." Farrah grabbed the leather photo album they'd looked through a dozen times and helped Mrs.

Janice into her wheelchair, then spread a crocheted green-and-white afghan over her lap.

"You know you made this beautiful blanket?" Farrah asked, lightly patting Mrs. Janice on the shoulder.

The woman looked at the hand-stitched blanket, confused. "I don't know how to do that mess."

Farrah laughed and grabbed Janice's yarn and well-worn crochet hooks, then stuck them in the tote bag that hung from the wheelchair's handle.

"Come on," she said, and pushed Mrs. Janice and her hobby supplies out the door and down the long, tiled hallway.

On the patio, Farrah removed her sweater to reveal short-sleeved scrubs. It was a hot one, but the overhead fans did a good job of circulating the air. Mrs. Janice's color instantly improved, which made Farrah's sweating worth the effort.

She pulled an iron patio chair beside Janice and flipped open the cover of the album. Mrs. Janice wasn't paying attention yet, as she had become enthralled with the multitudes of butterflies and other insects around the butterfly bushes in the grassy part of the outdoor courtyard. One monarch butterfly left the bush and flitted right in front of Mrs. Janice, and her aged face cracked into a wide smile.

"Wadn't that purdy?" she turned to Farrah and asked, awe in her voice.

"Just as pretty as you," Farrah offered, nudging the album her way. "Look."

Mrs. Janice's eyes flickered with recognition, but the notion didn't hold. Just as fast as it had come, it fled. "I should know these people's names..." she said, droning out the observation.

They were photos of Mrs. Janice and her husband, Hank, on their honeymoon. Mrs. Janice wore a light-colored, two-piece bikini and a 1960s beehive. How she got her hair to stay that teased and tall on the beach was a mystery—and probably a miracle.

In one photo by the Hatteras lighthouse, Hank hugged Mrs. Janice from behind, the wind whipping her beehive just a little looser. Her smile was genuine, in love.

On a better day, Mrs. Janice had told Farrah she was nineteen in these pictures, while Hank was twenty-three. Farrah couldn't help but think about Abbott. Though Hank had been a lanky redhead, his dimples weren't that different from Abbott's. And the sensation of love Hank had for Janice had no doubt been similar to the teenage infatuation Farrah and Abbott had shared. Yet Janice and Hank had made a life of it.

Could Abbott and Farrah have done the same, if she hadn't been so stubborn? She shook off the regretful thought. A cloud moved across the sun, darkening the hot patio, before bright rays broke through vibrantly again.

Farrah turned the page so Mrs. Janice could see the photos of their four newborns, all in their birthday suits, on their bellies, on a fluffy shag rug. They'd been born two or three years apart each, all in the 1960s. Mrs. Janice floated her hand over the page, awe in her voice as she said, "Oh." She touched each of the photos tenderly and her eyes glassed over. "What precious babies."

Slowly, she floated her finger down to the bottom right photo. Her voice light, cautious, she asked Farrah, "That one's in heaven, isn't she?"

Farrah wrapped her arm around Mrs. Janice's shoulder and nodded lightly.

Some things were never forgotten.

Janice didn't feel the pain today like she had the other days. She just petted the photo and smiled sadly, then turned the page. The rest of the album housed family memories starting a few years after her daughter had died. She wasn't in the picture-taking mood for a long while, she'd told Farrah on a better day. Not until it dawned on her that her other living children needed experiences with their mama.

Hank and Janice had taken their children to theme parks, beaches, and zoos. Inside the album were snapshots, all taken by Hank and Janice, of things they'd shared with their children, and later their grandchildren. Maybe it was just a grainy photo of a zebra at the zoo, but it had been important to Janice, indicative of a memory, a token of a moment spent in happy company. A reflection of youthful vigor and energy she'd used to take her children out and about.

At the end of the album came sadder photos. Hank's funeral, Janice's aging. Her grandchildren standing around her with a "Happy 80th Birthday, Grandma!" sign and enough candles to quickly cause a house fire. In the photo, she already looked lost.

By the time Janice had turned eighty, her family had serious concerns about her living alone. The last straw came when she left the burner on after heating her cat's food on an aluminum pie plate directly on the stove. It had burned and filled the house with smoke. Instead of calling the fire department, Janice had called the police and reported that someone had been smoking in her house.

They knew then that she needed assistance and moved her into Glade Village, but they were among the most faithful families when visiting time came. Janice was surrounded by loved ones almost every weekday afternoon and often on Sundays after church. It was a testament to how well she'd loved her descendants, that they came to visit her when she could no longer offer them anything of substance. When she could no longer remember the zebras at the zoo.

Farrah kept staring at the photos of a life well-lived long after Mrs. Janice had fished out her trusty crochet hook through habit and began stitching in the round, probably making a beanie or a beret. Skillfully and smoothly, her wrinkled hands wrapped yarn, hooked, and pulled through openings, creating a lovely line of stitches. From time to time, while her hands worked, her eyes would lazily float to the butterfly bushes and she'd smile, ever so slightly.

"Mrs. Janice has a visitor," the receptionist said after opening the patio door and peeking her head out. Farrah glanced at her watch. It was indeed visiting hours. She packed up the album and wheeled a still-crocheting Mrs. Janice into the common room, where Daniel and another one of her grandsons rose and greeted their grandma.

"I'll leave you all to it," Farrah said, tucking in Mrs. Janice's blankets. "The receptionist can page me when you're done."

Daniel thanked her. She had a good feeling with him now, after they'd profusely apologized to each other. She was thankful he was so easygoing and took it as what it was —an awkward mistake with a woman who just wasn't ready to date. Farrah had the sensation that he pitied her, but she didn't mind, as long as he didn't feel bad any longer.

They began their visit and Farrah exited the floral-decorated common room, saying hello to some other more independent patients sitting there reading or playing checkers. Mr. Mitchell, of course, was not one of these. She walked toward his room and almost ran into Dr. Smith head-on as she came out of his door, chart in hand.

"Oh, Farrah! I was just about to go find you." Dr. Smith's voice was full of compassion.

Farrah swallowed a lump in her throat, preparing herself for whatever lay ahead. "What is it? How's he doing?"

Dr. Smith's face pinched with regret. "I'm sorry, but it's definitely double pneumonia."

Farrah huffed out a breath. "What about the antibiotics? Are they not working? I thought—"

"Farrah." Dr. Smith placed a hand softly on her shoulder. "I know this is hard to deal with. It's a lot. He's been on that strain of antibiotics so many times that he must have built up a resistance to it. And he's allergic to so many others. I'm going to talk with the lung doctors at the hospital, but there aren't many more routes we can take. I've done about all I can." Dr. Smith paused, choosing her next words carefully. "You need to prepare… to lose the patient."

Farrah's throat closed up with the threat of tears. "W-When?" she stammered, fighting back a sob.

"I'm not sure. Not today, certainly. But many times, these types of illnesses are the beginning of the end. Especially when there's no other medicinal route we can take due to allergies and resistance." Her hand was still on Farrah's upper arm and growing clammy due to the nursing home's steady seventy-five degree temperature. "I'm sorry," Dr. Smith added with sincere empathy.

Farrah looked up at Dr. Smith's face. Well into her fifties, she had laugh lines that showed the joys she'd experienced and also two sharp creases between her eyebrows that betrayed the hours she'd spent in consternation, fretting over her patients, trying to investigate the best outcome. Dr. Smith had lost countless patients before. Indeed, death was the expected result for a palliative care physician's patients. Their prognoses were always terminal. Dr. Smith was used to it and focused on minimizing suffering.

But Farrah was not at all used to it. And she was having a hard time controlling her strong emotions and focusing only on the clinical facts. Her heart was in knots over sweet, frail Mr. Mitchell. She was one of his only visitors.

"Thank you, Doctor," she said, brushing past Dr. Smith and stepping toward Mr. Mitchell's door.

"Farrah," Dr. Smith said softly. "I wouldn't go in there if I were you. He is finally asleep after about thirty hours of wakefulness. He really needs some good rest."

Farrah nodded, tears filling her eyes as she looked at Mr. Mitchell's frail frame, declining in the hospital bed. "Okay," she managed to croak. He did need rest. Out of compassion, she gave up her selfish wish for a visit, her selfish desire to be the one who made him feel not alone. "Thank you, Dr. Smith."

"I talked to Jincey today," Abbott said, scratching at his five o'clock shadow with a brawny hand. He looked out into the blackness that was his back pasture as they sat on his screened-in porch under the soft golden glow of outdoor string lights.

He looked too handsome in this setting, and he had during their dinner date too. He'd grilled steaks and baked potatoes and set out a bagged side salad. Farrah had brought a seasonal blueberry pie her mother had conveniently made. During their meal, they'd kept the conversation friendly and light, with Abbott talking about the new calf and a side hobby of his—creating soaps, candles, and lip balms. The topics were enough to keep the conversation flowing.

Afterward, they'd settled into the back porch rocking chairs, a more intimate setting, and Abbott was holding back, not making many moves. A slight tension hung between them in stark contrast to the flirty moment they'd shared earlier in the day when he'd seemed fully smitten with her. A lot of it had to do with how he was probably reading her: reserved, restrained, solemn. Her spirit was heavy after learning of Mr. Mitchell's recent diagnosis. Try as she might, she couldn't separate the bad news from the romantic feelings of her dinner with Abbott.

There was no way for her to know for sure what was going on inside Abbott's head. She didn't want to push things too far or too fast. Last time, it had scared her, and this time, she wasn't sure Abbott fully trusted her. She remembered the look on his face the last time they'd talked at Pour Outcomes—the look that told her he wasn't convinced about her promise to open up more instead of closing him out like she'd always done.

"What did Jincey say?" Farrah asked, swaying her rocker with her foot, back and forth, holding her peach tea in her hands. The porch boards creaked beneath her, the sound reminding her of many summer nights spent talking about boys on her own porch's large swing with her mom and grandma. Talking with them about Abbott.

Abbott had made the peach tea decaffeinated, steeping the tea bags with dehydrated peaches he'd dried himself. Macon Farms' peaches. On the table between their rockers sat a crystal vase of deep indigo hydrangea blooms. Abbott probably stopped his truck upon seeing them along the road and clipped them for her. They reminded Farrah of her many runs down the gravel road toward the path that led to Quarry Creek. And, thus, of her many swims with Abbott.

"Well, she put her hand on my arm, for one thing," Abbott said and huffed out a laugh. She caught a glimpse of him from the side. His jaw clenched on and off as he chewed on a toothpick with his front teeth, the small piece of wood flitting up and down with each movement. "Other than that, she didn't say much. But she didn't deny anything either."

Farrah grunted in frustration. "I wish she and Jake could just be happy together. She's still after you and it makes no sense."

"She loves to stir the pot and doesn't like to be crossed. That's for sure."

"Yeah, but everyone deserves to be happy. Even chronically jealous people." They settled into a comfortable silence, looking out over the land lying in darkness under the sliver of moon. "This is all really weighing on me," Farrah admitted, her voice taking on a pained tremble. "Bobby and Amy came to see me this morning and wanted to call off the whole thing."

"What?" Abbott snapped his head to Farrah, his eyebrows scrunched together in shock.

"I can't blame them. They say their reputations are at stake. But we've already sold close to two thousand tickets across all of our locations. It would be so much to refund, and we'd have to wade through tons of receipt copies for those that paid with cash. It's going to take forever. They're technical things, but… gosh, I'm just so frustrated. If Jincey hadn't come along and started this drama, we could've done so much more for the Bells. I just wish she could see that they need the money, and step aside."

"I don't think she's affecting sales that much."

"Abbott… I saw people approaching to buy a ticket the

first day we sold, and one of her friends intercepted them. Then, they turned away without getting any."

"Yeah, but not many have done that. Don't forget that Jincey's reputation precedes her. Half the town doesn't trust her as far as they can throw her, but she's such a prominent figure and in charge of so much that they try to keep the peace." He sighed, leaning forward to rest his forearms on his thighs and wringing his hands. "Let me handle it. Don't worry about it anymore. I'll talk to Bobby and Amy and make them see what I see—a community of grateful people wanting to support them."

Farrah sighed and finished off her tea, then set the glass next to the hydrangeas. She reached out, gently fingering the delicate petals.

Abbott reached over and caught her hand in his, then pulled it to the armrest of his rocker, where he held it and looked into her eyes. She tingled all over. "Is everything else okay?" he asked softly. "How was work?"

Farrah swallowed hard. This wasn't a topic she wanted to broach, not with the news she'd just received about Mr. Mitchell's failing health. "It was… okay."

"Just okay?" He squeezed her hand.

"Yeah." She thought about how to word it. "My patient was really quiet."

"I bet that makes work kind of boring."

Farrah turned her head toward him, confused, and then realized he was trying to be understanding and supportive. He obviously had no idea that she wasn't referring to feeling restless on the job. She didn't mind being bored or when patients had a quiet night.

But in Mr. Mitchell's case, his quietness was a result of his body slowly succumbing to disease, something Abbott had no idea about, but which had completely monopolized her thoughts.

She would throw Abbott a bone. He had no way of knowing she had received such news, and he knew very little about what her job entailed. He was just trying to be there for her.

"It does help to have something to do, yes," Farrah said, meeting him in the middle. She ignored the churn of her stomach, the fight or flight reaction that made her want to clam up and go into her safe space—that spot where no one could rile her, where she could be alone with her thoughts, fears, and grief. "But what I meant is that it made me sad. Not bored. You know, that he was so quiet."

"Oh," Abbott said, understanding in his voice. He rubbed her thumb with his own. "They're dementia patients, correct?"

"Yes. But this one in particular… Well, he doesn't have many other visitors. It just hurts to see him… You know… dying."

Abbott stopped caressing her thumb and hand abruptly, and when she turned to look at him, his expression was serious. Pensive.

"I… wasn't aware you were losing a patient."

"Yeah," Farrah managed, tears threatening. What would he think of her if she descended into a blubbering mess?

"I'm sorry. Tell me about him, if you want."

Under a sudden burst of uncomfortable energy, she fidgeted in her seat and broke eye contact. If she started talking about Mrs. Janice and Mr. Mitchell, it would lead to talking about her move here, and ultimately Connor, and she just couldn't bear it. Though she was pleased with herself for opening up to him a little, she needed to retreat to her strong facade. It was way better than panicking again.

In response to Abbott, she shrugged listlessly, shaking

her head and looking out into the night for a while, fireflies blinking their messages sporadically as they floated in the humid air.

When she looked back at Abbott, his eyes seemed empty, tired. His attempt at a smile came off as a resigned acceptance.

Foregoing any more attempts at romance for the night, he released her hand, rubbed his thighs a few times and stood with a sigh.

"Come on," he said, his voice tight. "I can tell it's been a long day. I'll drive you home."

Their evening together was over.

An image of her teenage self running past the indigo hydrangeas and down the path to Quarry Creek flashed across her mind. In her memory, Abbott waited for her in the water, bare-chested, tan, and young. Smiling, he opened his arms with abandon, beckoning her. Not fearing her rejection or her silence.

She had wounded him by keeping him at arm's length when they were teens.

And she might even lose him again for the same reason.

All to not talk about the other man she'd lost.

Chapter Eighteen
TWO YEARS AGO

By the time the tail end of summer rolled in, the trial was finally over. The judge had ruled in Connor's favor, but the ghostwriter's negligence was only punished with a slap on the wrist—paying the court costs. It was a bittersweet ruling for a man who deserved to be held accountable for almost upending a major commercial artist's hard-won career with his carelessness.

In the few days since the trial had ended, Connor had made an effort to renew his focus on Farrah. He'd written her notes and helped out around the house. For that, she was grateful.

She expected Erin Matthews to go back to her lush, corporate office downtown and become a thing of the past. The gorgeous redhead unsettled her. She was a bit older than Farrah, single, perhaps more confident, and definitely not scared to speak her mind. Farrah sensed Connor's attraction to Erin. A subtle but enticing longing to know more about her, to be near to her. He was drawn to her. And that, more than anything, scared Farrah, because that was exactly how she had swept him off his feet a few years prior at the Oberg.

Farrah twisted her hair up and pinned it in place, then clasped on her dangly diamond earrings that had been a Christmas gift from Connor. Tonight she wore a little black dress, made mostly of silk, and dark green stilettos. She grabbed her matching clutch and flipped off the overhead lights. Connor was meeting her at seven at Marianne's Bistro to celebrate the ruling.

For Farrah, this Saturday night date was more to commemorate the fact that she could now have her husband back to herself. Erin was out of the picture, and she was ready to rebuild the foundation they had started so wonderfully, but that had suffered under the stresses of life. She had so much yet to see and do with Connor, and she certainly wasn't willing to throw in the towel because of a momentary breach of trust.

Tonight, she planned to talk to him frankly about Erin and what she thought was going on. She'd invite him to come clean, promising to work through whatever had happened—if anything—and attempt to forgive him, all for the sake of moving forward together. She'd recommend another extended trip at his beach house for a belated anniversary celebration. They'd gone so often in the first year they were married, but the visits since had dwindled. It would be relaxing and refreshing to go off together and just be alone.

Farrah drove her cargo van and parked in a garage, then clicked her way to Marianne's. It was five minutes after seven when she got inside, and she was worried Connor would be waiting on her, but she looked around the small lobby and didn't see him. Assuming he'd taken a table already, she approached the hostess, clad in black, with a tight low bun, the subtle glow of the bistro's evening light softening the girl's features.

"I think my husband is already here. It should be under Connor Dunes." Farrah said, and the girl's face brightened with recognition, then she looked at the list on her screen.

After clicking a few times, she landed on their reservation. No one could eat at Marianne's without a reservation booked several days in advance. The girl's face looked apologetic.

"I'm sorry, ma'am, but he's not inside yet. We do have your table ready, though. Would you like me to take you to it?"

The summer night air was thick in the lobby due to the front door of the establishment being frequently opened. Farrah swiped a sticky tendril of hair behind her ear, her silk dress clinging to her back.

"That'll be fine," she acquiesced. Connor would understand that she'd rather be in the air-conditioned dining room, even though they usually waited for the other to arrive before sitting down.

"Right this way."

Farrah followed the petite hostess inside the deep and moody twenties-inspired bistro interior. Low, green-glass lamps hung from the ceiling, and brass bars atop dark wood panels separated booths and tables. Always inclined to the nuances of aesthetics, Farrah had looked up the restaurant beforehand and seen pictures. Then she'd dressed to be cohesive with the interior design. She even wore hot-pink lipstick, which complimented the vases of roses and fresh, bright flowers on each table.

She waved cheerily at some gallery frequenters who brightened at seeing her, then snaked around, following the hostess back to a small table with two heavy oak chairs.

Farrah took the seat facing the other diners and the

door, then texted Connor to let him know she'd been seated. From her vantage, she would see Connor when he came in and wave him down easily in the rather dim interior. The waiter brought her a glass of water with ice and a basket with two gourmet breadsticks. He asked if she'd like to order, and she declined, saying she'd wait on her husband.

She took some time to look around the romantic atmosphere. She wasn't sure why Connor had picked this place. Sure, it was a special occasion, but they'd never been here together, and there were plenty of nice places they'd been before and loved.

Farrah's wait went on. She checked her phone. Seven thirty. Still no message or missed call. Her stomach was rumbling and the two small gourmet bread sticks were long gone. She ordered a chardonnay and some beef carpaccio with crostini as a starter, certain Connor would love that choice.

By the time eight o'clock rolled around, and her multiple calls and texts to Connor had gone unanswered, the plate of carpaccio was empty. Farrah downed the last drop of her chardonnay and tapped her foot impatiently, slumped in her chair. She blew away a small lock of hair that had fallen around her face and crossed her arms over her belly.

Yes, Connor was frequently a little late.

But never *this* late.

The waiter approached again, a look on his face that met somewhere between pity and worry. "Can I get anything else for you, ma'am?"

"Just the check," Farrah said. "I think my husband got held up at the studio."

Or by Erin.

The waiter obliged and Farrah shrugged off her fears

about Erin. After paying, she rose to leave and checked her phone obsessively for the hundredth time. Perfect reception, perfect Wi-Fi connection. Yet no messages or calls from Connor. Not that he'd text—he had an old flip phone that made texting cumbersome. He swore that technology inhibited his creative process, and Farrah could confirm it was true because he had completed so many more paintings since getting rid of his latest generation smartphone.

She sighed. She couldn't wait around any longer. If he showed up this late, he'd just have to eat alone.

As she walked toward the lobby of the restaurant, a familiar head of red hair caught her attention. Behind one of the oak separating walls topped by brass work, Farrah saw Erin Matthews dressed seductively, chatting with great elation to a person she couldn't see. Her heartbeat picked up speed and she swallowed a lump in her throat.

If it's Connor…

She took a sharp left and came up behind Erin, then emerged on the other side of the partition wall to find a handsome, clean-cut man of around forty whom she swore she'd met before. He and Erin held hands across the table. Farrah sighed just as Erin looked up, a little shocked.

"Farrah!" Erin said, letting go of the man's hand and standing to give her a hug, surprise all over her face. "Let me introduce you—this is my fiancé, Mark."

Fiancé?

"Oh! So nice to meet you," Farrah said, shaking his hand, her nerves overcoming her. She hoped they couldn't see or feel her hands trembling. "Well, actually, I think I met you before. One day when I took some food to my husband at his studio. When you were working on the case."

"Yeah, maybe so," Mark said and smiled. "Nice to officially meet, then."

"Oh, you know what? You're totally right!" Erin pawed at the air and let out a breathy laugh, taking her seat across from Mark. "I was so into Mark back then. Trying to get him to notice me, but he was just hunched over that MacBook!" Erin beamed her blinding smile, and Mark returned one just as perfect.

Farrah's relief grew as the adrenaline over Erin left her body, her heartbeat slowing down a bit. It had been Mark all along. Erin's sexy suits and work outfits, her insistence on working the case *as a team*. It had nothing to do with Connor. She was trying to snag younger, wealthy Mark.

Farrah realized she hadn't spoken and was thankful when Erin jumped back in. "You know, Connor really encouraged me with Mark. Thanks to him, we're engaged!" Erin showcased her ring, an elaborate, sparkly thing that took up almost her whole finger joint before she went on. "I was more focused on my career and stuff. But Connor assured me marriage was the best thing I could do for myself. So here we are."

Apparently Erin had been much closer with Connor in a friendship way than Farrah had realized. They'd been close enough for Connor to have advised her on personal matters. This was one of their relationship rules—never confide in or advise a person you're attracted to, because it opens a door to the heart, and feelings might grow. It was worrisome, yet Farrah was honored that Connor thought marriage was "the best thing." Peace suddenly reigned in her heart, and she let out her breath. Erin loved Mark and was not a threat.

"That's… great!" Farrah said, plastering on an excited grin. "Congratulations to you both." She nodded at Mark, who acknowledged her with another megawatt smile. Yes, Farrah was happy about Erin, but her head was spinning over something larger. Something unresolved.

Where in the world was Connor?

"Did you and Connor come here to celebrate the trial's outcome?" Erin asked, her nose wrinkling as she blazed her white smile.

"Um, yeah," Farrah said, and looked over her shoulder to her table. Connor still wasn't there.

"Awesome! I told him this was my favorite place, so I'm glad he got you in. Of course, he can eat anywhere he wants. He's Connor Dunes!" Erin giggled.

"It was nice to see you, Erin. Congrats again," Farrah said, then swooped away from the table as quickly as she could, probably leaving Erin confused at her quick departure.

Once outside, the hot, thick night air helped to ground her. Her mind spun around in frantic circles. Connor had forgotten their dinner that he had planned at Erin's favorite place.

Or maybe he didn't forget. Maybe he *had* developed feelings for Erin while he counseled her, and after hearing Erin was engaged and going there that night, he couldn't bear seeing her happy with her new beau.

"Surely not," Farrah whispered to herself, distraught. "It's a total stretch. There's no way."

But *something* had to be going on. And she had a very bad feeling about it.

Willing herself not to believe it, she paid for her parking and drove home, drained. After throwing off her stilettos, she crashed on her bed and covered herself up fully with her fluffy, white comforter. Once again, as she had so often of late, she sobbed until she'd let it all out. And then, she fell asleep.

<hr>

AT MIDNIGHT, Farrah's buzzing phone woke her from a deep sleep. It was Connor.

She clicked the green button, irate, and responded with one pointed word: "What?"

Silence came from the other end, then a faint cry.

She sat up in bed, pressing the phone to her ear. "Connor?"

He sobbed quietly into the phone.

"Connor? Do you need help? Did something happen?" Her mind immediately jumped to the worst possible outcome, that he'd had an accident and was trapped under his car, or that he had been mugged. He was always so trusting when he should have been a little less naive about how bad some people could be.

"Connor!" Farrah turned up the volume on her phone all the way to catch anything he might say. "Are you okay? Where are you?"

Connor drew in a wet, heavy breath. "I don't know."

"What do you mean you don't know?" Farrah's eyes darted around her room seeking a safe anchor. She was fully confused. The man on the phone had Connor's voice but none of Connor's confidence or self-assurance.

"I don't know where I am!" Connor belted out, distressed.

"Okay, okay. Calm down. Just… um." Farrah rubbed her hand on her forehead, thinking, then remembered he couldn't use GPS applications on his flip phone.

But she could.

"Read some signs around you, if there are any. I'll google them and come get you."

Connor drew a few more ragged breaths while sobbing. Then, he said, "Okay. There are a few here. Chip's Coffee… TrueYou Nails… and Litro Rooftop Bar."

Farrah's brow knitted together in confusion. She had

no idea what was happening. Charlotte was a big city, and getting lost was indeed possible. Yet, there was only one Litro and they'd been there at least three dozen times, most of those times with Connor driving. Instantly, she figured it out and smiled. What a stinker.

"Babe." Farrah sighed, laughing lightly at herself and rubbing her face in relief. "This is no time for a practical joke. You really scared me." She swung off her blanket and felt around for her heels, then popped them on. "*Yes*, I'll meet you at Litro. Even though you stood me up and I'm still mad. But I love you and I want to make things work."

There was only silence in response, so Farrah tried again. "I mean, what a way to invite your wife to go out with you." She chuckled into the void. Again, no response.

Then, quietly, he spoke. "Farrah… I'm not joking. I don't know where I am."

Chapter Nineteen

PRESENT DAY

Abbott drove Farrah to her house and surprised her by getting out of his truck when she did and filing behind her as she walked.

It was a little after ten, and all the lights in the house were off. Farrah moved purposefully slowly up her sidewalk, hoping he'd say something—anything. A quiet tension sat between them.

When she reached the top step of her stoop, the same spot where he'd broken up with her years ago, she turned to face him, catching him off guard. He had only a moment to react, and almost bumped into her but steadied himself, and let out a little laugh through his nose.

It was dark but Farrah could see that they were level in height since she was standing on the stoop. All around them, crickets and other night critters serenaded the night.

"What's the matter?" Abbott whispered.

She didn't answer, but her eyes welled up with tears. Somehow, though he couldn't see it, he knew.

"Bacon bit," he said sweetly. In short order, his hands landed on her waist. "Tell me." He took a step closer, and it was all Farrah needed to break down into full blown tears.

"I was having fun. Why'd you bring me home?" she asked. She might've clammed up on him, but she'd really been trying, and she definitely hadn't wanted the night to end. She'd just wanted to steer to safer topics—something relaxing. Something distracting.

"Farrah," Abbott droned, clicked his tongue, and looked down at his boots.

"No, I want an answer," Farrah demanded, crossing her arms over her chest.

"You want an answer? Fine. I was trying to make small talk about your patient, and you can't even seem to respond to that. You just gave me a shrug and looked out over the field."

"I told you I'd tell you everything when the time was right. I'm just not holding things together very well right now. Work is a sensitive subject, along with a dozen other things." Farrah let out a frustrated groan. "I'm scared for you to see me at my lowest, and I wonder what you'll think, because it might not be pretty."

"You can tell me anything. Farrah, I'm falling for you again. Can't you see that?"

Farrah was momentarily distracted from her frenzy, warmth spreading throughout her body at his admission.

"I'm really trying, Abbott. I don't want to leave you out anymore. I want to be different. And I want this awful situation to be easier than it is."

Abbott's face grew pained. He didn't say anything, he just grabbed her upper arms firmly and looked longingly into her eyes. Then he stepped even closer and slid his thick hands down her back, pulling her against his solid chest. He didn't take a moment to linger over her face, teasing, as he had in the bed of his truck. Instead, he planted a warm kiss right on her lips and held it there. She was pressed against him, melting like butter. He was firm, unwavering, where she was soft and vulnerable.

When he released her, he stayed close to her face and slid his hands into her hair on each side behind her ears, cradling her head as he whispered.

"Please, Farrah. Tell me you didn't feel anything."

Farrah looked into Abbott's brown eyes, barely visible in the night's darkness. "I felt everything," she admitted.

"Then I think you're ready for us. You're really going to throw all this away because you'd rather not talk?"

She searched his troubled eyes.

If she talked, she'd break.

But maybe that wasn't the worst that could happen.

As she'd realized before at his house, she didn't want to lose him, so she had to try, despite her overwhelm. Maybe when he understood the magnitude, he'd back off with the pressure and ultimatums. She took a deep breath and steadied herself.

"It's more than just saying if work was good or not, or if my patients are doing well or not. I'm in a bad situation, Abbott. There's a lot you don't know about. Unfathomable things, especially for a woman my age."

"Is it about your ex-husband?"

The words curdled Farrah's stomach, and Abbott, ever one to read her emotions, took a micro step backward and loosened his hands from her hair. He still stayed close, prepared to hear anything she had to say.

"Please, don't call him my ex," Farrah managed to say through gritted teeth.

Abbott huffed, frustrated. "Well, he is, isn't he?" He put his hands on his hips. Farrah remembered him well from years together. His impatience was flaring. "Don't tell me you still love the guy." Abbott looked at Farrah inquisitively, but his brow soon lowered. She couldn't answer, and his shock was palpable in his voice. "You're still in love with him?" The sound was similar to the fear and disappointment he'd felt when Farrah had told him she was going to UNCC. She knew what he'd looked like then, so even in the darkness where they stood, she could imagine his flushed face, full of hurt.

"I guess I should start by saying I didn't want the divorce."

"Because you loved him," Abbott stated matter-of-factly, but slightly annoyed.

"Yes, I loved him. A lot," Farrah admitted, tears threatening the dams of her eyes yet again.

"But he didn't love you."

A spark of anger lit within Farrah at this comment. "It wasn't like that. Connor *did* love me. It's just—"

"Then was there another woman? Because if so, it would explain—"

"How could you even—" Farrah interrupted him, but stopped suddenly, shaking her head briskly. Her blood boiled as she slowly lost control over her fears. She threw her hands up.

"Look, I know you're frustrated. I'm not giving you very much to go on. For all you know, anything could have happened in my marriage. I can't talk about this right now. But I assure you, he *loved* me. There's no question about that."

Abbott shook his head, frustrated. "None of this makes sense. If he loved you, then why did he leave you?"

Farrah balled her hands into fists, and when she spoke, her voice was thick with fury. "That's the same thing I've been asking myself about you all these years!" she bellowed. Her voice cut sharply through the otherwise peaceful night. "You blamed *me* for our breakup when you're the one that decided it. I would've stayed with you in spite of the distance! Now you're blaming me for not wanting to talk about one of the darkest periods of my life —hands down the worst thing I've ever gone through. Here I am trying my best to open up to you, and you're pouring salt in my wounds. I've had enough of this pressure from you."

The porch light flicked on and Mom opened the front door, then the creaky screen door. She stepped out and observed them, concern in her expression as she held the door open.

"Is everything okay?"

Farrah shook her head no. Abbott's face held a mixture of pain and confusion.

"I'm sorry, Barbara. I'll be on my way," Abbott said, an edgy tone to his voice. He turned and went to his truck, then cranked it and backed out.

Farrah watched him go, and the screen door slammed behind Mom, who came to stand at her daughter's side and circled her arm around her waist.

"I think I just made a mistake," Farrah admitted quietly.

"Well," Mom said, "I couldn't help but overhear. I came downstairs to get a glass of water." Silence descended between them, the crunch of Abbott's wheels on gravel almost too distant to make out. Mom spoke up again. "Just tell me how you feel now that he knows a little bit about your divorce and your love for Connor."

Farrah closed her eyes, looking inward. "Oddly... relieved. Like maybe I wanted him to know all along. I just wish the little bit I told him had gone better."

Mom turned to Farrah and pulled her in for a hug, the kind only mothers can give.

"Farrah, honey," Mom said into her ear, her speech

muffled by Farrah's thick hair, "if you want the man to trust you, you have to earn that trust."

"I do want him to trust me," she said, breaking down in tears. "I don't want to lose him."

Mom pulled away, holding her shoulders and tsking sympathetically. "Look, it's ten o'clock. You're tired, I'm tired. Let's sleep this off and have a good breakfast tomorrow. Then you can call him and fix things. It's as simple as telling him the truth, the whole truth, and nothing but the truth."

Farrah's mouth quaked with a smile, despite her streaming eyes. "So help me God."

"Come on, let's go in."

She followed her mom inside, then up the stairs, where she retreated into her room, feeling the sting of Abbott's absence.

It was clear that if she wanted him, she needed to tell him everything.

FARRAH WOKE the next morning in her childhood bedroom and reached over to lift her phone to see the time. Eleven thirty. She hadn't slept in this late in years. Her body must have needed it, especially since she had fallen asleep after midnight, rehashing her fight with Abbott and practicing what she'd say to him.

She scooted some pillows against her headboard and leaned her back on them while she checked her phone. More texts from Kia with adorable pictures of the nursery and updates on how everything was coming along.

She took some deep breaths before opening Abbott's texts, scared of what she might find:

> You were right about everything. I should
> have stayed with you. And I never should've
> blamed you. I'm falling in love with you
> again, Bacon.

Farrah tingled all over at being the object of his love. But his next text showed her the choice she needed to make:

> I don't know what is going on in your life,
> but I can't be left out of it. I don't care if it's
> not pretty. I want all of you. I want to build a
> real life with you, marry you someday, and
> all that. But it's impossible if you don't
> include me in the good and the bad. You've
> gotta let me know if I'm wasting my time
> loving you or not.

She didn't respond, because she couldn't discuss this via text. Even though opening up to him last night about her problems had left her in a fit of tears, she definitely felt better this morning. As if loosening the valve had freed months of pent-up tension.

Letting Abbott in to share a small piece of her burden had helped her. Her situation was more complicated than their teenage disagreement. Abbott would need to know about Connor and what had brought Farrah back home. He'd need to know everything, even if she broke down in the process. If he loved her, he'd be there. He'd stay.

She was ready, finally, to get everything off her chest.

She unlocked her phone and began to text him to ask if she could drop by to talk, but a call came through. It was Dr. Smith. For a second, she was worried she'd missed a shift at work, but it was her day off. Plus, Dr. Smith wasn't her superior, necessarily. The shift manager, Margaret, would have called her, not the physician.

She answered and their brief hellos revealed the tension in Dr. Smith's voice.

"I hate to have to be the one to tell you this, Farrah. But Mr. Mitchell is being moved to our palliative care unit on site. There's just nothing else I can do for him. I'm so sorry."

Farrah sat up in bed, heart pounding. "When's he being moved?"

"This afternoon."

"I can be there right now. I'll get ready, and—"

"Farrah, there's no need. Let the experts handle the move." Her voice was gentle, persuasive. The voice of someone seasoned in communicating news of impending death. "You can come later... as a visitor."

Farrah's tears fell hot and fast down her cheeks.

"Just bring your badge. No one will say anything. Or they better not. If they do, tell me, and I'll handle it."

"Thank you," Farrah croaked. "I'll be there later. And every day."

There was a beat of silence, and then, "Should I get Margaret to clear your schedule?"

"Yes," Farrah said, sniffing hard. "For the foreseeable future."

IF MR. MITCHELL was frail before, he was absolutely skeletal when Farrah arrived that evening to sit with him. He lay under blankets in the hospital bed, looking smaller than she remembered.

Occasionally, a bit of lorazepam was administered under his tongue to ease any anxiety he might feel, although they couldn't know if he was anxious or not. He just lay in bed, moaning or letting out a gurgling breath, his hands drawn, his jaw relaxed, and his dry lips cupped inward. The focus was on easing suffering, not fixing his maladies.

His imminent death was so hard for Farrah to wrap her head around.

She sat by his bed for hours, at times crying, at other times just holding his hand. CNAs and medical staff came in intermittently, but none of them said anything to Farrah about visitation hours being long over. Some just smiled at her sadly. They'd bend the rules for her.

Around ten o'clock, Farrah rose to leave. She would come back first thing in the morning. She grabbed her bag but threw it back down. Mr. Mitchell had his eyes open and they were fixed on her. She bolted back to his bedside and clutched his hand in hers.

His taut, pale face winced and his eyes glassed over. He moaned an exhausted sound.

"Are you trying to say something?" Farrah asked, wanting so badly to appear cheerful instead of heartbroken. She smiled at him as tears streamed incessantly down her cheeks.

Mr. Mitchell moaned again. His tongue and lips seemed to try to say something, but nothing intelligible came out.

He blinked his gray eyes a few times and rested his head back on his pillow, succumbing again to sleep.

"No, don't be gone," Farrah pleaded in a raspy whisper. She smoothed his sandy hair back away from his face. "Come back to me."

Mr. Mitchell snored softly in his sleep. Farrah watched him for a while, trying to see the man she had known so intimately. The man who had left this shell long ago.

She whispered as he slept. "Why won't you come back to me?"

Chapter Twenty
TWO YEARS AGO

A small nurse with curly hair opened the door to the waiting room while holding a clipboard and looking out over the sparsely filled chairs snuggled between faux plants and magazine-laden tables.

"Bryan Mitchell?" she called, looking around for her patient.

"That's us," Farrah said, grabbing Connor's elbow and escorting him to the nurse. "He goes by his middle name, Connor," she said. "Please put that on his chart."

"Yes, ma'am," the woman said, making a quick note. Then she led them to an empty office. "The doctor will be in shortly." She left the room, clipboard in hand, and closed the door behind her. Connor stared ahead blankly, his eyes bloodshot with worry as they had been for the past three weeks, since his frantic phone call to Farrah and the initial appointments she'd taken him to out of concern.

The large desk before them was populated with papers and files. A few photo frames sat with their backs to Farrah and Connor, special only to the doctor who called this desk his own.

The air-conditioning pushed strongly through the overhead vent, creating a comforting whir in the room. Farrah cradled her bare arms, pricked with goosebumps, and glanced out the window. Golden sun rained down over a blooming magnolia tree.

On a normal summer Friday, she and Connor might have been taking a dip in their pool or riding bikes before the gallery opened in the evening. It was their day to spend time together doing things they enjoyed. A day for more play and less work. But not today.

Farrah reached over and grabbed Connor's hand, looking his way. He met her gaze, his brow creased in consternation.

Dr. Ramboy came in, his black hair parted neatly on the side, a collared button-up visible under his white coat. He sat behind his desk after shaking their hands, a compassionate smile on his face as he began the consultation.

"Both genetic testing and scans confirm what I suspected. Connor, you have early-onset Alzheimer's disease. I'm terribly sorry to have to tell you this."

The words hit Farrah like a shockwave. Silence descended. Connor sat back in his chair, his worry turning to sadness. His lips parted and he looked as if he could not handle the news. Farrah squeezed his hand tighter.

"I'd like to answer your questions. I have all afternoon, so please, take your time," Dr. Ramboy offered.

Farrah had so many questions. They raced against each other, jumbling up in her mind. They wouldn't be organized, but she had to get them out.

"Will he ever get better? Is there a treatment?"

Dr. Ramboy's face was kind but apologetic. "Unfortunately, no. His progression is fast and aggressive."

"He was fine, though. How did this happen so suddenly?"

Dr. Ramboy smiled slightly, but it was a sad smile. He tented his fingers and leaned back in his chair with a creaking sound.

"Connor wasn't fine before the incident when he got lost. Were you, Connor?"

Connor shook his head, his bottom lip quivering and a tear sliding down his face. "I lose things all the time. I forget words. Sometimes I just smile at people because I can't process what they're saying. I'm no longer… myself." He broke down in silent sobs. Farrah threw her arm out to embrace him over his shoulders.

After a bit of reprieve, Dr. Ramboy spoke again. "Connor, I know your parents died young. You inherited the Alzheimer's genes from them. Did either of them have any mental decline before their deaths that you recall?"

"Oh yes," Connor said quickly. "Yes, definitely. Both. I was in my twenties, and I attributed it then to the normal dying process. Of course, they weren't in hospitals so they didn't get diagnoses close to death. We knew the diseases they had, but at the end a cousin took care of them both. They were poor mountain people. I supported them with my art teaching salary."

Farrah was cold. Stunned. She couldn't even will herself to cry, as her brain was in overdrive, trying to wrap itself around the situation.

"Doctor, how can he remember all that so perfectly, yet forget where he is? Or lose his keys? Forget he turned on the water? Leave the front door open? How?"

"Alzheimer's and dementia are diseases we don't yet fully understand." Dr. Ramboy hesitated, then added, "I must tell you, things will decline from this point on. Fairly quickly."

Farrah sucked in a breath.

"How long will I still be functional?" Connor asked, his face in anguish.

"It's hard to say," the doctor answered. "It's different for everyone. But you also have other diseases. You carry the genes for genetic cardiomyopathy and cystic fibrosis. I know you've been having some symptoms in regard to those illnesses as well."

Connor nodded solemnly.

"Doctor," Farrah started, reality setting in. "It sounds like there's no hope for my husband. What do you recommend we do?"

Dr. Ramboy smiled and his eyes grew glassy. He turned a picture frame around to show Farrah and Connor a photo of himself in his younger days with a woman who had to be his mother. She sat in a wheelchair with a happy but absent expression. They were at Disneyworld, both donning mouse ears. Beside the doctor was his wife, clinging to his arm, and his two pre-teen children smiling with braces on their teeth.

With empathy, he replied, "Enjoy the time you have left."

Chapter Twenty-One

***

Farrah left the gallery one afternoon, distraught as she had been all week since Connor's last appointment with the neurologist. Her thoughts raced as she drove home. For a while after his initial diagnosis, they had been all right. During the first few months, he'd only forgotten small things and was generally still able to live independently. Farrah had insisted he get a smartphone so she could track his location.

But then, his decline became abrupt. He would forget things about their house or about himself. Lifelong facts he'd always known. When he got turned around at the market on the corner and she had to rescue him only a block from home, she realized he'd need a caregiver with him when she couldn't be.

In the first month that Leslie worked at Farrah and Connor's home, she'd turned off the stove multiple times, as well as the shower, and discovered him outside on their lawn on four separate occasions, looking for something. Every time, he was looking for a different item. And each time, the item was something that was neatly stored in the spot where it always had been inside the house.

For the past month, it had seemed like Connor's cognitive decline grew worse every day. The devastating part was that he was still at the stage where he realized it was happening. He grew frustrated with himself, and often at night he descended into tears, apologetically telling Farrah he didn't want this for her.

It was heartbreaking, and she was never sure what version of him she would find when she walked in the door each night.

When she pulled in her driveway, Farrah saw a blue BMW next to Leslie's gray sedan. She parked and got out, inspecting the vehicle.

How could Connor possibly have company? He had no living family at all and few friends in the area. Perhaps someone he'd known all his life at the beach had come to see him after hearing of his diagnosis, if he'd told anyone.

Farrah hadn't—only her family. She needed to wrap her mind around it before the news went public. All she'd done was post on the gallery's social media platforms that she'd be spending less time at the Oberg for the foreseeable future. That may have been enough to get Connor's beach friends calling.

While handling the Oberg's business with the rest of the small staff, Ginny had graciously allowed Farrah to take off as much time as she needed. That had turned into Ginny pretty much taking over Farrah's position as an interim manager of late. Farrah just couldn't be away from Connor knowing how little time they had left. She had only gone into work for a few hours today to help Ginny with a specific exhibit related to a rather picky artist Farrah had worked with closely, but whom Ginny had never met.

She'd missed Connor all day and worried that she might come home to find he'd lost even more of his mind.

She walked inside the house, intrigued by who might be there, and heard soft voices coming from Connor's closed office door. She went to it quickly and threw open the door, not angrily, but worried.

Erin Matthews sat across from Connor's desk, laptop out, hands typing fervently, a pained and drawn expression on her face. She looked up to smile and say hi to Farrah, and Farrah could've sworn Erin had tears in her eyes.

What was she doing here crying in Connor's office? The court case was long over, and Farrah was happy with her out of their lives and wanted it to stay that way. Especially now that she had who knew how little time left to spend with Connor. She looked at Erin's hand, which sported a wedding band next to the engagement ring she'd shown off that night at Marianne's. The night Connor got lost.

Color must've risen to Farrah's face, because her cheeks were as hot as the sun had been that day. Still, she didn't want to upset Connor, so she concealed her discomfort and moved closer to him, then rubbed his shoulder warmly as he sat at his desk chair.

"Hi, Connor, did you have a good day?"

"Yes," he said, nodding, solemn. She could tell he was in a pretty good mental state just from his expression. That didn't mean he wouldn't forget some trivial thing later, but he seemed to be aware of who he was and what was going on.

Farrah glanced at the desk. All over its wooden surface were documents, files, details of Connor's assets and royalties. Erin continued to type and intermittently sort documents into several files beside her.

"A-Are you making a will?" Farrah stuttered.

Connor extended his hand and took Farrah's without answering at first. "No, we did that when we first married, and Erin has all that. Don't worry, honey, I'm still leaving you everything. You're going to be good and taken care of after I'm gone."

Farrah crouched down beside Connor. "Don't talk like that," she said. "We might have years left together. I've been making you those smoothies, and if you keep up with your mind-strengthening puzzles—"

"It's too late for all that. I just want you to go on and be happy." Connor's sea-glass green eyes looked grayer. Sadder.

"But I *am* happy. With you." Farrah clutched his chest. "I'm sure you can stay well for a long time. We don't have to give up. Fighting is the only way to win."

Connor patted Farrah's back. "Farrah, there's no way to win this."

The words hit her like bricks. She sobbed onto him, no longer caring that Erin was across the desk.

"You're so young… so beautiful," Connor started. "I know you want children. I want you to move on, to find somebody. I could be in this state for years—"

"No! Connor, no! I don't want anyone but you!" Farrah fell on him, clinging to him, unable to believe the way he was talking. It couldn't be over—not yet.

"Farrah, I'm setting you free. You don't deserve this life. I'm a burden now."

"What is happening? Are you divorcing me?"

Connor's stare into her eyes was sad, forcefully distant.

Cold.

Erin cleared her throat and Farrah looked up at her, wanting so badly to be angry. But the tears streaming down Erin's face and the compassion in her eyes softened

Farrah's dislike of her immediately. It was then that she looked down at Erin's round belly, swollen with new life.

"Farrah, why don't you have a seat?" Erin motioned next to Connor, and Farrah pulled a nearby chair beside where he sat at his desk. She took a seat, numb.

Through her tears, Erin explained that Connor had wanted to make sure his will was still up-to-date before he lost his mind completely, and he wanted Erin to have a copy of all of their assets and accounts, as well as contact information for his financial manager. Erin had made sure things were as he wanted them, and he had already signed the small changes they'd implemented.

With pain in her voice, she delivered the harshest blows. Erin would be Connor's guardian ad litem and would make all major decisions for him when he could no longer make them for himself. Farrah would be set free. He'd be moving to an assisted living facility in Charlotte in one month. Upon his death, he'd leave Farrah everything.

"I don't want to be free, and I don't want his money. I want *him*."

Erin's eyes drooped even more and she sighed, wet and thick. Farrah could tell this was one of the hardest things she'd ever done, just like it was one of the hardest conversations Farrah had ever been a part of.

"Connor has filed for separation. In the state of North Carolina, you have to be separated for one year before the divorce is finalized. That will be early June of next year."

Farrah's heart shattered, the pain in her chest physically heavy and sharp. She looked at Connor, but his eyes were dimmer, tired. He wanted her to be free to love someone else without guilt. But all she wanted was him.

"Honey, you're not a burden," she said to him through her tears. "I love you. And I'm not leaving you. What am I supposed to do without you?"

When he didn't answer, she turned to Erin. "How do you know this is what's best for him? Why do you get to make these decisions? I'm his *wife*."

Connor reached out and held Farrah's hand.

Erin replied, "I would never want this. Connor asked me, begged me—multiple times. You can read the emails from the past few months. This is what he's wanted, consistently, over time. And I have to honor his wishes. I have to honor exactly what my friend wants his life to look like for his still-living body after he leaves it." Erin choked on a sob.

"Yeah, I'm sure you do honor that for three hundred dollars an hour!" Farrah accused.

"Farrah," Connor pleaded, giving her hand a gentle squeeze.

Shaky, Erin grabbed her files, closed her laptop, and stored everything in her briefcase. After putting it on her shoulder, she stood, a pursed look on her face. She clutched her belly.

"No, Farrah. I'm doing this for free. As a friend."

She walked out, her face wet with sorrow.

Farrah and Connor sat alone at his desk in silence for what seemed like an eternity, the only noise the *tink-tink-tink* of Leslie refilling Connor's heart and lung medications in his daily dosage container.

"You really want this?" Farrah asked, turning to Connor.

He nodded. "I want this for *you*. More than anything. Please."

Farrah weighed her options. He couldn't *force* her to get a divorce, and he had no grounds to divorce her other than giving her so-called freedom that she didn't even want. She could fight him in court, and they'd probably side with her, being that Connor was literally losing his memory and his ability to make judicious and wise choices. If she really wanted to… she could win and get her way.

But she looked at her husband, the man she knew so intimately, and saw in his eyes the pleading and longing of a man who had so little left to give, other than last wishes and preferences. His mind was made up, and the last thing she wanted was to distress him further, to put him through a court battle. She would let him win this one out of respect. She'd let him end their marriage, if it was what he really wanted.

But if he thought for a second that she'd leave his side, despite the "freedom" he'd forced on her, he was sorely mistaken.

She swallowed her tears and let out a shaky, long breath.

"What nursing home are you moving to?"

"Mountain Glen. It's all paid for."

Farrah nodded, numb.

"Who's in the kitchen?" Connor asked.

"Leslie, your caregiver. She's refilling your medications."

Leslie had been there all day. Connor should have known she was the only person who would be in the kitchen messing with his meds. She did it every week. And yet, this information was irretrievable for him.

Still in his office, Farrah held his hand and leaned her head on his shoulder. If he was going to an assisted living home, she'd want to be there with him as much as possible. It sounded like it was time for a career change.

Farrah sat up and pulled out her phone then started googling. After some research, she decided a CNA position would be best, and she searched for classes nearby. So many options popped up. UNCC had a program, but the local community college offered a twelve-week course.

Farrah saved the page to sign up for it later that night. It was impulsive, but necessary. Not at all part of any plan she'd ever had.

She'd have to resign from the gallery she loved and devote herself to her husband while he was still alive, however many years they had left. Even if he wanted to set her free, she refused to leave his side. Divorced or not, she couldn't just walk away carefree like he wanted her to. She loved him, and her *till-death* vow meant something to her. She was determined to fulfill it.

"Want me to take you out for ice cream?" she asked. It was a hot day and she could use something cold and sweet.

"No," Connor said. "I'm tired."

"Okay. Let's get you in bed to rest."

They stood and walked hand in hand out of the office and up the stairs to the bedroom.

"Who's that in the kitchen?" Connor asked.

"Leslie," Farrah said. "She's refilling your medications."

She answered that question five more times that night about different things Leslie was doing.

Three months later, when Farrah finished her CNA course and took a job at Mountain Glen, Connor no longer remembered Leslie.

Or Farrah.

Chapter Twenty-Two
PRESENT DAY

❧

In just a couple days, the steady blip of Connor's monitors in the palliative care floor of Glade Village had become second nature to Farrah. If it wasn't there, she wouldn't have known what to do with herself. During the few fitful hours of sleep she got at night at her parents' house, she dreamed of the constant beeps and that she was checking his tubes and monitors.

Trying to help him.

When in real life, there was no saving him. Connor was long gone. In his place was Mr. Bryan Mitchell, a living shell once occupied by her husband.

Around the time Farrah petitioned Erin Matthews to allow her to move Connor to Whitetail Ridge so she could be closer to her family as she navigated the grief of slowly losing her husband, Connor had insisted his name was Bryan and that he was a teacher. He had reverted to a job he'd held in his young and free days.

He had no recollection of becoming Connor Dunes, a conglomeration of the middle name he'd always liked better and a beachy word that conveyed the feeling of his career painting coastal landscapes in oil. But when given a canvas and paints, it was like he'd never stopped creating. Art surged from him as if subconsciously. He could have no idea what day it was or what food he liked to eat, but his hand unleashed an ocean sunset on a canvas as if by third party design.

He developed strong preferences and would be adamant until he got his way. In earlier days of good mental health, he'd been easygoing. It wasn't so during his decline. He didn't like that his devoted CNA's last name was also Mitchell on her name tag. It confused him and made him irate. So she had taken a trip to the social security office one afternoon a few weeks after he moved to his first nursing home, and became, once again, Farrah Macon, and then asked for a new name tag.

Was she single? Divorced? Widowed, in a way? She wasn't sure. All she knew was it absolutely crushed her. Every morning she struggled just to get out of bed and keep going on with her life. To keep being there for the man who no longer remembered their magnetic attraction, their whirlwind love story.

And here he was in his last weeks or days. She couldn't miss any of it. She didn't want Mr. Mitchell to be alone. She rested her head on her propped-up arm and watched him struggle to breathe. She didn't know how long he could last in this state, and she was thankful that he seemed not to be in any pain. Her CNA training taught her that morphine was God's gift to a dying patient, and she made sure he had every dose he needed. As a result, his moaning had ceased, and he was at peace. Occasionally, he'd open his eyes. But not today. Today was a quiet, heavy day.

A knock on the doorframe startled her. It was Mom and Macy. Farrah rose and hugged each of them tight, holding on for a long time before letting them go. Macy handed Farrah a latte.

"I know you, and I can guess you're not sleeping a whole lot."

"Yeah." Farrah sighed.

She pulled up an extra chair and the three sat in silence, watching Mr. Mitchell's chest rise slowly, and fall quickly.

"Thank you for coming. I know you didn't see eye-to-eye with him in life, but I appreciate you being here in…" She couldn't bring herself to say "death."

"Nonsense, Farrah," Mom said, compassion and love all over her face. "I didn't see eye-to-eye with him because he wasn't diagnosed. I thought he was careless toward you, or worse." Mom shuddered and Farrah knew what she was getting at—Erin. "At the end of the day, I can tell you honestly that I appreciate that man because you loved him, and he was good to you." She reached across and grabbed Farrah's knee. "I'm sorry you didn't have more time with him."

The rims of Mom's eyes were red, and the whites were glassy, the signs of the kind of secondhand heartbreak a parent feels for their suffering child.

Farrah laid her hand on top of Mom's. "Thanks, Mom."

Mom got up, excusing herself to the restroom for a moment. Farrah turned to Macy. "So how was the farmers market today?"

"Good sales." Macy nodded.

"What about raffle tickets?"

Macy sighed. "There were some. Nothing like that first Tuesday. But I delegated all that over to Abbott and told him he'd need to handle it. I don't want you to worry about it either. You have bigger fish to fry."

Farrah felt a rush of relief that the raffle was in Abbott's capable hands. "How was he?"

"Who?"

"Abbott." Farrah's cheeks warmed.

Macy cocked her head slightly at Farrah and fought a smile. "He was fine. He asked about you."

"Hmm." Farrah rubbed her eyes in an attempt to escape her fatigue so she could say what she needed to. It didn't work. "Macy, this is important. Last time Abbott and I were together I kind of pulled back from him, and we fought. I hurt him a lot when we were teens by holding back. In a lot of ways, as an adult I've grown past that, but for some reason with this stuff with Connor… I've shut down like Fort Knox, and—"

"Shh…" Macy soothed Farrah, who had descended into tears, and rubbed her back. "This is a lot. Don't be so hard on yourself."

"But it wasn't fair to leave him out," Farrah managed, her voice thick from crying. "I was just scared of him seeing me… like *this*." Farrah blew her nose in a tissue and somewhat collected herself. "I've wanted to talk to him for days, but I've been so overwhelmed. Can you call him? Tell him it's important. Tell him"—Farrah sucked in a breath to calm her nerves—"that I'm ready to open up."

Macy hesitated, biting her lip, then spoke. "If you're sure… consider it done."

Farrah leaned on her sister's shoulder. "I love you, Macy."

Macy rested her head on Farrah's. "I love you too, sis." Then she got up and left the room to make the call.

THE REST of the day ticked by slowly as Farrah hoped Abbott would come. Daddy arrived to sit with her for a while after dinner. They watched Mr. Mitchell, and Daddy's eyes grew heavy with sadness for his daughter. Neither of them spoke. Farrah figured they didn't need to because their similar personalities understood each other, and that words would be better at another time.

Daddy left around nine when visiting hours ended, and Farrah lost hope of seeing Abbott that day, since the nursing home's visitation policy was very strict. She had been alone for an hour and extended the recliner that Dr. Smith had arranged next to Mr. Mitchell's bed. Farrah curled up on her side, holding his hand from time to time.

She caught herself nodding off. She needed to get home.

She packed her bag quietly and whispered a goodbye to Mr. Mitchell, then planted a kiss on his forehead. It was never easy to leave him, but she would come back first thing in the morning, and he'd have a dedicated team caring for him overnight, a team that would call her immediately if there were signs that he was passing.

She walked out to the parking lot and searched in her bag for her keys. When she approached her car and looked up, she saw a truck off to her right and a man outside it under a lamppost.

It was Abbott with understanding in his eyes. She approached him, standing squarely in front of him in the sticky night air. They exchanged quiet hellos.

"I'm sorry I couldn't come sooner. Had some issues with the cows."

"No, it's okay," Farrah said. "There was no real need."

"Yes, there is," Abbott offered, raising his brows. "You're ready to talk and I'm ready to listen."

Farrah looked down at her feet for a moment to avoid

breaking down. Abbott raised her chin up so her eyes met his.

"I can handle the ugly and the broken. Don't be afraid of melting down in front of me. I'm here for it."

Farrah stepped forward and wrapped her arms around him, sinking into him and almost letting the tears flow again, her tote bag long forgotten on the pavement beside them.

"Abbott," she whispered against his chest.

"Yeah?"

"Can we go down to Quarry Creek?"

Abbott sighed out a laugh. "I'll meet you there."

THE WALK through the woods hand-in-hand with Abbott was a lot different at twenty-nine than it had been at eighteen. For one, the dark stillness unnerved Farrah, whereas in the past she wouldn't have given it a second thought. But mostly, it was different because as a teenager, her sprints down to the creek had been marked by exhilaration to see Abbott and passion for him, in both body and soul. Now, in the place of those youthful driving forces stood melancholy and worry.

Each crunch of twigs and leaves underfoot took them closer to the swimming hole. Abbott reassured her as they walked, using his iPhone as a flashlight to see the trail before them. From time to time, the beam caught the white, reflective eyes of a forest critter, scurrying away.

"They're more scared of us than we are of them," Abbott said, giving her hand a squeeze.

The truth was, she was only a little cautious, but not at all scared. She couldn't be when she was with Abbott. Not to mention she was numb from everything going on. Emotionally spent.

They reached the dark shore of the creek, and their vision adjusted somewhat, enough to see what was sand, and water, and trees. The half-moon reflected brightly in the ripples of the swimming hole. Farrah remembered the summer they'd dammed it up as preteens, proud of themselves for having made their very own pool.

Abbott spread out a tarp he had brought from the back of his truck, and they sat on it looking out at the nighttime scene. Frogs croaked and crickets sang all around them in varying intensities and pitches, alto, soprano, and baritone. Farther up in the treetops, cicadas trilled a solid buzz as one.

Farrah reached for his hand in the dark and soon found it, rough and warm. She laced her fingers through his and took a breath for confidence.

"I'm so sorry I didn't let you into my current problems. You know I'm private, and I guess I thought if I kept this issue to myself there would be less pain. But that wasn't true." Farrah sniffled. "You deserve to know all of this." She took another deep, shaky breath as Abbott waited in silence, listening. "You remember when we first saw each other again at the farmers market? And you asked about my husband, and I told you we got divorced?"

"Yes, of course."

"Do you know who my husband is? *Was?*"

"Sure. Connor Dunes. The artist. My aunt has a framed beach print of his and a puzzle." Abbott paused. "He was a lucky guy to snag you. And, Farrah, I *am* sorry he left you. I know it hurt you, and—"

"No, Abbott. There's more to it than that." Farrah swallowed hard. "He had early-onset Alzheimer's disease. He lost his mind, divorced me to set me free, in his words, and then ultimately forgot me." Her voice crackled and broke on these last heartbreaking words. "I got him secretly moved to Glade Village, and I became a part-time CNA to take care of him. Now he has pneumonia on top of his other genetic diseases. He's on hospice and will leave us soon."

"Your patient… Oh, Farrah," he whispered, pulling her to his chest and wrapping his arms around her. Her face against his sternum, she let the hot tears flow. She shook in his arms as he rubbed her back, up and down. When she composed herself, he gave her a gentle squeeze and released her. She sat up and wiped her face. A wave of relief poured over her. Abbott knew the truth, and he was still here with her, his hand still on her shoulder in consolation. She no longer bore the burden alone.

"I'm so sorry," he finally muttered, low and tender. "The way I've been treating you… My impatience. I wish I'd known sooner."

"Abbott, it's okay." Farrah took a deep breath. "I'm sorry for not telling you. My heart wanted to, but things got in the way. It's not exactly easy to talk about this. But I know you probably have questions. I'll answer what I can."

"Actually, yes. Why isn't this all over the news?"

"Well," Farrah started, cracking a smile, "it kind of helps that I've been his publicist since we got married. Not that I'm qualified, but in the art world, it basically consists of releasing statements. Not many artists are on TMZ. I mean, have you ever seen Thomas Kinkade's face? Could you pick him out of a crowd if he were still alive?"

Abbott laughed despite the sad conversation. "No, but I could Bob Ross."

Farrah giggled. "Right, but Connor was never on TV. Never in the spotlight, really, despite being a household name for many people. I've been able to keep his illness discreet. I'll let his friends know this week, especially when he passes." Farrah grew somber again, the reality of Connor's end looming before her.

"And his family?"

"None. His parents were only children, and they're both deceased. No grandparents, not that a man his age would have grandparents anyway. No cousins. He was married in the nineties fresh out of high school, but it ended in an annulment. I wouldn't even know how to reach out to that first wife, or where she is. It was just him."

"No children?"

"Nope. He didn't want any." Farrah's heart panged. She remembered his decision that had crushed her in the moment, and she considered just how terrible it would be for a toddler, if they'd had one, to lose his or her father. She thought of Cash and Colton, so little and sweet, and how they would react if Elijah died. She shuddered. They'd certainly been better off without kids.

"Didn't you?"

"Yes. I still do."

Abbott hummed knowingly, then changed the subject. "So you really loved him."

"Yes," Farrah said. "It's why I couldn't just run to you and start fresh. I know I'm about to lose him… the shell of him."

"And I would never rush you, knowing this," Abbott said, turning his face close to her ear, tenderly cradling the small of her back. His hand was warm over her shirt, and rough. It snagged a bit on the fabric as he caressed her. "I've waited over a decade for you. I can wait another one, if needed."

Farrah humphed out her amusement. "It's so ironic, isn't it? He divorced me to set me free, precisely for this reason. So I could find someone and move on. He was convinced he was a burden. And now, I have you in the palm of my hand and instead of taking the opportunity, I just can't leave Connor's side." Farrah's tears returned, slow and silent with only a wet sniff betraying her in the dark. "I just loved him too much." This last sentence came out in a whisper.

They sat in silence for a while until Abbott spoke again. "I'm sorry he chose to handle things the way that he did."

"Me too," Farrah admitted quickly. "I think he wanted to make it easier on me, but it's only made it harder. He didn't realize there was no way I could fully separate the man I'd loved from Mr. Mitchell's vacant body. There was no way I could see him as the ex-husband that divorced me, and simply move on emotionally. As long as he's here, I'm going to be tied to him. With him, every day. And it's been a year of this. You'd think I would have accepted it a little more by now."

Abbott clicked his tongue a few times. "Grief is different for everyone." Farrah recalled that when he'd lost his grandmother in tenth grade he'd struggled. She had been like a mother to him. Meanwhile, his father had poured himself into work after losing his mom, barely shedding a tear other than at the funeral. It had been the start of a big disconnect between James Abbott Sr. and Jr.

"Besides," Abbott started again, "I can tell by the way you talk about him that you loved him with everything you had. You were a great wife to him—still are. You're so loyal. Even in death. It's an example for me and so many. An example of honoring your vows. I'm proud of you. Seeing your commitment to him, and your openness with me… It gives me hope. I know somewhere down the line we could explore something and make it work." Abbott thought a moment and then added, "Thank you, Farrah. For telling me all this. Thank you for letting me in."

Farrah leaned over and rested her head on Abbott's shoulder, seeking comfort, but also giving in to her tiredness. She appreciated Abbott more than ever. She had been so afraid of this moment, and all for nothing. He was so understanding, not expecting anything from her at all.

"Thank you, Abbott. Everything you just said means more than you know."

Abbott hesitated, and when he spoke, his voice was quiet and a little unsure. "Remember how you loved *me*?"

Farrah smiled, remembering herself wrapped around Abbott in the swimming hole where they now looked. "Yeah."

"Was it the same?"

She sighed. "Yes. I don't know if that hurts you, but I can't lie to you. Yes. I loved him as much as I loved you."

Abbott laughed a little. "It doesn't hurt me," he said. "It makes me feel better. I was doubting if what we had was on that level. If it was real."

"It was real," Farrah admitted softly.

It's still real, she wanted to say. Instead, she rested her head more comfortably on him. There would be a time for her to move forward with Abbott. Her healing would show her when that was.

She must've fallen asleep, because a while later Abbott roused her with a gruff whisper.

"Come on. Let's get you home." He stood and crouched, offering her his back. She climbed on and he carried her through the dark woods, holding her thighs tight against his muscular sides. He smelled of lavender and laundry detergent. He'd mentioned he'd been making soaps. Maybe it was the scent of one he'd concocted. She smiled thinking about the big, muscular, softie juxtaposition that was Abbott.

"Anything I should know about the basket?" Farrah asked, suddenly remembering the raffle.

"Yes, actually. I've somewhat convinced Amy and Bobby. They're calmer now, at least, and not wanting to cancel it. The drawing has been moved to this Friday at the amphitheater."

"Wait, what? I thought it was next Tuesday at the market." Abbott's steps caused Farrah to jostle up and down, slightly jarring her voice.

"*You-know-who* stepped in and complained, citing the maximum capacity of the farmers market lot. Our ticket sales exceeded it—greatly. I don't know how she knew that. Maybe there's a mole."

"No, *she's* the mole. A good old-fashioned busybody." Farrah rolled her eyes. "Who paid for the amphitheater reservation? Hopefully not Amy and Bobby's earnings."

"I did," Abbott said. "Don't worry about anything. Just worry about Connor. I've got everything under control. I've already followed up with Chuck at the newspaper to get information out about the drawing both in print and on socials. The winner doesn't have to be present to win, they just need to turn in their winning stub within seven business days. But you knew that—it was in the contract my lawyer drew up. The one you signed."

Farrah grew sheepish and probably red in the face. She had been far more concentrated on how his trim body looked leaning over the table near her than the stipulations of their contract.

"Right," Farrah said.

Abbott slowed. "Hop down."

She lowered herself onto the ground and they walked side-by-side toward the edge of the woods. They reached the gravel road where their cars were parked in the grass off the shoulder. Abbott walked Farrah to hers, but before she got in, she turned to him, grasping his upper arms with her hands. He, in turn, held her at the elbows, looking down into her face as a cool night wind blew under the starry expanse.

"If I were an honest man," Abbott said, "I'd tell you I want to kiss you. Badly. But I'm not going to. I know you need time and space. I'll be here waiting when you're ready."

A tingle ran through Farrah. She wanted to be kissed, probably as badly as he wanted to kiss her. But Abbott was right and had voiced exactly what she needed. She was losing what was left of her husband and needed to be by his side bright and early in the morning. She needed to see off the body that was clinging to life before she could close the chapter and move on, despite Connor's wishes and the easy path he'd made for her to do so.

She let Abbott go and stepped back.

"Goodnight, Abbott," Farrah said. "And thanks."

"Goodnight," Abbott said. "And, Farrah? I'm sorry for pressuring you. I understand now. If he was so important to you, he's important to me too. I promise I'll come by another day and sit with you… and him."

Farrah smiled with gratitude and nodded, then climbed into her driver's seat. She did a three-point turn to head in the direction of home. As she pulled away, she looked in her rearview mirror. Abbott was slightly illuminated in the dim, warm glow of her taillights, watching her go.

Chapter Twenty-Three

"I can't believe this is really it," Kia said, rubbing her growing belly. She sat, legs parted as pregnant women do, in the Oberg's main office as Farrah packed up some special personal items.

She hadn't been to the gallery for months, but she'd needed to get a few things she'd left behind. Who knew how many years Connor would be in decline in Whitetail Ridge at Glade Village nursing home. Alzheimer's could be a very slow process, and it was already proving so. She had prepared to move back home permanently, for the long haul.

This meant collecting her diplomas, certifications, awards, and accolades to transfer to a box she'd store in Mom and Daddy's attic, and leave the Oberg free of any trace of her. Ginny would resume her role full-time. But she'd already told Farrah she could come back at any time. *"I'd absolutely love it if you came back and stole this job from me,"* Ginny had said during their last phone call.

Farrah could only hope. But wanting to be back at the

gallery meant losing Connor, and she definitely didn't want that. It was a hopeless, grief-filled situation no matter how she looked at it.

"Yep," Farrah said to Kia, not at all peppy but trying to sound it. "But this transfer is going to be good for Mr. Mitchell and me. I need to be closer to my family."

Kia groaned. "It's still so hard for me to hear you call him that."

Farrah smiled as she dug through her clutter, throwing out things that didn't matter and setting aside things that she wanted to keep. She was extremely organized at home. Everything was in its place, even in her storage rooms. But at the office, her creative wheels went crazy, making it a less-than-tidy place. Especially in her desk area, where her projects table and lockers teemed with ideas, some in full execution mode and others barely started. Neat-freak Ginny would appreciate Farrah's desk area and art lockers being nice and tidy when she left.

"Believe it or not, it helps me to call him Mr. Mitchell. It's what he wants to be called because in his mind, that's who he thinks he is. He has reverted to when he was twenty-six and teaching college art classes as a recent master's graduate, though every day, according to him, he teaches a different subject. It's sweet, how he thinks of himself that way." Farrah smiled lightly. "And it helps me to separate him from the man I loved, the man who's left."

"Phew," Kia said, dabbing at the corners of her eyes with a tissue. "Don't mind me. My hormones have me extra emotional." She clutched her belly and the two shared a laugh. "How was your meeting with Erin yesterday?"

Farrah scrunched her nose, searching for words, while she pulled out a big pile of documents and projects from a forgotten locker. She began sorting through them. "Bad. I learned that my divorce was finalized."

"Oh, Farrah…"

"But it was also good. She's been amazingly supportive." Farrah stopped sorting and turned to Kia. "I really think she loved Connor as a friend. I believe her now when she says she never wanted to be his guardian ad litem and she'd rather it had been me. She's done everything I've asked, even allowing him this transfer to my hometown."

"But why? I mean, I'm glad she's been so cooperative, but there's nothing in it for her."

"Beats me," Farrah says. "She and I didn't have the best start, and some things she says and does still irk me. But I think she is trying to be a friend by honoring his wishes. That's how she puts it, anyway. You have to respect that."

"Did you ever find out if there was anything going on between them?"

Farrah thought back to a few tough conversations she'd had with Connor and Erin on separate occasions. Back then, that possibility had seemed like the be-all and end-all of her pain and worry. Now, fears about Connor's fidelity seemed like small apples.

"I asked them both," she went on. "They adamantly denied it. Erin even with tears in her eyes." Farrah let out a small huff, remembering the tension of that discussion with Erin, when she'd asked her to meet her at the corner coffee shop to clear the air. "Honestly, Kia, I believe them. And I have peace, especially because Erin's married with a kid now. I think it was all in my head and distracted me from what was really happening with Connor's decline. She was into Mark— another lawyer on the case, whom she married—the whole time."

Silence settled over them. Kia seemed deep in thought as Farrah sorted papers, graphs, and various projects.

Farrah shot a look to Kia. Her friend's brows were knitted together, and she wore a slight frown while rubbing her belly and staring at the cowhide rug.

"What are you thinking about?"

"Nothing," Kia blurted, then her face softened. "And everything… I mean, where are you going to stay?"

"Mom and Daddy's. They didn't even hesitate when I asked."

Kia offered a soft hum in response. "Sounds like you've got it all worked out."

Farrah humphed. "Feels like the opposite."

"Hey. Everything's gonna be all right," Kia offered in consolation.

Farrah sighed. "I wish that were true."

Silence again as they both thought, and Farrah worked.

She crouched on all fours and looked into the back of a locker. There was an eleven-by-fourteen or so leather portfolio. She extended her arm to the back and could barely reach it.

"Gosh! I might need your long arms, Kia," Farrah teased.

"There's no way I could get down on the floor with this giant belly," Kia said.

Painstakingly, Farrah pulled out the leather portfolio. She opened it and slid out a canvas she had long ago misplaced, and gasped.

"What? What is it?" Kia asked.

"*Sandcastle Girl!*" Farrah flipped the small painting around for Kia to see. "It's me. The week we fell in love."

She ran her fingers over Connor's beautiful strokes, so full of color and life. So contrasting to how he himself was decaying at this very moment in time in a nearby nursing home bed. The beauty of the painting and the pain of remembering those perfect days were inseparable, and yet, her prevailing feeling was joy at finding it again, no matter how emotional it made her.

She clutched the painting to her chest, tears streaming, and smiled up at the ceiling. "Oh, thank you, God! And thank you, Connor!"

Chapter Twenty-Four

It was a beautiful Friday for the raffle drawing, even though Farrah did not want to be there. Bright sun shone down on the hundreds of people making their way to the amphitheater across the green grass, folding chairs or blanket in hand. A sound team was preparing two microphones as Farrah and Abbott stood off to the side of the stage, nervous as two groundhogs caught in a garden. The nerves drained Farrah even more, and she was already exhausted.

She had spent Wednesday and Thursday by Mr. Mitchell's side as he slowly declined, only going home once to sleep for six hours and take a shower. By Thursday night, he only moaned and sputtered out short, labored breaths.

Earlier in the morning before leaving for the raffle, Dr. Smith had called Farrah to let her know that Mr. Mitchell was actively passing, which meant the end was near, but there was no reason to think it would be today. He'd pass when he was supposed to, and his vitals seemed okay, considering the circumstances. So when Macy came by insisting that Farrah head to the drawing, she made herself go.

"It'll just be two hours at most. I'll stay with him the whole time, and you can come right back afterward," Macy had said. *"I know this project means a lot to you, and I want you to see the end of it."*

After hearing her sister's reasoning, Farrah had decided to go, but only for Amy and Bobby. She was the face of the project, and it had come under so much scrutiny that she needed to be there, proudly supporting them. So she had driven home, taken a shower and run some curl cream through her hair, which bunched up in beachy waves. Then she threw on a simple yellow cotton dress and sandals, and headed to the drawing.

It wasn't long until some country music started to play over the crowd, now relaxing into their positions. Abbott, clicker in hand, counted them.

"Seems there are around six hundred people."

"Wow," Farrah remarked. That was a big show of support for the Bells. She looked down on the front row, and Amy waved at her, while Bobby smiled her way. Amy jerked her thumb over her shoulder, mouthing the words *oh my gosh!* Farrah nodded emphatically, eyes wide. Amy was right to be surprised—it was a lot of people. Still, they'd sold nearly two thousand tickets, so Farrah figured a lot of those who had bought were working or otherwise unable to come.

"Maybe we should have hosted this on a Saturday, instead of a Friday, or a Tuesday as we originally planned," Farrah suggested. "I'm sure a lot of people couldn't come due to work."

"I tried." Abbott shook his head, annoyed, but not at Farrah. "Guess which rotary club member handles the renting of the amphitheater?"

She didn't need to guess. It made sense that Jincey

wouldn't want the drawing to be a success, so she'd relegated them to a weekday.

"Some people just should *not* be given power."

Abbott laughed. "If she wasn't given it, she'd take it. One way or another."

"How do we get the word out about the seven-day window to claim the prize if the winner isn't here?"

"The town newspaper is posting on social media with the winning ticket number all week and telling about the due diligence period. I'm sure the winner will come forward."

Abbott amazed Farrah. He had put in countless man hours, calling, texting, organizing, and dealing with Jincey —all for Bobby and Amy. Or maybe it had all been for her. She looked up at him, his tan, stubbly face so attractive under the bill of his ball cap.

"And if not, we'll host a second drawing next week."

Farrah surveyed the audience once more, looking for familiar faces. Off in the distance, Jake the Cop stood near his parked patrol car, on assignment for crowd control. A few other local cops were doing the same sort of task. She was glad to have the help, though it looked like the crowd was completely calm. Everyone seemed excited and eager for the drawing.

A stagehand approached and tapped Abbott on his arm. "Mr. Abbott?" He turned around to meet the young man and accepted a microphone from him. "It's five past eleven."

Abbott gave a little jolt, thanked the boy, and turned back to Farrah, breathing out his nerves. "I guess this is it."

He walked to center stage as the music faded, and he greeted the crowd with a rowdy hello. If he was still nervous, he hid it well. His voice boomed out across the crowd with enthusiasm and confidence. The excitement was palpable, in spite of the hot rays pouring down on them all. Many people fanned themselves with papers or sat under umbrellas.

"And we've been so proud of this community, helping Bobby and Amy in this way. We know Bobby has kept our tractors and mowers running, and Amy and the others at her salon keep us looking our best. Bobby's the last person that deserves a health trial or a bad financial situation, and that's why we're so glad to help him with this benefit basket. We're proud to announce that we've sold just under two thousand tickets, and after taxes and small business expenses, we'll be able to pay nearly one hundred thousand dollars toward the Bells' medical debt to hopefully help save their house and land."

Abbott had to pause because the crowd before him cheered uproariously. Farrah was happy with the number and clapped with a smile on her face. But it wasn't the full amount. She'd hoped to erase the problem for them completely, not just cut it in half. She glanced at Bobby and Amy, clapping and smiling from the front row, much like she was. Maybe, internally, they also worried that it wasn't enough.

Abbott went on. "So we can proudly say the fundraiser was a massive success. I'd like to thank Farrah Macon for coming up with this amazing idea." He turned to Farrah, motioning with his hand, and the crowd applauded, causing her cheeks to warm even more than the temperature had done. Abbott's eyes twinkled as he looked at her.

"And, of course, all the people who donated, whose names and businesses are listed on the back of your ticket stubs—a round of applause for those that provided the basket items!" The crowd erupted with some standing and then tapered off into silence again.

"Thanks to all who contributed by buying a ticket in

exchange for a chance to win the gift basket of a lifetime. Lastly, thank you to the rotary club that rented us this fantastic amphitheater…" Abbott seemed to struggle to come up with some words that wouldn't sound too much like an insult. "It… wasn't in our plans, but thank you to Jincey Taylor for pointing out the, um, *need* to relocate in order to… uh… *save* our fundraiser." A noticeable giggle and murmur arose throughout the audience.

Apparently taking the mention as a summoning, an angry Jincey appeared out of nowhere and elbowed her way through the crowd, beelining toward the stage in a bright orange romper and black platform shoes. Her hair was teased to Tennessee and her large gold earrings jingled as she approached the stage. "Wait just a minute!" she called as she walked, still a ways off.

Farrah looked toward the crowd control officers. Jake the Cop had started a swift jog toward Jincey and the stage. Farrah couldn't help but think how sad it was that he had to spend the morning chasing after his headstrong wife. Sad or not, he was too far off to stop her, and she was nearly to the steps.

Abbott shot Farrah a nervous glance as people pointed and questioned what was happening. Farrah twirled her fingers at him, motioning for him to keep going and come up with something to distract from Jincey's interruption. But how?

Jincey began stomping up the steps to the platform. Jake ran, dodging camping chairs and picnic spots, hurdling over labradoodles, and begging her to stop.

"Jincey, don't!" he called, and the crowd quelled a bit to hear him. "Let's just go home. It ain't worth it." She ignored him completely, and the crowd's chattering picked up again.

Panting, she marched across the stage and toward the

other mic, then flipped it on, as if she were a scheduled part of the raffle drawing.

Abbott launched into action. "Uh, without further ado, I suppose we'll draw the ticket—"

"No you won't, neither!" The speakers screeched at Jincey's shrill outburst into the mic.

Gasps ensued from the crowd and from Farrah too. Her heart raced.

Jincey's hands shook and her face was redder than a garden tomato. "I'll have you know that I've tried to limit this little enterprise for good reason!"

"Jincey, what are you on about?" Abbott asked, confused.

"Shush!" she called to him, then spat out to her husband who was jogging up the side steps onto the stage, "Leave me alone, Jake. Let me say my piece!" Poor Jake stopped mid-run and slouched, defeated, as he glanced between Farrah and Abbott and Jincey.

Abbott laid into her, fired up at being disrespected. "Don't shush me, I—"

"The painting is stolen!" Jincey cried out dramatically into the mic. All at once, the hundreds of people in attendance went silent, turning to one another in surprise, and some murmurs arose from the crowd. Jincey extended her arm, pointing at Farrah.

"That woman, Farrah Macon, stole it from her ex-husband, the famous artist Connor Dunes!"

All eyes shifted to Farrah. Having so many judging gazes on her made her suddenly very hot, and she trembled with anxiety.

"That's ridiculous!" Abbott barked into the mic. "He was her husband. He gave it to her, and she—"

"Then why did I hear her telling Amy Bell that he wouldn't even know she was donating it, and that she wasn't even going to ask him permission? Huh?" Jincey took a step toward Abbott as she said this and poked him in the chest. Farrah's blood began to boil. That was close, but not precisely what she had said to Amy when Jincey was eavesdropping. She hated a lot of things, but manipulating the truth to shock and confuse others was one of the worst.

Farrah spoke low to Jincey, away from the mic. "That's *not* what I said, and you know it."

"Well, that's what I heard!" Jincey said into the mic, bobbing her head from side to side like a high school mean girl.

Farrah walked over to Abbott and swiped his mic, much to his surprise.

"Farrah, you don't need this. Let me handle it," he pleaded, eyes sorrowful. It was true that he had the good-guy, crowd-pleasing persona that could quell this uprising, but Farrah had to handle this herself. She was being lied about, yet again, and she had to defend herself the only way she could: with the truth.

"I've got this," she said aside to Abbott, then turned to the crowd. Abbott's hand landed supportively on her back, letting her know he was there if she needed him to take over.

"The painting isn't stolen," she said calmly to the crowd. "It was a gift—"

"Convenient story!" Jincey accused.

"It's the truth!" Farrah turned to her, steaming mad. "That's me in the picture. My husband painted *me* at the beach the week we fell in love." The crowd quieted, and the murmuring noise was different, understanding, calmer. This enraged Jincey, who turned a deeper shade of rage. She gritted her teeth and snarled.

"I'll show *you* the truth!"

"I can explain everything," Farrah said, trying to remain calm, again turning to the crowd.

She was just about to open up and reveal the truth about Connor's dementia, when Jincey lunged forward in a fast flash of electric orange. She extended her arm and grabbed Farrah's microphone, trying to wrestle it out of her hand while crying, "I don't think so!"

"Just let me say what I need to say," Farrah said while pulling back on the mic. Jincey pulled hard and Farrah's grip slipped, as did her feet. She lost her balance, falling into Abbott, as the microphone slammed onto the cement stage, cracking and sparking from the force of the impact. As Abbott stabilized her, Farrah caught a glimpse of Jincey looking at the broken mic, smiling in victory.

"Jincey, what is wrong with you?" Farrah asked, horrified.

The question snapped Jincey out of whatever trance she was in. Her eyes grew wide and she looked out at the crowd, realizing everyone was watching in sustained suspense. "I… I only meant…"

Stagehands rushed around to secure the area and the crowd's nervous chatter at the scene unfolding grew to a steady rumble.

"Are you okay?" Abbott asked, cradling Farrah's face.

"Yeah, are you?"

"Yeah."

He lowered his forehead to rest on hers, just for a moment, before enveloping her in a hug. As close as they were in their public embrace, Farrah was certain her secret of loving Abbott was on display for everyone within a three-town radius. But she didn't care.

Their moment was broken when Jake jumped forward and addressed a frazzled-looking Jincey with a furrowed brow. He looked as surprised to be saying what he was saying as everyone else was to hear it.

"Mrs. Jincey Taylor, y-you have just committed destruction of p-private property… I'll have to t-take you down to the station." His eyebrows were up in the heavens, and he stuttered a bit under his blonde mustache, his voice breaking at times like that of a prepubescent teen.

Jincey's mouth dropped open in shock, and then Jake cuffed her wrists with newfound bravado. Jincey's eyes just about bugged out of her head as Jake recited her Miranda rights. But there was something behind the look they held. Was it respect, at last, for her husband? Farrah couldn't tell, but she hoped so.

With a blip of a siren, Jake's fellow officer pulled the patrol car around and Jake loaded Jincey in the back, a resigned look on her face, black streaks of mascara on her cheeks.

"She always did like orange," Abbott quipped, but wiped his smile off when he saw Farrah's solemn face. "Too soon?"

"Just a little," she said, forcing a smile to put him at ease. The truth was, she wasn't at all in a laughing mood.

As the cop car drove off, a small round of applause rose. An explanation was still needed in order to regain trust. The sound crew re-checked the good mic, and Farrah saw wariness on the faces of those gathered.

She asked for the mic from Abbott and he placed his arm around her shoulders as she spoke.

"I'm so sorry about all that. There's been a misunderstanding. It's true that Connor Dunes doesn't know I'm donating the painting," she said, fighting tears. "But it's not because I stole it. It's because he has Alzheimer's disease and doesn't remember the painting… or me… or even himself."

She paused to collect herself and wiped hot tears from her cheeks.

"I can do this if you need me to," Abbott whispered. She declined with a slight shake of her head and spoke again to the crowd.

"When he found out about his prognosis, he divorced me to set me free. I know it seems strange, but he was nineteen years older than me. Even so, I loved him and never expected to lose him so quickly. He was a wonderful husband," she said, recalling his face during better times and choking on a sob.

"He was good to me. And he named me as his sole benefactor after his death, which means *Sandcastle Girl* will be mine. I can get his lawyer to confirm it, if whoever wins is concerned." Some supportive noises came from the crowd and a few compassionately shook their heads. "He's still alive, but only for a short time more. He's in palliative care at Glade Village. They expect him to pass anytime. That's why I'm back in town. Even though he wanted to set me free, I can't leave him."

A few people dabbed at their eyes with hankies and the silence was thick. Farrah sensed people believed the truth and were no longer worried about Jincey's claims. She glanced at Bobby and Amy who smiled and nodded at her from the front row. She needed to tie this back into the basket and make it about the Bells again. It never should have been about her. Still, she had gotten it all out, and she was lighter from having told the truth instead of keeping it in.

"There will always be naysayers and critics," Farrah started again, pulling herself together and wiping away her last tears. "But Connor wasn't like that. He loved helping people, and so do I. Today is about the Bells. So what do you say? Should there be a drawing or not?"

Clapping and hollering arose from the audience along with a chant of "draw that ticket!" Farrah and Abbott exchanged a look, laughing together.

"I guess I'll hand it over to Mr. Abbott, here, to do the honors."

She gave him the microphone and he shook the gigantic ticket jar. The people gathered looked at him intensely, each hoping to win but trying to manage their expectations.

"The first stub number is for a fifty-dollar cash gift," he said. "One zero four six."

Immediately, a middle-aged woman stood and waved, then made her way to the front to collect her prize, smiling and content not to go away empty handed, even though she'd spent more than the prize value on her ticket. At the end of the day, it was all about helping the Bells.

"The second is for a one-hundred-and-fifty-dollar cash gift," Abbott said, drawing another ticket. "Zero four four zero."

"Yeehaw!" a man called from the far right, then walked up and claimed his envelope, shaking it in the air triumphantly. Clapping peppered the audience. A slight wind blew, and Abbott looked over at Farrah. Gears were turning in his mind. He turned back to the crowd.

"Now for the big drawing… the basket, complete with the authentic Connor Dunes painting, *Sandcastle Girl*… I'd like Farrah Macon, the original sandcastle girl, to do the honors." Abbott handed Farrah the mic, grinning slyly. She stepped forward and accepted it. Slowly, applause rose from the townspeople on the amphitheater lawn. When she raised the large plastic jar with the stubs in it, cheering and whistling broke out. Energy was high. Jincey was gone. Everything was fine.

Farrah reached far into the jar and pulled out a ticket

stub. All noise settled. It was so quiet that the cars on the faraway highway were audible, as well as the chirping and cawing of various forest birds. Farrah read loudly and confidently the winning ticket's number.

"Zero one eight two."

A minute or so went by, and no one stood. She waited as people in the crowd checked their stubs yet again, shaking their heads to neighbors to confirm they hadn't won.

"I guess they're not here," Abbott leaned in and said to Farrah, shrugging.

"Well, I'll call it again," she stage-whispered to him. "You have to call it several times."

He nodded, but with low enthusiasm.

"Zero one eight two?" she called and waited. "That was, zero one eight two."

No one approached. A few calls of "They're not here," arose. The crowd looked on to see what Farrah would do. She looked at Abbott.

"Let's draw a different one," he said in a low tone, pushing the mic a little bit away from her mouth so he wouldn't be heard.

"What? Why? That's not how this works." Farrah turned back to the crowd, many of whom were already packing up. Some people had walked over to shake Bobby and Amy's hands and wish them well. Others, wanting to have won something, left disappointed.

"Okay, folks," Farrah addressed them. "Looks like the winner isn't here. The person who won has a window of due diligence to bring in their stub. If that isn't completed in seven days, we'll draw a new ticket."

Abbott reached for the mic, and she handed it over. "Check social media, the paper, and the Macon Farms market stand on Tuesday for updates. If the winner comes forward, even anonymously, we'll announce it through those means. Thank you all for coming and for supporting the Bells." A light applause rose from those who were still in attendance and packing up.

"Thank you all!" Farrah said into the mic Abbott held. She looked over at Amy and Bobby, and Amy shot her a happy thumbs up. At least the Bells thought it went well.

Abbott flipped off the mic and turned to Farrah, his brow furrowed as he chewed on his lower lip.

"What's wrong?" she asked, rubbing his upper arm.

"Well… actually," he started, breaking into a forcefully carefree smile, but he stopped talking almost right away, because her phone rang loudly from her pocket.

Farrah pulled it out. On seeing Macy's name, she swiped to answer.

"Come back, quick. His breathing is shallow and his vitals are weak." Macy's voice was frantic and apologetic. "I waited ten minutes to see if he'd improve before calling. I'm so sorry, Farrah. I should've called you earlier."

"Macy," Farrah began. "It's fine. Calm down. I'm on my way." She hung up.

"It's Mr. Mitchell," she said to Abbott. She hastily pocketed her phone and pulled out her keys, jogging past Abbott.

The parking lot was congested with people leaving. She'd need to get out of there quickly, but it looked like she'd face some major traffic.

"Farrah!" Abbott called, and she stopped and turned on her heels, sparing him a few seconds she didn't have. "I have four-wheel drive and I'm parked over there." He pointed out his truck next to a dirt embankment that connected with the semi-busy state highway that ran through Whitetail Ridge. "Want to do some off-roading?"

It should've been funny, but it provoked her to tears.

She nodded, and the signal was enough for him to break into a run and grab her hand, guiding her to the truck.

When he cranked it and effortlessly—and probably illegally—crested the embankment and screeched out onto the highway, she prayed she'd get there in time to be with Connor in his final moments. So he wouldn't die alone. So he'd know he was loved.

Abbott was proving she could trust him with the hard and the ugly. Even the hardest and the ugliest.

Chapter Twenty-Five

PRESENT DAY

"I love you," Farrah said to Connor, alone in his hospice room. She hadn't stopped crying since she had arrived, almost all her tears dripping over his weathered hand clutched between both of hers. That hand that had held her and helped her for a few wonderful years.

"You were so good to me. And I'm here with you now. You're not alone. You are loved, and you meant so much to me. I'm so grateful that I got to have you as a husband. I'd pick you again and again and again."

She went on that way for the whole afternoon. In case he forgot, she repeated herself often so he'd know how she felt, at least in the present. Connor didn't respond, and she didn't expect him to. He struggled to pull in a breath, then went silent for a while, then struggled to pull in another. He was close to the end. Oh, so close.

Toward the evening, a knock came on the door frame and she looked up to see Abbott standing there with a milkshake from Grill Out. She could bet money it was strawberry cheesecake. She smiled through her tears, and he set it on the side table before pulling up a seat next to Farrah and observing Connor.

Farrah didn't stop speaking. Abbott was all in and could hear anything she needed to say.

"I'm still here," she whispered to Connor, weak from talking and crying all day. "I've never left your side. Even when you wanted me to, you stinker." Farrah laughed. "I'm right here. I love you."

Her stomach rumbled with hunger. She eyed the milkshake longingly, but she couldn't live with herself if Connor felt alone while she indulged in a sweet treat.

Abbott's hand rested on her shoulder during her brief pause. "I'll sit with him," he offered. "And talk to him."

Farrah's chest filled with warmth. She reached over and hugged Abbott, mouthing a thank you through her tears. She addressed Connor one more time, sniffing hard before beginning. "My friend Abbott is going to talk to you for a little bit. I'm still here." Connor's gray eyes remained absently directed toward the opposite wall, his curled-in mouth agape.

Farrah stood and grabbed her milkshake. Abbott shifted to her empty seat, and to her surprise, he grabbed Connor's hand, then leaned in to talk to him like a friend.

He looked for a moment like he wasn't exactly sure what to say. But when he started, his kindness shattered Farrah.

"I figure I'll tell you a little about the Farrah I knew, since you loved her so much. I don't blame you for loving her." He shot Farrah a glance and nodded at her milkshake, urging her to drink. She did. It was heavenly. Tart and sweet and rich—just what she needed.

"She's pretty incredible. You know she loved you so much that she left this great town to build a life with you? She didn't know that when she chose to move to Charlotte.

But meeting and loving you was the plan for her life. It was her honor to be your wife. She was so proud of you."

Abbott stopped for a moment and cleared his throat. "Let me tell you a little story you might not know. Me and Farrah were neighbors, in a way. Grew up on the same country road, about a mile and a half apart. When we were kids, maybe eleven or twelve, she snuck out one night."

Oh no. He was *not* telling that story. Farrah laughed, remembering. It was certainly one she'd never told Connor.

"She came to my window," Abbott continued, "and opened it up. I woke up with the creaking of the panes. She tried to convince me to go out to my dad's pasture and do some cow tipping. I told her that was just an urban legend, but she insisted that night was the night to try it.

"So we headed out to where the cows were asleep. It might've been two in the morning. Their pen was pure mud and manure—that was the way my dad kept them. And we snuck up on a cow that was dozing while standing up as they sometimes do, and we pushed with all our might. That cow didn't even budge. I said, 'I told you so,' and she got mad and yelled at me right in the pen. Well, the cow woke up and started mooing and horning the ground, pawing with her forefeet, throwing dirt all around us. She was in fight mode.

"I grabbed Farrah's hand and told her we had to run, quick. Her eyes were as wide as two full moons, and she knew not to question me anymore. The only problem was, her rubber boots got stuck in the muck and she had to run across the pen barefoot. She smelled awful, so we ran down to the creek and she washed off. Then I walked her home and went back to my house. And I think that night was one of the highlights of my childhood. All because of her."

Connor showed no signs of understanding or recognition. His breaths were growing shallower and weaker.

Farrah's human needs pressed within her. She'd been in the room for hours on end. She peeked out the door and into the hallway just as Abbott started another childhood story. She eyed the bathroom longingly. Knowing Connor was not alone, she jogged down the hall, intent on not missing any of his last moments. When finished, she washed her hands the quickest she ever had and jogged back to his door, but paused outside when Abbott's silence made her fear she'd missed Connor's passing.

To her relief, she quickly realized Abbott was still talking to a barely-there Connor, he was just taking his time. He was saying different things, the type of things that don't come quickly to the tongue.

She snuck inside the doorframe, leaning her exhausted body on it, and listened.

"And I reckon I have a lot to thank you for. Mostly for loving her." Abbott paused and rubbed Connor's weathered hand with his thumb. "For making her happy, what short time you could." There was thick silence as Abbott looked down at Connor. Farrah thought about cutting in and taking over, but Abbott spoke again. "And, Connor, I'm determined. If she'll have me, I'd be glad to pick up where you left off… to love her… take care of her. Support her dreams, like you would have if you'd been able."

Farrah's throat contracted at Abbott's sweet words, and she swallowed hard.

"*If she'll have me…*" One day, she would. She wanted nothing more than to have Abbott. But her heart had to do a bit of work first.

Farrah came up behind Abbott and placed her hands on his back. It was time for her to take over. Every minute they were closer to the end.

"Thank you, Abbott. For the milkshake. And for your words."

He correctly understood that she needed to be alone. He rose and faced her, holding her hands. "Call if you need me. I can come back, any hour. Day or night."

She thanked him again and took the seat he had left vacant. He slipped out of the room, now dim and quiet, as all of Connor's medicines, drips, and monitors except the morphine were off. Farrah felt an expectant peace that she couldn't explain. She was excited for him to no longer suffer. She was ready for him to find the peace he longed for. The healing he needed.

She held his hand but rested her head on her arm, relaxing her upper body. She continued to tell him how much she loved him, how very much he had meant to her.

At some point, she must have fallen asleep.

Because at about three o'clock in the morning, she woke up to find that Connor was no longer with her.

Chapter Twenty-Six
PRESENT DAY

❧

Under Daddy's arm, Farrah exited the graveside service for Connor, leading Mom, Macy, her brother-in-law Elijah, and her nephews out to the parking lot of the countryside cemetery. The day was cooler, less humid. As if nature knew that mild, dry days were Connor's favorites.

The visitation and indoor funeral several hours before had been full of acquaintances and friends of Connor's that Farrah had contacted, some traveling from the beach town he'd called home for decades. While their marriage and especially Connor's disease had been kept private, and Farrah had never wanted anything about it online, the day after Connor died, she had posted on his website and social media accounts of his passing, sparking hundreds of comments from concerned followers who had been wondering why he'd had a years' long absence online. A local news station from Charlotte and another from Wilmington set up cameras in the parking lot and filmed a segment about Connor, but the journalists remained respectful and kept their distance.

Ginny had come, reminding Farrah as she hugged her in the visitation line that she'd get through this and that she could come back to the Oberg at any time. Noticeably, Erin Matthews wasn't there, and Kia was on bedrest due to preeclampsia.

The graveside service outdoors had been small and intimate. It was also brief and special. Her parents' pastor shared some of Connor's favorite verses, and they all sang a hymn together. Now, with the service concluded, Farrah stood with her family giving her goodbyes, as they hadn't arranged for a post-funeral meal or gathering.

Even though her family would leave, Farrah would hang around a bit. Because Abbott had been there the whole time. He'd come to the funeral and stayed by the graveside. Some men looked out of place in a black suit and tie, but not Abbott. He stood off to the side, lingering near his truck with his hands in his pockets. She could tell he wanted to talk but didn't want to impose on her grieving process.

After giving her nephews the biggest squeeze ever and watching her family's cars turn out of the parking lot and onto the main road, she made her way to Abbott, her black summer dress flitting in the dry breeze.

She stopped just short of him and looked up at him, suddenly exhausted.

"How you doing, Bacon?"

"I'm… okay." She nodded as if she had just decided this. "It's been a long few days."

"Yeah, you've had to meet with half the town, I bet." Abbott eyed her. "You look nice, if that helps. And the services were great."

"They were," Farrah agreed. They had been perfect. "I think Connor would have loved the way everything turned out."

"Yeah," Abbott said, looking out over the cemetery. The day grew bright as the sun pushed through clouds. He slid on his sunglasses and looked even better than he had before.

Silence settled over them, except for the honking of Canada geese flying overhead and landing on the cemetery's large pond.

"Abbott… I know I wasn't upfront with you as a teen, and I know that hurt you."

He turned his shaded eyes toward her, fully engaged in what she was saying. The magnetic energy between them was thick. If Farrah longed to fall into his arms for comfort, she could bet he wanted to reach out and embrace her just as badly. She held back, and he did too.

"You know all that's forgiven," Abbott said, his voice gravelly.

"And I thank you for that. But I want to be really clear and upfront here so we both know where we stand."

Abbott cocked his head, waiting. Farrah went on.

"Remember last time? When you wrote me that note I never read, telling me to reach out when I was ready?"

Abbott's mouth stretched into a lopsided grin. "I seem to recall."

"Well, let's do that again. Only this time, I really will reach out."

Abbott laughed through his nose, a gentle and understanding smile on his face. "So you're telling me you need time."

"Yes… time to work through the fact that my husband is really gone."

It was one of the truest things Farrah could say, because even though Connor's diagnosis and demise had been a years' long process, she had never fully lost hope. She was just too optimistic to accept that he was beyond help while he was alive, much as she fought to do so. As long as he had been breathing, a small voice in the back of her mind had whispered *what if?* But now, all hope of his earthly recovery was gone, and she would be able to start the process of assimilating his death.

Farrah went on. "Time, also, to figure out how I can feel like a widow and not be one." She laughed, self-deprecatingly.

Abbott unpocketed his hand, placing it safely on her upper arm, giving her a slight rub. "Take all the time you need," he said, reassuring her. "I'll wait. Days, weeks, months, years. I'll be here."

"Thank you, Abbott." Farrah smiled and turned to go, then remembered something and spun on her heels.

"With the chaos of the past few days, I've missed the news and I forgot to ask Macy—what became of the raffle basket?"

"Oh," Abbott said, raising his brows above the line of his sunglasses and looking as if she'd put him on the spot. "Um, yeah. About that. The winner came forward and claimed it."

"Oh, that's great! Who was it? Was it that CEO guy who bought twenty tickets?"

Abbott scratched the side of his head above his ear and winced. "No, but… they want to remain anonymous." He shrugged.

Farrah couldn't tell if he was keeping something from her or just unhappy with the person who won it. Something was off, though.

"What about *Sandcastle Girl?* Did you get it from Mom and Daddy's house and deliver it and—"

Abbott held up his hand. "It's all taken care of."

Farrah sighed. She had a hard time when others organized and planned in her stead. "Well, good then. I'm glad it all turned out okay."

"More than okay. One hundred thousand is a great amount."

Abbott seemed genuinely pleased, but there was still ninety thousand dollars left for the Bells to pay. She doubted that knocking out only half their debt could really help the Bells in the long run, as far as keeping their house. She couldn't hide her disappointment and looked down at her feet.

"That's still short of saving the farm."

Abbott reached out, grabbed her chin, and raised her face up. "Chin up, buttercup. I already talked to the Bells and they're ecstatic. They're hosting a giant community-wide cookout at the public park next Saturday with a thousand dollars of the proceeds. They said they've got enough to put down that they can squeeze by and make ends meet and stay in their house."

"It's just hard for me to be happy when I know we might have made more if Jincey hadn't intervened."

Abbott's head bobbed with his scoffing laugh. "You know she spent a night in jail for what she did, and had to pay a fine? She came to see me and apologized."

Farrah snickered and shook her head. "She's still coming to see you. A married woman visiting a single, attractive man."

She couldn't help but notice that Abbott straightened a little when she said *attractive*. A smile played at his lips, and he brushed off the sleeves of his suit, suddenly nervous.

"Actually, I set things straight with her." Farrah wasn't convinced, but Abbott pressed the matter. "I think you'll be surprised when you talk to her again."

"Ha! After the stunt she pulled, I doubt we'll talk

again." Farrah turned and walked toward her car, leaving him and his truck behind.

"Oh, she'll come see you," Abbott called after her. "She told me she was going to when things settle down."

"I'll believe it when I see it," Farrah said more to herself than to Abbott.

She loaded up and headed for her parents' house, ready to put on some pajamas and start her grieving process. The burial had been the final punctuation of the whole act. It was all over. Connor was at peace.

And now it was time to accept and heal.

Chapter Twenty-Seven
PRESENT DAY

Two weeks had gone by since the funeral, and Farrah sat waiting on her porch swing watching the gravel road for any sign of an approaching car. She had a batch of lavender honey lemonade ready, the fragrant buds picked fresh from the garden. In a nearby dish was some peach cobbler, Mom's recipe, covered with a linen dish towel to keep away the flies. At any moment, Erin Matthews would arrive, and she'd inform Farrah of her financial state and what to expect going forward.

A breeze blew, swishing the long branches of the front yard willow and rustling the great oaks around the house, creating a calming shushing noise. The wind chimes sang their tunes. She closed her eyes and rocked, just being present in the moment.

She was so relaxed that she almost missed the crunch of gravel coming from the driveway. She sprang into action and approached the car, which wasn't a blue BMW.

It was a large, big-rimmed, black SUV with tinted windows. And out of it popped the tiniest, orangest woman.

Jincey.

She sheepishly approached Farrah, a small smile on her face, and extended a large Tupperware container toward her.

"I made you a pound cake," she said with her country twang.

Farrah took it, unsure of what to say.

"It ain't poison," Jincey blurted, throwing her hand out by means of explanation.

"Um, thank you," Farrah managed. "You really didn't have to do this."

Jincey sighed dramatically. "Yes, I did too. I'm sorry, Farrah. Truth is, it really irked me that you had such a good idea. I couldn't stand not heading something up for once. So I'm sorry. I acted all out of sorts." It was a sweet apology and she seemed to mean it. "And then there's Abbott and me… we never got over each other. Teenage love and whatnot."

Farrah stifled a laugh, but Jincey was none the wiser.

"He told me the other day that it was for real over. And to tell you the truth, I felt relieved. I opened up to Jake, told him what was going on. We're going to counseling. And I think we're gonna be okay."

Farrah broke into a smile. "That's great, Jincey. I'm happy for you."

"Me too," she admitted, her orange earrings jangling with each enthusiastic nod. "I reckon it took a night in the slammer to make me come to my senses." She giggled, a tingly little sound, not unlike the windchime. "I really thought I was doing the right thing and jumped the gun to intervene. I never knew you was going through all that."

"Yeah. I didn't tell anybody, really."

"Well, I am sorry. But, Farrah, I do have a question."

Her brow was scrunched over her nose. "Wadn't it hard to give away that paintin'?"

Farrah sighed out a laugh. "More than you know," she said. "But I did it for the Bells. Amy and Bobby… They're so important to so many."

Jincey nodded, a newfound sweetness on her face. She rubbed Farrah's shoulder. "You're a good person, Farrah Macon. Better than most." Just then, Erin's blue beamer pulled into the driveway. "Looks like you got company. I'll leave you to it."

Farrah thanked Jincey and watched as she pulled out and left. Erin hopped out and unloaded a box of files from her trunk, then carried it up to the porch.

"Was that the girl you mentioned from the raffle? The one who—"

"No comment," Farrah said playfully and gave Erin a hug. "I figured we could visit outside, since it's so pretty."

She led Erin to a table and they sat in the warm summer breeze. A bit of an awkward silence ensued as Farrah served the lemonade and peach cobbler.

"What a treat. I didn't know you were feeding me."

"Of course."

"I'm sorry I wasn't at the funeral, Farrah. It was my daughter's birthday. I'd planned it months ago and the venue was nonrefundable—"

"Erin, don't worry about it." They ate for a while in silence, but the awkwardness was fading. Somehow, Farrah was confident again. Not scared. She was ready to be friends with Erin, because she had been a friend to Connor. "Tell me about the party. Did she get a smash cake?"

Erin gushed as she told Farrah all about her daughter and how she barely touched the expensive cake, how the balloon arch kept falling down, how the Princess Shasta actress didn't look anything like the cartoon. Somewhere in her vibrant story, Farrah began chuckling along with Erin's misfortunes. They were laughing together. And it was nice.

Before long, they'd finished their food and drinks. "I suppose we should get down to business," Erin announced.

She leafed through the files in the box and pulled out one that included Connor's last will and testament. She handed a copy to Farrah, then read it aloud.

As Farrah had expected, he'd donated a large chunk of his fortune to Alzheimer's research and art therapy foundations, as well as designated a few of his privately owned works to certain museums as gifts for their lifelong patronage and enduring friendship.

But everything else, he'd left to Farrah.

"Everything?"

"Everything."

"Royalties? The house? The collection?"

"The Charlotte house and the beach house, royalties, even his 1976 Chevrolet Impala. Any artwork not explicitly donated in his will is now yours."

"So… how much am I worth? After his donations to other organizations?"

Erin rifled through another file, then flipped over a document to show Farrah. "It's an estimation of all combined assets. Art fluctuates."

Farrah gasped. "That's a lot."

"Yeah," Erin said breathily, nodding along with Farrah. "I want you to meet with Connor's investment manager about this. I'll get his name and number to you right now. He's handled all of Connor's assets for years. You'll have to pay taxes on your properties every year, as well as make this money last your whole life, which would probably best be done by rolling enough of it over to a high-yield savings account, so you get a continual interest income to live off.

Of course, royalties will continue. Besides all that, do you plan on working, or staying here, or..."

Farrah ran numbers in her head as Erin texted her the wealth manager's information. Farrah knew a lot about savings accounts, interest, and investing just because she was savvy in that way. The wealth Connor had left her would be enough for her to move back to Charlotte and become an owner of the Oberg. She could pay off Amy and Bobby's remaining debt and probably her nephews' college and still not have to worry about living expenses, especially working at the gallery.

But is that what I really want?

Being close to Mom and Daddy and substantially closer to Macy, Elijah, and the boys had been so wonderful during the short time she'd been back home in Whitetail Ridge. The town had really grown on her.

And even as she tried her best to reason logically and dispassionately, she couldn't fully ignore the handsome, stubbly farmer's face that popped into her mind every time she thought of leaving. She worried about how he would feel about her moving far away, since that was the trigger that had made him leave her when they were teens.

Back then, being so young, she'd known she couldn't sacrifice her dreams for another person.

But now, as an adult, after all she'd been through, she wondered if there could be a way for both of them to find their fulfillment and purpose in Whitetail Ridge.

"I need to talk to my boss, Ginny," Farrah admitted. "She sees me as a protégé, and I feel like I owe it to her to take up my old position. But now it just seems so..."

"So what?" Erin asked after Farrah didn't speak up for a few beats.

"It feels like something from long ago. Something that went with someone I used to be. Not who I am now."

Farrah sighed. "But it'll be fine. I'll go back to work and all those good feelings will return, I'm sure. I'm meant for that job."

Farrah forced a smile, but her heart squeezed as she thought about Abbott being so far away. She couldn't grab food after work with him or find him on her couch after a long day working the land, watching football when she got home.

"It'll be fine," Farrah repeated one more time to convince Erin, or perhaps herself.

"Hmm." Erin's smile was simple and full of understanding. "If you say so."

AFTER ERIN HAD PACKED up and gone, leaving Farrah with the news that she was a wealthy woman, Farrah headed upstairs, hoping to crash on her childhood bed. She had spent a good deal of time healing in bed the past couple weeks, and it was a great room to watch the sunset from.

She headed that way but stopped short. A paper was peeking out from under her bed skirt. Stooping down to pick it up, she flipped it over and saw that it was part of one of the symbols for the raffle basket. It was a sheet of paper explaining to the winner how to claim the free house cleaning. She was supposed to have pasted it on the back of the vacuum symbol, but in the busyness of everything, it must have slipped her mind.

Suddenly, her heart hammered. It was the perfect excuse to call Abbott.

Truth be told, she missed him. She had wanted to call him every day since the funeral but had resisted until she was sure she was ready. However, if she called him about the basket, she could tell him she was thinking about moving back to Charlotte and gauge his reaction—and at least she'd hear his voice, which might satisfy the desire for closeness she craved.

She pulled out her phone and pressed his name to call him, then lay back on her bed, looking out over the forest line and distant Pilot Mountain through her window.

With each ring, she grew more nervous. Finally, on the fourth or fifth, he answered. He seemed to have been in the middle of something, because some rustling noises and shutting of doors sounded in the background through the phone.

"I wasn't going to answer, but then I saw it was you," came his honest reply.

"Abbott," Farrah breathed out. "I've missed you."

His silence said everything. He was probably wondering if she was ready, or if she was calling for another reason.

"What you need, Bacon bit?" He was obviously protecting himself, so he was sticking to the point.

"I was cleaning my room"—*great, already starting out by lying*—"and I came across the instructions for claiming the free house cleaning. I wanted you to relay them to the winner of the basket."

Abbott skipped a beat or two before answering. "Um, yeah. I guess I can do that."

He guesses he can?

"It's simple. Just give the winner my number and tell them to text me to claim it."

"Wait, *you're* offering the house cleaning?" Abbott chuckled lightly.

"Hey, don't knock me. I was the head custodian for the Oberg for two years. I can make a toilet sparkle. And I vacuum in *all* the corners."

Abbott laughed again, a throaty, genuine sound. "All right. I'll tell him."

"Great." Farrah caught a glimpse of herself in her vanity mirror, grinning like a fool. "And there's something else."

"Okay?" His voice was tentative, hopeful.

"First off, you were right—Jincey came by to apologize, and I really think she meant it."

"Oh ye of little faith," Abbott quipped.

"And secondly, I met with Erin, Connor's lawyer, today."

"Oh." He sounded surprised. "How did that go?"

"Besides a sizable charity donation, he left me everything. I'm…" She wondered how to put it. "I guess I'm wealthy."

Abbott laughed again. "Congratulations. But just know I liked you before all the fame and fortune."

Her cheeks reddened at his flirtation. "Yeah, I know." She fiddled with the yarn ties on her patchwork quilt, then shifted to sitting, her old mattress creaking with the movement. Now was the moment. "I wanted you to know before anyone else that I'm moving back to Charlotte. I resigned this week from Glade Village, and today I found out Connor also left me the house, and my gallery job is there, so it just makes sense." She held her breath, unsure how he would react.

When Abbott spoke, he seemed to be trying to control his voice. "That's wonderful, Farrah. I'm happy for you."

"Thank you," she said. "But this doesn't mean my part of the deal is off. I'll still let you know when I'm ready, if the distance isn't an issue for you."

He wasted no time putting her at ease. "Distance ain't an issue. I love you, Farrah. But your healing is an issue. Take all the time you need."

His support made her want to fast-forward through her healing process and run up the road and into his arms. But she needed to *feel* ready to explore a life with Abbott, not just receive his comfort. She was close, but not quite there yet.

"So you'll let the winner know?"

"Uh-huh," he mumbled. Why did she get the funny feeling he was hiding something?

"Thanks, Abbott."

"Sure thing."

When she hung up, she thought back to their whole conversation. He'd told her yet again that he loved her. When was she going to tell him? Because the feeling was definitely there.

"Time will tell," she said to herself, as she had a hundred times in the weeks since Connor had died. "Just give yourself time."

Besides, she couldn't take on too much in one day, and she still had one last call to make.

She dialed Ginny's number, and she answered on the second ring. After a few how-have-you-beens, Farrah posed the question she'd imagined asking for months.

"Are you ready for me to come back to the Oberg?"

Ginny's bombastic cackle was enough of an answer in itself.

"Honey, I've been ready."

Chapter Twenty-Eight

PRESENT DAY

⁂

Early August brought Abbott's thirtieth birthday. Farrah's would come this weekend. As an early celebration a week ago, they'd shared a cup of coffee at Donna's before she left for Charlotte. He'd given her a friendly hug when they'd departed, holding back from any romance, and she'd tried to quell the tug in her chest as they drove apart in separate cars.

Thirty. It seemed monumental to Farrah.

Kia had bemoaned turning thirty, but Farrah was ready. She took the change in number as an open door to allow herself to step into the life she wanted, even if she wasn't fully healed. She'd come to realize in the few days she'd been back in Charlotte that her emotions fluctuated a hundred times within a day. She was learning to embrace this as normal, instead of rushing herself to get past it.

She'd grown wiser through her grief and understood now that mourning happened at its own pace. She'd joined a grief share group at a local church, and they'd had their first meeting this week. Seeing people a year or two out from the initial loss still struggling with pain and depression helped her understand that she could not put her life on hold if she wanted to have a chance to be happy.

Every day, she missed Abbott more, and even if her feelings for him were coming at the "wrong" time, she wanted the comfort of his arms and his steadfastness to help her through her grieving process.

She was unsure how to reconcile the job she loved, the boss she felt obligated to, and the man she couldn't live without. Ginny had hinted multiple times that she was ready to sell Farrah her part of the Oberg, but Farrah just couldn't bring herself to accept. She hoped Ginny wasn't offended by her switching the subject or brushing off her insistence every time she brought it up. Buying into the gallery seemed very final, and Farrah wasn't ready to close anything yet. She needed to explore the longing in her heart, the aching yearn every time she thought about Abbott or home.

Something would happen—some sort of catalyst—that would make clear the path she needed to choose: Charlotte or Whitetail Ridge. And if that last domino tumbled the way she wanted it to, she'd give Abbott the call she so badly wanted to make and let him know she was ready to open her heart to him. She was just waiting and praying for a sign.

"Did you want to keep these?" Ginny called from the other side of the room, her wispy gray waves held back with a bandana. She was holding up some cardboard portfolios.

"Confirm that they're empty, then toss them," Farrah said. They were cleaning out a storage room together before Farrah resumed managerial control of the Oberg the next week.

The other minority-stake owners, like Ginny, were also aging and longing for retirement. They were all so happy

Farrah was back to run things, though Vlad and the other staff, including the interns, had done a marvelous job assisting and learning from Ginny. Many of the stakeholders had plans for their golden years, including Ginny, who was over-the-moon to have her first grandchild. *"Maybe this one will like art,"* she'd mused to Farrah earlier in the day.

Farrah had been able to make it to the hospital the same day Zinnia was born. Seeing Kia as a mother holding her sweet peanut of a baby girl with loving, doting Travis by her side gave Farrah a glimmer of hope for her own future. She was so happy for them and wanted so badly what they had, especially when she got to hold Zinnia for the first time and stare into her sweet, sweet face. She was nine pounds of pudgy, pink preciousness, and Auntie Farrah was smitten.

Ginny was ecstatic, despite the darker moments of missing Keith and wishing he could meet their grandchild. But she didn't let the nostalgia weigh her down. She kept pressing forward, excitedly planning on helping overnight with the baby sometimes so Kia could rest. She'd still bought a ticket to France for October since she figured the baby would be sleeping well enough by then for her to escape for a few weeks and see some old friends.

As they sorted boxes and filled a dumpster, the doorbell rang. Some days, they only opened to the public in the evenings, which was still a few hours away.

"I'll get it," Ginny hollered and jogged out. Soon she returned with a large, padded shipping envelope. "It's addressed to you," she said. "What did you order?"

"Nothing," Farrah said, a bit caught off guard. Ginny handed her the package and went back to work. It must have been a mistake or some old subscription Farrah had forgotten about. She hadn't announced to anyone that she was back at the gallery. She looked for a return address but could only find a nameless P.O. Box from Winston.

But the sender knew *her*. It was addressed to Farrah Macon on the Certified Mail shipping label with the gallery's address below it. "How strange," she remarked, then ripped into the package and pulled out its contents, wrapped in more bubble wrap.

She peeled back the protective layer and gasped.

"What is it?" Ginny said, running again to her side. When she saw, she put her arm around Farrah, gripping her in support, mouth agape.

Someone had mailed her *Sandcastle Girl*.

In an instant, the memories of that beachy balcony and her husband in his white linen shirt came flooding back to her. His sandy hair, his tanned face, and cool-guy smirk. What wonderful moments they'd had. Goodness, she was so thankful for the memories.

A few tears had trailed down her cheeks. She smacked at them with the back of her hand. "Excuse me just a second," she said to Ginny, who gave her shoulder a light squeeze. Farrah carried *Sandcastle Girl* back to the office and placed it on an easel away from the sun.

She called the only person who would fully understand: Macy.

"Did you win the basket?!" Farrah asked, half accusatory, as soon as Macy answered.

"What? No. Did you?"

"Why would you ask me that?" Farrah scoffed at her sister, as sisters do.

"Because I just got a completely anonymous package with the dog symbol from the basket. Pansy gets a free grooming. Isn't that awesome?"

Farrah's mind raced. Anyone would know she was the model in *Sandcastle Girl* and that it was important to her because it was a gift of time and creation from her husband—she had announced exactly that in front of hundreds of people at the amphitheater when the winning ticket for the raffle basket was drawn. But who would know that Macy had a labradoodle with a particularly thick coat that required frequent grooming? Pansy was almost always at the Gatewoods' house in their large fenced-in back yard or with Macy's mother-in-law in Winston when they traveled, so not many people in Whitetail Ridge had even seen the dog.

"And get this"—Macy interrupted her thoughts—"Jincey got the cabin stay in the mail. She called me to claim it this week! She and Jake are taking a much-needed couple's weekend in September."

"Oh my gosh." Farrah gasped. "Macy, I got something too. Whoever won the basket sent me *Sandcastle Girl*."

"Are you kidding me?" Macy's shocked tone sent an excited shiver through Farrah.

"Dead serious. Look, I need you to do some investigating. You're at the farmers market, right?"

"It *is* Tuesday, isn't it?" Macy said smugly. "And you *did* just abandon me to help Mom at the market stand alone, if I recall correctly." Farrah playfully rolled her eyes. But the truth was, she'd love to be back at the Tuesday market with her family.

"All right, enough of that. I need you to ask the people who donated if they also got mysterious, anonymous packages with symbols from the raffle basket in them. Call me later after you do a little digging."

"You got it!"

Farrah hung up feeling all out of sorts. She was excited to have her painting back and added framing it to her to-do list for the week. She'd never let it out of her sight again. It would go on a special, permanent collection wall in the Oberg's upstairs gallery space. She'd have a plaque made in Connor's memory, and thousands of people would enjoy Farrah and Connor's beachy moment for years to come. The thought brought a wide smile to her face. She stood, then ran to meet Ginny and help her again. The gallery was opening soon, and they'd have to get to a stopping point and make themselves presentable.

But Ginny wasn't in the storage room anymore. Farrah looked for her, and then found her in the main gallery, staring at a portrait of a jazz musician in oil.

Farrah stood beside her. "Is everything okay?"

Ginny smiled ruefully and looked at Farrah. "You tell me." Farrah was worried for a moment that she had offended her boss and friend, but the look behind Ginny's eyes was as kind as ever. "You don't want this, Farrah." Ginny motioned around her beloved gallery.

"Of course I do." Farrah tried desperately to come up with some reasons to defend herself but came up short. She sputtered, "I-I'm good at this, and you need me, and—"

"No," Ginny said gently, shaking her head, and coming to face Farrah. She placed a hand on each of her cheeks. "That's where you're wrong. I can put out an ad and find another manager, train them just like I trained you. I could sell this place to someone very capable within a matter of weeks. Don't think I haven't had offers. I've kept you around because I love you like a daughter. But I won't have your sense of duty to me keeping you from what really matters." Ginny released Farrah's face, which was now warm and probably pink with emotion.

There was no use denying it. Ginny had sensed unspoken things, the truth that Farrah had pushed behind her. "I-I'm sorry, Ginny."

"Don't be. Listen..." Ginny pulled some paperwork

out of her pocket and showed it to Farrah. "Recognize this?"

Farrah skimmed over the document. "Of course. I signed for you to display my collection of Connor's artwork here at the Oberg."

Ginny took the document back and slowly ripped it in half. "The deal's off."

"Ginny, I—"

"Go back to Whitetail Ridge and open up a Connor Dunes gallery there. People will travel to see his work, buy his merch. You can charge admission, or even set up a little café inside to keep money flowing. The possibilities are endless." Ginny sucked in a breath, her eyes twinkling and full of hope. "Farrah, you can still do what you want, and love who you want. Because that's what matters most. Love." Ginny stuffed the ripped document back in her pocket. Then she took Farrah's hands. "You don't have to choose one or the other. You can have it all, Farrah."

Farrah fell into Ginny's hug. She whispered a muffled thank-you into her hair. Ginny squeezed her back.

Just then, Farrah's phone rang in her pocket, and she pulled back to glance at its screen. It was Macy. "So sorry. I've got to take this."

Ginny nodded, a twinkle in her eyes, and Farrah stepped into the office.

"Farrah, you're not going to believe this. It's just like you said—every single person I talked to that donated an item to the basket got something in the mail this week. All twenty gifts are accounted for, either by someone telling me they'd received it, or relating what they heard others had gotten."

Farrah's heart was beating out of her chest. The only hypothesis that made any sense was that Abbott had won the basket and distributed the gifts. He was the only other person with access to the donors list. It explained every-thing: his shortness on the phone, him wanting her to draw a different ticket right away, his poor ability to lie, his not telling her who had won the basket.

He'd know about Pansy, and he'd know that Jincey and Jake needed a romantic getaway. Most of all, he'd want her to have her painting back, even if it was worth thousands.

One question would resolve the mystery. Depending on the answer, she'd tell him she was ready.

It would be her catalyst, the sign she was praying for.

Trepidatiously, she asked her question clearly through the phone. "Macy, what did Abbott get?"

"I didn't see him," Macy began, "but Amy said he received the free house cleaning."

Heat rushed to Farrah's cheeks and she swallowed hard. Secret generosity. It was the last domino to tumble. It was time to let herself love Abbott.

She glanced over at *Sandcastle Girl* and felt peace. Farrah moving on was what Connor had envisioned when he'd made his rash and hurtful decision to divorce her. He wanted this for her. So she could no longer hold back in honor of him.

She was ready.

"Thank you, Macy. I've got a call to make."

As soon as she hung up, she called Abbott, then called him again. Ring after ring after ring, he didn't answer. When she'd gotten his voicemail four times, she pocketed her phone and keys and ran to find Ginny.

"I know it's late notice, but can you handle things alone tonight?" she asked, breathless.

"Sure. Why? Are you all right?"

"More than all right. I have to go take care of some-thing back home."

Ginny wasn't a clairvoyant, but she smiled coyly whenever Farrah talked about Abbott, even if Farrah only mentioned his name. Now, that same smile played at Ginny's lips.

She planted her hands on Farrah's shoulders and beamed. "Go get him."

NEARLY TWO HOURS LATER, Farrah knocked on Abbott's door over and over, to no avail. She walked around to the back of the house and knocked again. When she saw that wouldn't work, she peeked in his garage. His truck wasn't there. He was obviously either out for his birthday, or more likely, working. It was odd that he didn't answer his phone and hadn't called her back, and to top things off, she'd driven an hour and a half just to knock on a door to no answer.

She walked back around to the front porch and sat on the stoop. After thirty minutes or so of waiting and checking her phone and trying to call him again, she grew frustrated. Then she realized she hadn't actually tried the doorknobs. She stood up and walked to the front door, hopeful. The bottom knob twisted easily, and she pushed.

But the door was locked at the top deadbolt. She groaned.

"Darnit, I didn't come here for nothing," she said to herself, trying the two porch windows. They didn't budge.

She then circled around the property, trying every window she could reach. She figured if she could get inside, even if she tripped off an alarm, she could call Jake. He owed her too much for her part in saving his marriage to take her down to the station.

Fearless, she climbed up on a patio chair and, to her surprise, a small window opened. She removed the screen, worried for a moment that her hips might be too wide to fit through, but with some shimmying and core strength, her now bare feet landed on… a wet towel?

She was in his bathroom, and man, it was totally fitting for a bachelor pad.

More importantly, no alarm sounded. She walked into the hallway, trying to come up with a plan.

He's got to have some cleaning supplies around here, she thought, snooping in his closets. When she got to the kitchen, she slung open what she thought was a food pantry and found a rechargeable vacuum and mop bucket, as well as cleaning supplies, detergent, sponges, and rags. *Bingo!*

Outside in the hot summer sky, thunder rumbled. Since she had broken into his house, the sky had grown dimmer, both from the weather and the evening's advancing. She flipped on some lights and told his house speaker to play some country music, volume four. Then she got to work, throwing in a load of laundry first, then wiping down every surface, vacuuming, and mopping. She found his phone charging on the kitchen counter. That explained a lot.

After she'd finished her first chores, she changed his sheets, made the bed, and folded the laundry. Once she'd tidied the living room, the rain was pelting, and she crashed on the sofa with one of Abbott's blankets and succumbed to an evening nap.

She woke when the front door opened with a jangle of keys. She sat up straight and saw a wet-headed Abbott stopped in his tracks, staring at her with his mouth agape.

"Am I seeing things?" he finally said, his gray T-shirt clinging to him.

"Happy birthday! Since you never claimed the free house cleaning," Farrah began, moving toward him slowly, "I came to hold up my end of the bargain."

He took a few steps toward her, too, cautiously reading her. "I never would've asked you to do this. We had a cow escape, and I'm dirtying the floor all over again." He kicked off his boots and stepped onto the rug, standing just inches from her, looking down at her face.

She searched his eyes. "Why'd you do it?"

"Do what?" he asked, playing innocent.

She cocked her head and pursed her lips.

"Okay, fine. It was me. I wanted you to have your painting back. It wasn't right that you gave that up for someone else. Especially since you paid off all their debt."

"How'd you know I did that?" she asked. She'd tried to be secretive.

Abbott raised one eyebrow. "Who else just received a huge inheritance and could have covered the remaining balance so quickly? It was amazing of you to do that."

Farrah's cheeks warmed. "Thank you," she said. "And the other raffle gifts? Jincey's?"

He smiled, dimples making their handsome appearance. "I just wanted more than one person to win something. And honestly, I gave that to Jincey so she wouldn't go snooping around. Imagine if she found out I won. She'd claim a conflict of interest and come after me for real." He chuckled and so did Farrah. Then they grew serious, locked in each other's gazes, the energy of their potential surging between them.

Slowly, carefully, she placed a hand on his chest and another on his arm. She took a step toward him, tilting her face near his.

"I'm ready," she whispered. "And I love you."

Abbott didn't waste a second. His mouth met hers as his hands pressed into her back. He kissed her with everything he had. After a few minutes, he pulled back and rested his forehead on hers. "After all these years, our moment finally came."

"Mm-hmm," Farrah said, smiling blissfully. She closed her eyes and melted into Abbott's embrace.

"You got anywhere to be tonight?" Abbott whispered.

"Nowhere but here," she said. "And I'm planning to stay."

"Today? Tonight? What do you mean?" His eyes twinkled with anticipation.

"I'm moving back. I don't know when, but soon. I just have a few loose ends to tie up at the gallery, and—"

Abbott kissed her again, then released her. "You don't know how happy this makes me."

"No, you don't know how happy this makes *me*."

"Oh, are we going to argue now about who's happier?"

"We can, if you'd like."

Farrah hugged him around his waist and rested her head on his chest, as he planted a kiss on the top of her head. Everything was exactly as it should be.

Epilogue
FOUR MONTHS LATER

"Where are you heading now?" Kia asked, strapping her tiny daughter into her car seat. They'd enjoyed a late breakfast together and then visited the new Connor Dunes gallery and gelato shop in White-tail Ridge. Ginny had promised to come up soon but hadn't been able to make it today. Farrah couldn't go very long without seeing little Zinnia, so she'd invited Kia to spend the day and get to know her small town and see the new gallery, featuring *Sandcastle Girl*'s final spot. It was framed on a central wall with museum lighting so every guest who entered would see the sentimental piece and read the brief tribute to Connor.

"Um. Judging by the location Abbott just shared, it looks like I'm going to Amy and Bobby's backyard," Farrah said, giggling. "It's just a few minutes away. He told me he has a surprise for me, but who knows what it could be in my neighbor's field."

"Well, I think it's romantic." Kia laughed, opening her car's door.

"I guess so." *It totally is.*

She and Kia said their goodbyes, taking their time to give extra good hugs, and Farrah hopped in the van to go meet Abbott. During the drive, she racked her brain trying to figure out why he was asking her to meet him at the Bells'.

When she pulled up to Amy and Bobby's, they were standing at the entrance of their driveway, blocking her. She rolled down her passenger window, her brow scrunched in mock offense.

"No entry! Keep going!" They pointed and directed her farther down the gravel road, mischievous smiles on display.

"Fine, then," she said, laughing and waving them off.

As she drove toward Abbott's, she noticed a brand-new gravel driveway off to the right with a big poster with an oversize arrow painted on it.

"Guessing this is for me," she said to herself and turned down the freshly laid gravel and drove a few minutes until she arrived at a clearing—the back of the Bells' land—and saw Abbott standing in the middle of it.

She parked and hopped out of the car, curious and excited. Long gone was the heat of summer. A gentle, crisp breeze blew. She approached Abbott who stood with a picnic blanket and basket behind him, complete with her favorite bottle of red.

"Abbott… what is this?" She clutched her necklace that she had made from the sea glass Connor gave her in her engagement ring and chewed on her lip.

"It's my new tract of land."

"You bought it from Bobby and Amy?"

Abbott nodded, overjoyed. "It was their idea. Bobby's getting too old to work it, and it's perfect."

"Perfect for what?" Farrah grinned.

"Oh, I don't know… driving my old Tacoma out here

and sleeping in the bed of it with my old quilts and eating my Nabs."

She laughed. "Really?"

"Nah." He swiped at the air. "It's perfect for the type of farming I want to do. You got your dream, and I got mine. Well… I *think* I got mine. I've got to ask you something first."

She was about to ask him what exactly that meant, but she didn't have time because he dropped onto one knee. The breeze tickled his dark curls as his ruddy face stared up at hers, resolution in his handsome eyes.

"Farrah, I love you. We've waited so long for this moment. From lovestruck teenagers, to grieving, complicated adults, here we are. I love every part of you, and I want you to spend the rest of your life with me here. I want us to dream together about your gallery and my farm. I want us to have children and grow old together, like you deserve. You were such a faithful wife to Connor, even up until the very last moments. And I want to give you what you gave him in return. Will you marry me?"

He slid a gold band with a sparkling diamond on her ring finger. It was breathtaking. She looked down at him kneeling there, so vulnerable, so loving, and she remembered how she'd always envisioned her engagement: Abbott on one knee with a diamond. And how perfect that it was happening in Whitetail Ridge in the middle of their very own field.

"Yes," Farrah said. "Yes, I will."

He stood and lifted her up, spinning her around, not unlike he used to do when they were teens. He set her down, then kissed her hard, and they held each other for several moments, taking in the awe and comfort and bliss of the moment.

"I just have a few requests," Farrah said, pulling back to look in his eyes.

"Anything you want."

"Okay, well, no destination wedding. Connor and I did ours in the Bahamas, and no guests other than my parents could make it. I want to do things differently."

"Of course. What's the second thing?"

"I want peach trees on this property. Lots of them."

He laughed, shaking his head. "That's a given."

He pressed his lips to hers again, and she melted into his arms.

"Oh, and Abbott?" she mused, again breaking their kiss. "One thing I did right and want to do again."

"What's that?" He looked down at her, smiling, humoring her.

"I want to get married quickly." She ran her hands into his thick, curly hair. "I don't want to waste any time since I had to wait so long for this to happen. You know, you kept making it so hard on me and playing hard to get."

Abbott kicked his head back, laughing. "Bacon bit, you have no idea." He kissed her again, soft and warm. "No idea at all."

THE END

Acknowledgments

Thank you from the bottom of my heart to Jenny Hale at Harpeth Road for taking me on. I'm so happy to be a part of the family! My gratitude as well to my brilliant Harpeth Road editors: Elizabeth Mazer, Charlotte Hayes-Clemens, Liz Hurst, and Jodi Hughes, whose line edit was possibly the best thing that ever happened to this book. To the wonderful Emma Sherk, Two Seas Agency, and all my HR author sisters, a hearty thank you. Melie Williams, thanks for your lovely performance on the audiobook. To Vanessa Mendozzi for the amazing cover, and to all other behind-the-scenes contributors to *The Silver Lining*, thank you.

A heap of gratitude for help in the early stages of this manuscript goes to Haleigh Wenger, Brielle Porter, and Deb McCormick for beta reading. To my agent Colleen Oefelein, I appreciate your feedback on this and your effort to find it a publishing home.

Thank you to my family, Jonathan, Alastair, and Ander, for your love and support. A special thanks to Amy Medwin for inspiring Amy Bell in this book, raspy laugh and all. Forever thankful—you know why! Thanks to my extended family and friends near and far who've supported me on this journey. Much gratitude to Ashley Mitchell for real estate knowledge and for lending your last name to one of my favorite characters ever, and to Sarah Moore for information about cows and fences. Thank you to Chantal Mullen for inspiring a farmers market setting—though this time, without any sausage making.

A Letter from Audrey

Hello!

Thank you so much for picking up my novel, *The Silver Lining*. I hope it warmed your heart and made you believe in the power of second chances.

If you'd like to know when my next book is out, you can sign up for new Harpeth Road release alerts for my novels here:

Sign up to be the first to hear about new **HR** releases and updates from Audrey Lancho: https://www. harpethroad.com/audrey-lancho-newsletter-signup

I won't share your information with anyone else, and I'll only email you a quick message whenever new books come out or go on sale.

If you did enjoy *The Silver Lining*, I'd be so thankful if you'd write a review online. Getting feedback from readers helps to persuade others to pick up my book for the first time. It's one of the biggest gifts you could give me.

Warmly,

Audrey Lancho

P.S. Did you find the Spain Easter eggs in the text, as well
as all the names that start with A?

9 781963 483239